Destiny Reclaimed

FELICIA JEDLICKA

Book 2

For those who kiss frogs.

More titles by FELICIA JEDLICKA

DESTINY REJECTED
DESTINY RECLAIMED
DESTINY RAZED
DESTINY RESTORED

DÉJÀ VU

SAVE THE HUMANS

THE NECROMANCER'S CHILD

SISTER WITCHES
THE DEVIL'S SHADOW
THE DEVIL'S SOUL

THE NEBRASKA APOCALYPSE NOVELS
CORN COWS AND THE APOCALYPSE
COW TIPPING AFTER THE APOCALYPSE
CORN HUSKING AFTER THE APOCALYPSE

THE WARDEN SERIES
SUCCESSORS
RIVALS
LOVERS AND LIARS
BAD BLOOD
TENANTS AND TYRANTS
THE RING BEARER
GODS AND MONSTERS
BEASTS AND BURDENS
MAGIC AND MAYHEM
FORK IN THE ROAD
DETAILS AND DEADLINES

Destiny Reclaimed

Felicia Jedlicka

BABY BLUES

I dropped the third blue-tinted lollipop to the counter and stared at it. The congealed candy slapped against the stainless steel and my irritation for its unprecedented color change rose. I looked at Rayne sitting in the seat next to me and expressed my disappointment in him with a jaw-cocked scowl.

He was by far the most beautiful man I'd ever encountered. It was as if someone had crossed a burly mountain man with an upscale pretty-boy model. The blend of the two gave him a robust physique, but with the benefit of a chiseled jaw line and fantastic hair.

His dark auburn locks were a little long and, as of late, he had been dragging them back with an extra dose of hair gel. However, that still left little tufts of curled hair peeking around his ears and down the back of his neck. His narrow sage-green eyes and thick eyebrows made him look menacing. Not to mention sexy as hell.

I hadn't thought about our age difference, but I assumed, over time, I would notice the fine lines around his eyes and mouth a little more. Besides nearly a decade between our bodily age, Rayne had spent nearly a decade in a hypersleep coma. I had waited a long time for my Sleeping Beauty to wake up and I was looking forward to, once and for all, living happily ever after with him. Of course, that was before I'd realized he was a lying jerk-face.

As I continued to fantasize about stuffing lollipops down his throat, I noticed a cold ire drowning out the shock on his face. It wasn't until his eyes reached a brazen simmer that I realized he wasn't disappointed with the positive pregnancy result, but furious.

I narrowed my glare at him, questioning the audacity he had to be mad at me. After all, *he* was the one who'd told me he was sterile. Had I known he was still packing fertile ammunition, I would've taken far more precautions to protect myself from an inconvenient pregnancy.

Not that I was entirely against children. In fact, after meeting my sister, I had considered starting a family of my own someday. Unfortunately, with my father's people ever so vigilant of my DNA potential, I was reluctant to partake in that particular white-picket-fence scenario.

I opened my mouth to chastise Rayne for his selfish arrogance, but a muffled *clunk* drew my attention away from him. Ayil and Terrin were in the freezer compartment, reassigning my egglettes with new untraceable names. The work had apparently resulted in a dispute because Terrin had wrapped his hand around Ayil's neck and pressed him against the glass door.

"Son of a bitch," I grumbled and rushed over to break them up. I slid back the freezer door, but it did nothing to alleviate Ayil's elevated position. Terrin barely flinched at having to take on Ayil's full weight with one hand.

My former bodyguard was a 6-foot gattaw—a race referenced many times in human folklore as the "crocodile bulls." Their leathery, pebbled, avocado skin made them look reptilian, but they were technically humanoid. The two black horns that grew from their foreheads earned them the "bull" moniker, but it was their strength that had provoked my ancestors to enslave their race for labor—an intrepid feat that had barely lasted a decade since the gattaw, though loyal and honorable to a fault, were not above violence when provoked.

"What the hell are you doing?" I asked Terrin.

"Proving a point," Terrin said simply. He wasn't angry so much as frustrated with the young man gripped in his taloned fingers. He was accustomed to being a leader and, as such, did not like his orders being questioned by someone he could crush with his bare hands.

I looked at Ayil to discern if he was turning blue yet. His toffee skin was turning red, but so far, Terrin was not creating a deficit in his airway. This was just Terrin's way of flexing his muscles—and the inevitable result of their increasingly tenuous relationship.

Ayil had been working as a slave prostitute when I met him. The guy who'd owned him was a hardcore asshole who had dominated him for years. The abuse left Ayil sensitive to overbearing men. Though working as my dedicated cabin boy had put some much-needed meat on his bones, Ayil was still no match for Terrin. As such, his only defense was juvenile defiance. Terrin prided himself on his civil authority, but even a buzzing fly will piss someone off, eventually. Now the fly was finally getting swatted.

"Let him go," I demanded.

"Not until he understands who is in charge."

"Kit, would you tell this asshole," Ayil rasped under his grip, "that this is only going to make me hard." Ayil released his grip on Terrin's wrist to grab his crotch.

Terrin let out a scoffing hiss and dropped Ayil to the floor of the lab. "Must you be so distasteful?" He stomped out of the freezer while I assisted Ayil to his feet.

Ayil coughed and turned his attention to me. The satisfied smirk on his face told me he knew very well who was in charge, and he had figured out how to push his buttons. I did my best to contain my smile, but Ayil always had a way of making me see the funny side of life.

"Was it you?" Rayne asked from behind me. Before I could respond, or even see who he was talking to, he shoved past me and grabbed hold of Ayil. He pushed him back against the opposing side of the glass freezer door, twisting his shirt up into his neck. "How long has this been going on?"

"What the shit, man?" Ayil squawked as he tried to maneuver out of his grip.

"Rayne, leave him alone." I pressed in behind him, trying to pull his shoulder back. He released one hand and shoved me back. The forceful push sent me wheeling, nearly ready to topple to the ground. Terrin caught me around the waist and helped me secure my footing.

"What's going on?" Terrin asked.

"I have no freaking clue," I said.

"Bullshit!" Rayne looked back at me; his contemptuous glare made my heart seize. "How could you do this to me? I came back for you! And you..." Rayne turned his attention back to Ayil, baring his teeth in a wretched grimace. "I saved you—and your son! And this is how you repay me? By sleeping with my wife?"

Ayil's mouth dropped. His eyes flickered over Rayne, growing wide with the same shock I was feeling. He looked back at me with baseless guilt on his face. He had no idea what had prompted this accusation, but he was certain he had done something to warrant it. Mortified, he accepted his punishment before he even raised a defense.

"Ayil and I are not sleeping together." I tried to pull Rayne's grip off my friend. He reached around to shove me again, but Terrin grabbed his arm. Rayne stared at him, debating his options—so few as they were with Terrin's loyalty on my side. All four of us stood there tangled up in each other's arms, exchanging glances, and trying to decide who was right and who was gonna get punched in the face.

Terrin was the first to move. He reached around and pulled Rayne's fist away from Ayil's chin. It was a rather mercurial character shift since only moments ago, he had been instigating the violence. "If we can't discuss this like friends, then at least we should argue like gentlemen."

To my surprise, Rayne released his grip on Ayil. He didn't retaliate against Terrin's presumption of control. However, as he moved away, Rayne cuffed my shoulder with his.

"I can't believe you're continuing with this machination," I said, following him. "You know damn well I didn't sleep with Ayil."

Rayne whipped around and threw a finger in my face. "You damn well slept with somebody!"

"Yeah, you, you idiot! If I had known you were lying out of your ass, we wouldn't be in this situation."

"What situation are we in, exactly?" Terrin asked.

Rayne stomped over to the workstation we had been sitting at and scooped up the blue lollipops. "This is the situation we're in." He waved the candy for all of us to see. "Now which one of you is responsible for this?" He narrowed his accusing eyes at Terrin. "Is my baby going to be green?"

"Baby!" Ayil jumped to my side and looked at my stomach as if it might balloon before his very eyes. "You're pregnant?"

I motioned to the nefarious blue lollipops. "Apparently."

"Since when?" he asked.

"Knowledge wise? Since about two minutes ago."

"You haven't answered my question, Terrin." Rayne approached the gattaw, persisting to interrogate him, even though his suspicions were outlandish. I had learned early in my puppy-love stage that Terrin and I were not meant to be a couple. *Biologically incompatible*, I believe the phrase was.

Terrin calmly turned his attention to the irrational man before him. Rayne was tense and ready for a fight. Though I was certain Terrin would have no trouble thwarting a physical attack, Rayne was likely carrying a few knives on him. And Rayne was lethal with a blade.

"Did you sleep with her?" Rayne whispered.

Terrin's normally implacable expression gave way to a small conspiratorial smile. "Since Mallory is clearly still alive, and not without the function of her reproductive system, I think it's clear I did not sleep with your wife."

"There are other ways," Rayne said with a low, rumbling voice.

Terrin's smile broadened and he chuckled. It was a rare treat to hear the deep resonance of his laughter, but in this situation it sounded mordant. "Indeed, but none I am interested in at present."

"At present?" Rayne queried. "What is that supposed to mean?"

"Stop this." I moved to break them apart, but my presence did little to hinder the stalemate. "Just admit it, Rayne. You lied about being sterile and now I'm pregnant."

"I did not lie!" He yelled at me with so much fury that I tucked behind Terrin. "I have been sterile all of my life. If you are pregnant, it is not by me, you traitorous bitch."

The words hit me as hard as a punch, and I was certain I would've preferred a fist in my gut over the knife in my heart. I backed away from both of them. I wanted to curl into a ball and cry, but I wouldn't give him the satisfaction. "Fine," I said with an all-encompassing surrender. "My life leaves plenty of room for odd circumstances. How it happened isn't really the issue. You obviously have no desire to be part of this and you're determined to abandon your duties. So please, don't waste my time any further."

"What are you talking about?" Rayne narrowed his eyes at me.

"Mallory," Terrin whispered. "Let's not do this here. Don't say something you will regret later."

"Whether you are the father or not, you clearly don't want to be," I said, ignoring Terrin's advice. "That is what you're saying, isn't it?" Rayne balked at the suggestion. "Just go then. Disappear again. I came after you once. I won't do it again."

I watched Rayne mulling over my suggestion. I had hurt him as much as he had hurt me, and there wasn't likely going to be a resolution anytime soon. Short of a paternity test in nine months, neither one of us was going to have proof the other was lying.

Rayne looked at the lollipops in his hand, as if he was picturing three little baby boys, perhaps one for each of my suspected and confirmed lovers. He moved back to the counter and slapped them back down. He looked at me once more, disappointment cutting through his sadness. I didn't understand how something could break so easily. One flippin' lollipop and it was anarchy.

My eyes watered as he turned to leave. I wanted to scream and beg him to stop, plead my ignorance and rationalize a thousand different ways I might have come into contact with some errant sperm, but I wasn't sure he would believe any of them now.

"Wait," Ayil chimed in. "You're not seriously going to leave?" Rayne stopped, but he didn't turn around. "This is ridiculous. Obviously, this is some misunderstanding that needs to be investigated. You'll just throw away everything we've been through because of... because of..."

"An affair?" Rayne suggested and turned to face him.

I turned from his view to wipe a tear out of my eye. "I didn't cheat on you," I whispered. "You're the only man I've ever been with."

"When you say sterile," Terrin said, "do you mean effectively sterile or completely sterile?"

Rayne shook his head. "I don't know what you call it. I just know they don't swim. They're dead in the water. Short of forcibly implanting them, they won't work."

"And you're positive this isn't something someone told you to prevent you from attaching yourself to a woman? Perhaps your uncle—"

"No!" Rayne yelled.

"Prove it," Ayil said.

"Prove what?" He glared at him.

"This is a fertilization clinic." Ayil motioned to the room. "I'm sure one of these brainiacs can figure out how to use a microscope." Ayil moved over to one of the metal shelving units and grabbed a small plastic container with a blue lid. He tossed it across the lab. Rayne caught it against his chest and looked down at it.

"You want me to give you a sample of my semen?" Ayil clicked his tongue and winked at him. "Right now? In the middle of a burglary?" He looked at me, pleading for a suspension of the threatened task.

"There's some rooms down the hall." I motioned toward the depository rooms.

He rolled the container around in his fingers for a moment. "Why don't you show me the way?"

"I wouldn't want to contaminate the sample with sperm from my various lovers," I scolded him and he frowned. "They have reading material. I'm sure you'll do fine on your own. Might as well get used to it," I murmured and perked my eyebrow at him.

He clenched his jaw and stormed out of the room. I wasn't sure what to hope for when he returned. If he was telling the truth, then I had a lot of questions about where I might've come into contact with someone else's sperm—a question I didn't really want to think about, let alone find the answer to. However, if he had been lying, then I wasn't really sure how much of anything he had told me was true. After all, it wasn't the first time he had lied to me about his past.

Motility

Rayne returned to the lab a good deal more relaxed than when he had left. His private tryst had no doubt put a damper on his aggression. He slapped the plastic cup down on the counter next to a microscope and sat down in one of the twirly chairs. "I bet you couldn't wait to get your hands on it. Dig in, baby."

I looked at Ayil and motioned to the container. He grimaced and backed away. "Don't look at me. I came up with the idea. One of you guys can do the scientific shit."

Terrin cleared his throat and moved over to the microscope. He took a sample of Rayne's donation with a cotton applicator and dabbed it on a glass slide. He slipped it under the lens and fiddled around with the dials, trying to get a proper view on the screen.

I moved around to see the evidence for myself. Rayne scooted up behind me and wrapped an arm around my waist. I tried to pry his fingers off of me, but he pulled himself in behind me, bracing me to his chest. "You missed some good fun."

I shrugged. "I'm sure the magazines were very stimulating."

He pushed his face closer to my ear. "I didn't need the magazines. I just pictured you," he whispered.

"Stop flirting with me," I whispered back. "After what you said, your balls should be black and blue, let alone blue."

"I wasn't lying to you. I am sterile."

"Yes, you are," Terrin announced as he drew back from the microscope and turned the view screen to display the evidence.

I frowned as I looked at the magnified solution, populated with tiny little translucent spots. I wasn't sure I understood the specifics of conception beyond sperm plus egg equals 20 years of financial obligation. However, as I looked a little longer, I noticed the normally spry DNA carriers were completely immobile. In addition to that, the little buggers lacked their telltale tails. Without it, they were dead in the water. Therefore, just as Rayne said, short of injecting them directly into an egg, they couldn't produce a child.

Rayne's arms went slack and dropped away from me. His efforts towards making up with me were being put on hold. I moved away from him and sat down in one of the twirly chairs on the opposite side of the scope. I looked to Terrin. "I didn't," I whispered. "I swear to God." I knew I couldn't convince Rayne, but I needed *someone* to believe me.

He nodded. "I know, but of course, that still leaves us with a questionable paternity."

"Are you a sleepwalker?" Ayil asked. We all looked at him with perturbed expressions. "I'm just saying... Sometimes I have pretty vivid dreams. Maybe you took a ride on the night train." He motioned to his crotch.

"As much as I would like to dismiss Ayil's theory outright," Terrin said, "it is possible we are entertaining an abnormal conception." Terrin crossed his arms and moved back to the microscope. "I'm going to need another sample."

Rayne laughed. "Oh boy. I don't know how it works in your world, Terrin, but on the human end of things, once the shades are drawn, there's no getting them open again until morning—or at least a couple hours."

"That's very disappointing for you, but that's not what I mean." Terrin looked at me. "I need a sample from Mallory."

I chuckled. "A sample of what?"

"Your lubrication."

I felt my face instantly blush. "You want my…"

"Vaginal discharge," he specified, adding more rouge to my cheeks.

"Can't I just spit on it?"

"I'm afraid not. And it needs to be fresh."

"What does that mean?" I squawked.

"It means," Rayne said from across the microscope, "that you might want to peruse those magazines, so you're good and wet before you take your sample."

Ayil stepped up behind me and offered me a small plastic container with the blue lid, like the one he had given to Rayne. I stared at the over-sized container with wide eyes. "Give me that," Terrin chastised him and handed me a set of cotton swabs. "Bring it back quickly. If it dries, it's useless."

I sighed and slumped over, giving in to the embarrassment. I slipped off my seat and made the short journey down the hall.

Virility

I cringed as I looked over the pornographic material in the room. Most of it was designed to appeal to male desires. I was surrounded by images of animalistic fornication that not only demeaned women, but belittled the reputation of the men who were forced to maintain the illusion that they liked it. I wasn't entirely clear on what men liked or didn't like, but I was quite certain the images displayed in magazines preyed exclusively on the enthusiasm for predacious sexual scenarios, rather than the actual enjoyment of it.

I glanced at the lewd pictures posted on the walls. There were a number of species on display. They depicted the same graphic positions as the human material. I examined the structural detail of the abnormal female bodies before me. Similar to my own, and yet different enough in the details to make inter-species relationships nearly impossible.

"Is that working for you?" Rayne's voice made me jump. I turned around and found him standing in the door.

"What are you doing?"

"Checking on you." He came in and shut the door behind him. "I remembered there weren't a lot of women-friendly magazines. At least not of the heterosexual variety." He took a seat in the chair I had been sitting on. The hard plastic was uncomfortable, but given the assignment of the room, it was appropriate.

"So." I shrugged and leaned against the wall. "I can manage on my own."

He smiled. "Why didn't you believe me? About being sterile."

"*You* don't believe *me*."

"I'm starting to." He took a breath and leaned over his knees. "I'm sorry about what I said. I know I must have hurt your feelings pretty good if you're willing to kick me out of your life entirely."

"I don't want to kick you out of my life, but I meant what I said. If I'm pregnant and you don't want to be a part of this—"

"It was never my decision to be sterile," he snapped and stood up. "I don't entirely understand what's going on here, but if you're sincere about your loyalty to me, then, of course, I want to be a part of this."

"Even if the baby isn't yours?"

He moved forward and wrapped his arms around me. "As long as *you* are mine, that's all that matters to me. I'm certainly not going to leave you to raise a child by yourself."

"I'm not sure if you're being noble by suggesting I couldn't do it." He chuckled and kissed my forehead. He reached down and unsnapped my pants. "What are you doing?"

"I'm going to get a sample brewing for you." He smirked as he dipped his hands past my underwear and manipulated my desires.

I gasped and leaned my head back to enjoy his offering. A thought occurred to me, and I frowned. "You're going to get me all worked up and then leave, aren't you?"

He leaned in close to my ear and whispered seductively. "Oh, yes, I am."

Fertility

Despite Rayne's declaration to leave me high and... wet, he actually finished me off twice over before running my collected lubricant samples back to the lab. I shuffled in shortly after the delivery, feeling a little embarrassed but altogether relaxed. Ayil gave me a sly smile as I tucked my hands in my pockets and tried to look innocuous. I glanced at Rayne and saw a mischievous smirk hiding in his eyes. He was pleased as can be to have sedated me with his lovingly brutal attentions.

"Interesting," Terrin announced and stood back from the microscope. He turned the screen for all of us to see. I moved around the long counter to observe what the slide showed.

We were once again looking at a sample of Rayne's sperm, but the frozen little dots had now unfurled tails from their bodies. They were darting through the fluid like heat-seeking missiles. Short of jumping off the slide, they were determined to get to their destination. Conception or death, and I got the feeling from the vigor in their pace that die was not an option.

"What exactly are we looking at?" Ayil asked.

"This is a sample of Rayne's ejaculate with the addition of Mallory's sample," Terrin answered. "I'm not a fertility expert, but it would seem Rayne's otherwise sterile semen has been activated by Mallory's discharge."

"Ew," Ayil added quietly as he stared at the screen.

Either because of my recent activities, or the realization that I really was pregnant, I became a little light-headed. I stumbled back from the counter and took a few cleansing breaths. "Holy crap," I said. "I'm going to have a baby."

"It would appear so," Terrin responded diplomatically. I turned and looked at him. He was thinking the same thing I was. He was thinking about the danger already involved in being me, and how adding the burden of pregnancy was like adding gasoline to an already raging fire. The risks were still the same, but how much harder would my father's people look for me when they found out I was pregnant? If they discovered the oddity of Rayne's condition, he would be put on that list right along with me. My husband, my child, and I would be the most wanted trio in the galaxy.

No Deposit

With my little egglettes safely disguised under a different name and the drama of my baby daddy behind us, we made our way out of the fertility clinic via the alley door we had originally sneaked in through. As we weaved our way through the refuse, Rayne slipped his fingers into mine and squeezed my hand. I looked up at him to smile at his affectionate gesture, but the frown and determined stare on his face told me he wasn't being romantic. Rayne's eyes had locked onto something at the end of the alley. I couldn't see past Terrin's broad shoulders to assess the risk ahead of us, but I noticed he had a firm grip on his copper sword.

"What the balls is this?" Ayil mumbled from beside Terrin. "Friends of yours?"

"Associates," Terrin answered with a degree of displeasure bleeding into his voice. He stopped midway through the alley, and we stopped with him. "What are you doing here, Sis?" Terrin asked whoever was in front of him.

I peeked around his back, desperate to get a view of whoever he had designated *sis*. I wasn't aware of Terrin having any relatives beyond his parents and, as far as I knew, his mother had already passed. Besides the tall, muscular female gattaw standing at the far end of the alley, there were eight male gattaw blocking our exit. Each of them was dressed in a long, red trench coat. The style seemed to be more of a uniform than a fashion statement. Whoever these people were, they were part of an organized group.

"I think you know exactly why I'm here, Terrin." She turned her sinister gaze on me. "Give me the girl and I'll let the other two live."

Rayne released my hand and pulled a pair of knives from behind his back.

"You shouldn't have come here," Terrin said. "I told you not to come after her."

"You told me a lot of things, and then you betrayed us."

"I didn't betray you. I had obligations."

"Obligations that put a human ahead of your people."

"Obligations to a friend."

"And what am I, Terrin?"

"That depends on why you're here."

The woman smiled broadly, exposing her ample canines and dark gums. It looked more like a snarl, and the shift in Terrin's stance confirmed my suspicions. "You may have obligations to her mother, but I have obligations to her father." She drew her copper sword and her crew followed her lead.

Terrin dragged his sword from its sheath. "Get her out of here," he said, not taking his eyes off the woman. "Ayil," he specified.

Ayil looked back at me and then at the knives in Rayne's hands. There were only two people in our group capable of fighting a gattaw. Unfortunately, we were on the losing end of that character trait.

Ayil slipped past Rayne, grabbed my arm, and pulled me deeper into the alley. The only way out was the way we had come—which we had already locked behind us—or one of the other random doors leading into the alleyway. Ayil chose one of them, but it was locked.

"Shit." He tugged me down to the next one, but it was also locked.

A series of war cries took my attention back to the battle. The men were storming into a fight. Terrin slashed through three of them, knocking each attacker to the side. Rayne took his opportunities, one at a time, to bury his blades into their chests and necks as they faltered. Terrin fought the next two men, who were tactically more prepared. Splitting his attention between the duo, Terrin narrowly avoided their slashing swords. Rayne struggled with another who was dodging his deadly blows with ease. While they were occupied, the remaining two gattaw slipped past their defensive line and headed straight for us.

"Go!" Ayil shoved me forward toward the wall.

"Where?" I stared at the door-less brick wall.

"Here!" Ayil lifted a metal hatch at my waist. It was big enough to fit through, but it certainly wasn't designed for people. Before I could question the smell coming from inside Ayil's foot shoved me forward.

I tumbled into the darkness. My hands squeaked on the surrounding metal as I tried to slow my accelerating descent. Ayil's echoing howl signaled he had joined me in the chute.

My palm grazed something wet and I lost all my potential for traction. I careened down the progressively slimier path until I ejected into open air. For a moment, I was flying, but gravity swiftly took hold and I was falling.

I landed on my back with an audible *squelch*. The trash pile beneath me exuded freshly squeezed liquid in response to my body pressure. I was drenched down to my underwear in God knows what. The sickening smell of rotting food entered my nose, threatening to activate my gag reflex.

I struggled to find purchase on the unstable heap. I could barely roll, let alone stand up. Ayil's final yowl alerted me to his arrival. He landed on top of me, stalling my mobility and pressing me deeper into the garbage sludge.

"Oh!" Ayil groaned on top of me. "What the hell is this?"

"I think we came down a garbage chute," I answered.

"No, I mean specifically. What the hell is *this*?" He raised one of his hands, showing me the bluish slime hanging from it. He whipped his hand, trying to fling the sticky blob off. The viscous material stretched like a rubber band and attached itself to the rim of the over-sized bin we were lying in. He yanked back on it to release himself from the incessant booger, but the material only stretched, maintaining a connection with him as well as the bin. "Dammit," he protested.

I looked around the gigantic room. We were several floors beneath the alley in what looked to be a disposal warehouse. The chute we had come from was one of many feeding into the area. Each had their own designated container. I could only surmise from the facility's size that it accommodated for the garbage of several blocks of the city above.

There was a clanking sound above us, and we both looked up to the chute that supplied our container. The metal tube shuddered as if a heavy deposit was coming down it.

Ayil looked back at me, fearful but determined. "Come on!" He leaped to his feet, far more agile in the refuse than me. He grabbed my hand, inconsiderately adding his blue goo to my already filthy body. With a good deal of effort, he helped pry me upright. "Oh, crap." He stared at something behind me.

I looked over my shoulder to see what his concern was. A stringy trail of gummy blue tendrils led from my back to the pile of garbage I had just extracted myself from. I wasn't sure if this was a problem or not, but I still gave Ayil a worried look. He shook his head and pulled me forward. Whatever concerns we had about the sticky substance, it was a very distant second to our concerns about the gattaw who crashed down in the bin behind us.

We flopped over the rim of the container and landed on the concrete below. Ayil dropped my hand and we sprinted away from our pursuers. The blue snot waggled between our hands, refusing to release either of us from its sticky embrace. I glanced back as we distanced the bin, but even with several yards between me and the origin of the blue goo, there were still sticky threads stretching out behind me. A trail of breadcrumbs and then some.

"Where the hell is the door?" Ayil hissed as we maneuvered between another set of bins.

"It's probably an automated facility. The only way out is how the garbage gets out."

"And how is that?"

I scanned the room for a gigantic machine capable of accommodating the sizable bins that would be inserted into it. "There." I pointed to the far corner of the room, where I saw a massive piece of machinery that towered nearly to the ceiling. Much as I suspected, it was a trash compactor on an industrial scale. We ran toward it, dodging the occasional overflow of garbage—not that we could stink any more than we already did.

Footsteps pounded on the concrete behind us. The gattaw had to be following my interminable trail of blue goo, but there was nothing I could do to stop it. If it had hung on this long, the substance wasn't likely to release me anytime soon.

We reached the compactor and Ayil searched for an exit. I, on the other hand, slowed to a complete stop, as if someone had put my brakes on. I looked back and found my blue webbing had compacted into several tight cords. It was no longer a sticky matrix, but rather several taut rubber bands about to snap.

The sound of metal squeaked from the other side of the machine as something shifted into place. "There's a loading elevator." Ayil looked back at me, surprised by my lagging effort to keep up with him. "Kit, move your ass!" he yelled.

"I'm trying!" I shouted, fighting against the tension behind me with the weight of my body. I could feel the goo tugging on my skin. Whatever this substance was, it had reached its limit, and short of soaking myself in solvent—or losing a layer of skin—I was stuck.

"Look out!" Ayil ran toward me, but it was too late. A copper blade landed against my neck. "Leave her alone." Ayil didn't stop his attack until the second gattaw arrived and blocked his path to me.

"Don't be stupid, boy," the gattaw holding me hostage said. "We only want the girl. There is no need for bloodshed."

"No need, but it's probably gonna happen." Ayil's beautiful brown eyes flickered with sinister intent. He wasn't half as strong as either of the men, but that wouldn't stop him from stepping up to the challenge.

I shook my head, begging him not to hurt himself for my sake and especially not for the sake of his ego. He dipped his brow in disappointment, but he refrained from attacking. "Why are you doing this?" I asked. Despite the threat of the blade against my neck, I shifted my position. The gattaw naturally assumed I was struggling and tightened his grip on my shoulder. What he didn't understand was that I was using all of my strength to stay still. The tugging sensation on my back was intensifying.

"We have an obligation to uphold," my captor said.

"You know they want me dead, don't you?"

"They only want you dead because they can't catch you. If it weren't for Terrin's feeble heart, we would've had you long ago."

"And you think better late than never is going to win you a prize?" I grounded out through clenched teeth as I exerted myself to maintain my stable position.

"We will deliver you as promised. What they do with you after that is up to them."

"And here I thought gattaw were a proud sort."

"Our pride lies in our duty, not infatuation." The gattaw holding me turned his gaze down on me. I looked up at him, more than a little perturbed by his interpretation of Terrin's devotion to me.

"Love doesn't make you feeble, you know. It makes you—" The material holding me went from rigid to retractile in an instant. My feet flew out from beneath me and I launched backward like a parachute had just opened behind me. My captor stumbled after me, but he had no chance of keeping up with my forceful reversal.

I was happy to rid myself of the exigent threat to my body. However, I was increasingly less appreciative of my impromptu escape when I discovered that my reverse path was going to traverse several directional changes at high velocity.

I grunted and yelped as my body collided with nearly every container we had passed on our way through the facility. I tucked myself into a ball and relaxed my muscles, allowing myself to ricochet off the metal trash bins with a little more ease. After a few more tinny *thunks*, I slid across the open concrete floor, slowing to a stop next to the bin I had originally crawled out of.

I half expected my body to retract up the side of it and splotch back into the garbage, but the force pulling on my back had stopped. It was replaced by a new tension tugging on my hand. I examined the fibers straining at their maximum reach all the way back to their origin—Ayil's hand. I was once again at the end of a rubber band.

"No, no, no, no, no, no, no," I whined as I braced my feet on the concrete, trying to prevent another trip on the blue-goo-train. My shoes slipped and I groaned, dreading the next round of bruises.

I yipped as the connection reached its full capacity and shot me forward. Though the bond was smaller, it had no trouble dragging me over the floor. I hit a patch of garbage and the slippery mess left me skiing through the basement. I bounced my feet off the containers as I went by, maintaining a more bipedal trajectory this time, and saving myself from a great deal of pain.

Halfway through my return trip, I met up with the gattaw who had been holding me captive. As unprepared as he had been for my initial exit, he was even less prepared for my return. A well-timed kick upon passing slammed him into a garbage bin and knocked his sword out of his hand.

When I arrived back at the compactor, I found Ayil narrowly avoiding the slashing sword of his opponent. Without a pistol to balance the fight, the gattaw was likely just toying with him.

Ayil's eyes widened as I slid toward them both at tremendous speed, drawn to the last thing he had shared our bluish goo with. He jumped clear of my collision course, leaving me with only one landing pad. I slammed into the back of his opponent. The six-foot mound of muscle and bone felt about as good as the walls of iron I had already run into. I wasn't sure I could do much damage to him, but the sudden hit to his back was enough to unsteady him. I wrapped my legs around him, holding myself in place before the next round of live-action Pong could begin.

While he was still distracted, Ayil kicked the short sword from the gattaw's hand. He snagged it from the floor and stood before the man, eyes flaring with anger I rarely saw from him. Still struggling with his added appendage—me—the gattaw couldn't defend against Ayil's attack.

The blade went into his lower abdomen. A painful wound, but possibly a merciful one if he could survive long enough to get medical help. He careened forward, cradling his stomach.

The goo on my back started to seize and tighten again. I pawed at the gattaw's red trench coat, trying to maintain my position, but my fingers lost grip. My legs were still latched around his waist, but that wouldn't last long either.

Before I could be ripped away again, the connection snapped. I flopped down on top of the moaning gattaw. I looked back and saw that Ayil had severed my blue rubber band with the short sword.

He helped me up and we ran to the loading elevator. We rode it back up to the ground level, where we had left Rayne and Terrin.

No Return

Ayil and I stepped out of the elevator and made our way out of the alley. We immediately took a turn and started back toward our shuttle. With any luck Rayne and Terrin were already there waiting for us. As clever as we had been up to that point, we hadn't even realized we were only a block away from where we had started.

Green heads in red trench coats spilled out of the alley ahead of us. Ayil cursed and veered immediately to his left, pulling me along with him. We shuffled across the street between stilled cars that were waiting for the traffic light to change.

"Did they see us?" Ayil asked.

I peeked over his shoulder, but no one was watching us. They were far too interested in their recent captive. "Rayne," I gasped and pushed against Ayil's herding arm.

"Don't," he said and pushed me against the wall of the building across the street from them. He braced himself in front of me, blocking both our faces from any onlookers.

Rayne struggled against the two gattaw dragging him from the alley. He had taken more than a few punches, but I suspected the blood covering his shirt was not his own. One of the gattaw leaned over to say something to him. He must not have liked what he had to say because his response was to headbutt him. The gattaw stumbled back, holding his nose. After he recovered, he kicked Rayne in the stomach, causing him to cough and sputter. I bit my lip, trying not to cry out his name or something just as melodramatic.

"You can't help them. You know you can't," Ayil warned me.

I saw more movement in the alley, and I watched two more gattaw arriving with their second captive. Bloody and beaten, Terrin sagged in the men's arms as they dragged him along. I didn't even realize I was moving forward until Ayil pressed his hand into my chest, forcing me back against the wall. He shook his head.

I was surprised to see Terrin had taken such a beating. He had no doubt put up a good fight, but with the attackers sharing his muscular advantage, he hadn't had a chance. Adding to that the resentment his former partners must have felt, he was probably lucky to be alive.

"Where is she?" I scarcely heard the female gattaw over the din of the mobilized traffic.

"How the fuck should I know?" Rayne spat at her feet. "Long gone, hopefully."

"Where's your shuttle?"

"Go fuck yourself, you gat bitch!" he yelled at her.

"If you're not useful, then you're expendable." She raised her copper sword above her head and held it a moment for Rayne's eyes to focus in on the threat. I expected her to say something about cooperation, or compliance, but the sword careened down at his chest without further monologue.

"No!" I screamed, heedless of my safety, or Ayil's.

Rayne's eyes shot across the street, pinpointing my struggle in Ayil's lassoed arms. The female gattaw turned and saw me as well. She looked positively dumbfounded.

As stupidity goes, this would have gone down as one of my record-holding moments. After such an effort was made to assist my escape, I had only made it forty feet away. My only saving grace was the green light returning the traffic between us to its usual break-neck speed.

The leader lowered her sword and sauntered to the edge of the busy street. She looked across the expanse of passing vehicles between us. The rushing rapids of the heavy metal river were impassable... for now.

"Release them and I'll go with you," I yelled across to her. "Voluntarily."

The woman looked at me with a certain curiosity. I was no doubt a spectacle to her, risking myself for something as stupid as love.

"What the hell are you doing?" Ayil screeched in my ear.

"She was about to kill him," I explained, since he hadn't technically seen the threat from his angle.

"And now she'll kill all of us," he hissed and gripped me tighter around the waist, as if he might simply pick me up and carry me down the street to safety.

"I'll make you a deal," the female gattaw hollered across the street. "I'll let you save one of them."

"No, let them both go."

The woman closed her eyes and took a slow breath. "I am not your childhood playmate, Mallory. You can't just bat your eyes and get your way. Your guard dog has already killed two of my men. Someone is going to have to pay for that. I'm willing to settle for one, but if you don't cooperate, I will kill them both right along with your sidekick there."

"Sidekick?" Ayil mumbled and stood up a little straighter beside me.

"So, which one is it going to be? Who do you want to live?"

"You would really kill your own brother?" I asked.

"Brother?" She laughed. "Terrin is not my brother."

"He called you Sis."

"Short for Sicily. I assure you, my relationship with Terrin is definitely not familial."

I frowned, losing my only hope that Terrin might be safe with this woman. I gulped and looked at Rayne. He was furious I was trying to be the hero, but I couldn't stand the idea of losing him, even though I was only reversing that pain onto him. Suddenly, my self-sacrifice was a little more self than sacrifice.

The light down the street turned red, and the cars bunched up in front of us, opening our brimming mechanical barrier for a pedestrian crossing. "Rayne. I choose Rayne. Release him, and I'll come over to you."

"Why don't you both cross at the same time?" She waved her finger and her men dragged Rayne to the edge of the street with her. She did the same to the others and they brought Terrin forward as well. She pulled up his heavy head by his horns and pressed her copper sword against his neck. "Assuming everyone makes it across the street appropriately, I won't be forced to make you watch your bodyguard die."

I winced and took a failed step forward. Ayil's grip wouldn't cease. I looked back and saw him exchanging silent plots with my husband. I could almost see the plan forming between them. They weren't going to let me go. They were going to risk their lives anyway and get Terrin killed.

It was damned noble. It really was. And I appreciated it. I mean, after all, I was risking my life for them. It didn't surprise me that they would un-save their lives to re-save me, but at some point, somebody had to get us out of this situation.

The light changed to green and the cars crept forward. Every vehicle accelerated before the path in front of them had cleared. With every honk, they demanded the laws of physics to change.

Ayil grabbed my arm, opened the door to a nearby taxi, shoved me inside, and toppled in behind me. "Go, go, go," he yelled at the driver.

"Ayil!" I screamed, and shoved him off me. "Stop!" I yelled out the back window as the cab took off. The cab immediately jolted to a stop, and I flopped against the back of the passenger seat.

"No, go!" Ayil insisted.

The driver took off again, with urgent speed. "Stop, stop, stop!" I bellowed, and the vehicle lurched to a stop. I reached for the door, but it was still locked since the driver was not in a parked position. I took the next best option, and climbed through the open sunroof.

"Dammit, Kit!" Ayil grabbed me around the waist and yanked me back down. "Why do you have to make it so hard to save you?"

"Funny, I was thinking the same thing about you," I grunted and pulled myself back up, despite the weight of his body hanging around my waist.

He gave up pulling and joined me in the confined rectangle of the sunroof. "Look at me! Terrin would not want you to sacrifice yourself for him. Neither would Rayne. Just come with me."

"What's the point then?" I grimaced as I tried to breathed against the pressure of our bodies squished into the hole. "Don't you see? You three idiots are the only reason I've made it this far. I need you, but you guys don't need me."

Ayil frowned and dipped his brow. "Fuck you, Kit." I blinked at him. "You realize if you give yourself up now, we'll just have to turn around and save you again?"

I shrugged and nodded. "If you're not too busy. That would be nice."

Ayil glanced down the street where Rayne and Terrin were still primed for their death sentence. "Well, I guess I'm dead either way."

Ayil shifted out of the way, allowing me the space I needed to climb out of the cab. He insisted the driver hold his position. I toppled down to the street where a line of cars had built up behind us. Adding to the honking, there were several shaking fists and more than a few shouted curse words.

I walked back on the sidewalk until I was in line for the exchange. The light turned red and the cars bunched up again. I stepped out into the stilled traffic and meandered through the vehicles. On the other side, Rayne was instructed to do the same with a rough poke in the back.

I watched him inch his way across the street, watching my every move as we approached each other. I could see the tension building in his eyes, knitting his brow. I looked to Sicily and the blade she had pressed up against Terrin's neck. A slight cut was already forming from the pressure she held it with. I shook my head at Rayne, silently begging him not to do anything to jeopardize Terrin's life. His jaw clenched, frustrated by my undisciplined reverence for life.

When I reached the other side, two of Sicily's men grabbed me and tethered my arms against their chests. She moved over to me, taking in my features like a cannibal's menu.

"Sicily!" Rayne yelled from across the street. The cars began to move again, minus the holdup of the faithful taxi driver. "If you harm her in any way, your death will not be quick."

"You mean like this?" Sicily's hand whipped across my face. I could feel the heat of the slap, followed by the sting of her generous nails, which practically qualified as claws. "You shouldn't be making threats you can't back up."

When my vision cleared, I looked across the street at Rayne. The angry defiance I expected to see had disappeared. Something cool, calm, and creepy had taken hold of him. I wasn't sure if Sicily knew what my husband was capable of, but I certainly did. She was very fortunate to be on the opposite side of the street from him.

Rayne turned his attention to me. His reprimanding irritation clouded the sympathy he should have had for my situation. I was supposed to be long gone, having fled to the safety of our ship. Unfortunately, I was now in the clutches of Terrin's outraged former employees, about to be dragged off—hopefully alive—to my father's people. Perhaps it was a good thing I was on the opposite side of the street as well.

His Ex

A rather crowded car ride later and we arrived at Sicily's shuttle. Strapped in painfully tight, the trip out of the atmosphere was a little bumpier than I had expected. I could see Terrin belted in across from me, still unconscious and breathing shallowly. The only good thing about the situation was that his throat was still intact.

After docking with the main ship, the men gruffly unbuckled Terrin and dragged him away. "Don't hurt him," I pleaded with Sicily as she passed by. She paused and looked at me. One of her men moved to undo my straps, but she waved him away and attended to me by herself.

I noted her bulbous, elongated nails as she unfastened my safety restraints. She had painted them bright copper to match her sword. She offered me her hand to assist my rise, and I reluctantly accepted, if only to keep up the appearance of cooperation. "You really do care for him, don't you?" she asked.

I debated my options, but there wasn't much point in hiding my connection to Terrin. I had known him since I was young, something I was sure his coworkers were aware of when they took their positions to help hunt me down.

I imagined there wasn't much about my life they weren't aware of. "With all of my heart."

She smiled introspectively and led me out of the shuttle. As I followed her into the main bay, I was once again awestruck by the size of the ship. It was an odd choice of vessel for bounty hunting, since speed was a primary concern. However, since one perk of the career field was acquiring the vehicles of their detainees, it was often necessary to have additional storage space. "I was always under the impression you had a bit of a crush on Terrin," Sicily began to monologue ahead of me. "It doesn't surprise me. Our species always did attract a certain *type*." She glanced back at me, making sure I had heard her.

"And what *type* is that?" I asked.

"The type that thinks they can circumvent their human physiology." She chuckled at her joke. "What about you, Mallory? Did you think your body could withstand a male gattaw?"

I bit my cheek, stifling the insults my *type* liked to brandish when bitches got in their face. Rather than getting into a yelling match with a woman I desperately needed to suck up to, I took the conversation in a more civil direction. "It was never about that," I admitted to her. "My fantasies of Terrin in those days were childish. I dreamed of castles and white knights, dancing and stolen kisses. It was never about sex. He was my first real friend," I said wistfully. Even as the words left my mouth, I considered how true they were. And how pathetic. And quite possibly how delusional.

"And what about now?" Sicily asked. "Are your fantasies still about holding Terrin's hand, or have they advanced to other body parts?" Sicily smirked over her shoulder at me. I glared at her despite having opened the can of worms on this conversation. "Don't worry, you're not the only woman to fall in love with an unattainable man. Even I have fallen victim to that trap. The burden of a gender more than a species, I think."

I nodded in agreement. "What's it like?" I asked, drawing a little closer to her, so she didn't have to keep looking back at me.

"What's what like?" she asked as we turned into a narrow corridor.

I looked around in case somebody was following us. "Sex—I mean for you. For a female gattaw."

Sicily snorted. "Don't you think we've had enough girl talk for now?"

"Is it painful?" I persisted.

"You really want to know?"

"The only gattaw I have ever interacted with was Terrin. We kind of stopped the sex education course at *incompatible*."

She smiled. "Yes, I imagine that does put a damper on one's curiosity."

"So, just between us girls..." I prodded further.

"No, it doesn't hurt. Actually, I think you would describe it as ticklish." She stopped at one of the doors in the corridor and punched a number into the keypad beside it. The door slid open and I looked inside. It was apparently my containment cell. Better than a coffin, but not by much. "It's too bad you'll never have an opportunity to experience Terrin." She leaned on the door, crossing her arms as she looked me over. "He really is an exquisite lover. I'm not sure if you knew this about gattaw, but it's not uncommon for a male to have several wives. It's the only way to ensure any of them get any sleep. And Terrin is no exception." She giggled, thoroughly pleased with her taunting.

"You had a relationship with him, then?" I asked. She nodded. "Does that mean you won't hurt him?"

She considered that for a moment. "I'll keep him alive for leverage. You obviously won't misbehave if you know his life is on the line." I looked to my feet, ashamed that I had just handed her my resume of weaknesses. "However, if you should somehow flee captivity, I will kill him." She motioned to my quarters.

I frowned and stepped inside the dimly lit room. I turned back and looked at her. "Was he the unattainable man for you too?" I asked. Sicily stiffened, as if she realized she had given away a secret she hadn't intended to. "Since you had his bed, it must have been his heart he wouldn't give you." Sicily's mouth twisted in anger. "It's too bad you'll never have the opportunity to experience Terrin's true affection."

"Careful, Princess, I'm sure there are plenty of my men in my employ willing to show you exactly what a gattaw sex life has to offer you."

I tipped my head in thought. "It must really piss you off that he chose my company over your pussy." My face erupted in pain. I stumbled back and held my throbbing mouth. It occurred to me that I had never been punched in the face before. I had earned myself a slap on multiple occasions, but this was my first punch.

An achievement I shouldn't have claimed to be proud of and yet...

I looked back at Sicily, licking away the blood from my fat lip. "Worth it," I mumbled to her.

She yanked the door shut, placing me inside the nearly vacant cube with literally only a pot to piss in. I slumped down against the cold metallic wall and hugged my knees. I was about to relax into my boredom when a piercing siren ignited my eardrums into a frenzy. I clamped my hands over my ears, instantly regretting my success at irritating Sicily.

Phone Home

Later that day—or perhaps it was the next day—the door to my cell slid open. Since I wasn't being offered the luxury of a sleep pod, I was forced to endure the long trip home in boredom. I assumed Sicily had made it her mission to watch my slow descent into madness. Without a bed or even a decent amount of light to assist my vacant stares, my boredom was sure to make me suicidal in less than a week. Thankfully, my grasp on time was getting a little sketchy, so I didn't have to shred my shirt into a noose just yet.

I squinted against the light streaming in from the hall and tried to determine who the body frame in the door was. It was difficult to tell the difference between a female and a male gattaw to begin with, let alone in a blinding light transition.

As my eyes adjusted, I made out Sicily's face. I frowned and turned away, but she persisted in joining me in my shadowy confinement. "What now?"

"Is that any way to talk to your only visitor?" Sicily said with undue cheerfulness and stopped beside me.

I squinted up at her. "I'm not sure you count as a visitor, since you're also my captor."

"I wasn't talking about me."

I looked at the door, hoping to see Terrin step through. I waited, but no one entered. I looked back at Sicily. "Is this your idea of a joke?"

"Not at all." She bent down and I scrambled to get away from her. "Relax, I'm handing you a telecom." She reached out her hand, displaying the small rectangular screen.

I frowned at it. "Who's calling?"

"Press connect and find out." The small smile perched on her face told me she was pleased with the surprise she had in store for me.

I took the device from her and activated the screen. After a moment of reconfiguring, an image came into focus. My brow dipped, and my eyes immediately turned tearful. "Daddy?" His face seemed so much older than the last time I had seen him. His balding head was developing age spots, and he looked a little thinner.

"Mallory? Is that really you?"

"Yes, it's me." I pressed the device to my forehead, trying in vain to get closer to the image. I desperately wanted to have some physical connection with him.

"That woman... She said she has taken you captive and wants to collect on your bounty. Is that true?"

I pulled the screen back. "Yes."

"Has she hurt you?"

"No. We're practically best friends now. We have a sleepover scheduled next week."

My father's brow dipped as he looked over my image. "Mallory."

I shook my head. "Not in any way that counts." As I stared at the screen, my father's eyes glistened with tears. The guilt of all the years passed ripped my heart in two. I had missed so much time with him. I wouldn't have traded my adventures traveling in space for anything, but that didn't mean I didn't miss my family. "I'm so sorry, Daddy," I blubbered. "This is all my fault. Everything. I never meant to hurt you."

"I know. I've made my own mistakes." His eyes turned downward for a moment. "Unfortunately, we don't have the option of turning back the clock." Richard leaned into the camera. "My sweet girl, I love you so much. You know I would do anything, pay anything, give my life, to see you home safe and sound," he asked almost forcefully.

I nodded. "Yes."

"You also know there are many things beyond my control. Outside of my jurisdiction."

"Yes." My lip quivered.

"They've declared you a traitor. If you return, they will put you on trial. If convicted..." Richard glanced away from the screen, presumably at whomever was in the room with him, listening in on our conversation. When his eyes returned to me, he was no longer sad. For the first time in perhaps my entire life, I could see anger in his normally subdued expression. "You must never come back here, Mallory. The Coalition has been lying to us. All of us! They are going to kill—" The image shifted, as my father's words cut off. A second later, his face returned. "Keep away, Mallory!" he yelled. The camera shifted to the ceiling, then to the floor where several pairs of boots and shoes were dancing about, no doubt wrestling for the telecom. "It's all a lie!"

I heard a *thunk* and the screen dropped to the floor, showing the red Persian rug in my father's study and a limp arm in the distance.

"Daddy?" I yelled at the screen. "Daddy!" The image shifted as someone picked up the device. I spotted a gattaw in the background before it shifted onto a new face, or perhaps in this case an old one. "Chancellor?"

Chancellor Agate was the man behind the man behind the Coalition. My father may have been voted in by the people, but as with most political positions, there were always men in the shadows, pulling strings with money and connections. Agate was one such man.

He was a little younger than my father, with slicked back reddish-blond hair and sage-green eyes. In the long-confined days of my youth, I'd longed to catch a glimpse of him when he visited my father. Though I had never glommed on to him in the same way I had Terrin, he still qualified as one of my first crushes.

The years since our last interaction had not aged him well. His once smooth skin was pale and uneven. It looked tacky, as if he had put on makeup to cover the irregularities. The skin on his cheeks creased like crepe paper when he smiled at me. "Hello, Mallory," he said in a dulcet tone that hadn't changed a bit. It called to my memories, drawing up the good with the bad.

"What's going on? What have you done to my father?"

"He'll be all right." Agate glanced down at the floor before giving me a longing look. "This has gotten out of hand—for all of us. I think you know that."

"You're the one trying to kill me."

"Mmm." Agate pinched his lips together and shook his head. "It was always my intention to bring you back safe and sound. However, after a six-year hunt, some delegates became concerned you would use your genetic value against us." Agate clicked his tongue, chiding my presumed disloyalty. "They believed if we couldn't have you, that no one should."

"And now?"

"Now the Coalition is finally in agreement. You are to be brought back to Vagari and answer for your crimes."

"What crimes?"

"High treason and theft."

"Theft? I didn't steal anything."

"You took your DNA."

"You can't prosecute me for theft of my own body."

"Not initially. That's why it was so difficult to get the support we needed. But now we have proof that you have been stealing from us."

"Proof of what?"

"I know about the egg banks, Mallory." I cringed. Terrin was right to be concerned about my side income. That was the reason for my bounty stipulations being changed from "alive and unharmed" to "alive or with proof of death." The Coalition was trying to stop me from spreading my DNA across the galaxy.

"So?" I didn't bother denying it, since my face was confirming the truth. "In what world are my eggs your property?"

Agate smirked at me. There was a knowing gleam in his eye. "Let's skip the legalities and assume they are. Now that we can prove you've been selling them, we're able to make a case for military involvement."

"What does that mean?"

Agate chuckled. "It means the last seven years have been a picnic compared to what I am about to throw at you. If I were you, Mallory, I would forget what your father said and come home willingly to stand trial. Surrendering to me will be your only chance at survival now."

I stared at the screen, unable to muster the bravado necessary for a sarcastic response. I knew as well as anyone that the Coalition wielded a formidable military. Though my mother commanded an army of billions, the Coalition was backed by advanced weaponry and a replenishable supply of biomechanoid soldiers.

Sicily took the device from my hands. "I'll deliver her as promised. When will I receive my payment?" She frowned and clicked a few buttons, trying to reestablish the connection. "Hello? Asshole hung up on me," she grumbled. "He'd better not stiff me."

I turned to her and debated how much she needed to know about the course my bounty had taken over the last few months. Apparently, my father's government hadn't been using every resource to find me until now. I wasn't just a runaway anymore; I was a fugitive. That meant hit men were no longer my only enemies. Every private citizen with loyalties to the Coalition was going to be keeping an eye out for me.

"There are a lot of people eager to get their hands on me," I told Sicily.

"Well, they are going to have to stand in line, because the only person who's getting their hands on you is the one who's paying the bounty." She headed to the door, gripping the handle to close it.

"Sicily." She paused to look at me. "I know you won't believe me, but I'm going to tell you this, so I don't have to feel guilty about it later."

"What's that?"

"If you take me anywhere near my home planet, you will be signing a death warrant for me and every member of your crew, including yourself."

Sicily laughed loudly. "Do you come by that ego naturally? Or are you just deluded by your credit stamp?"

"You're walking into a trap."

"Don't you worry, Princess. I can handle a few overeager bounty hunters."

"Best case scenario for you is bounty hunters. Next best are the hitmen."

"They don't send hitmen after runaways."

"They do when they are afraid my DNA will fall into enemy hands."

Sicily scoffed and headed to the door. She stopped in the frame and turned back. "What's the worst-case scenario?"

"The Coalition arrives and kills every last member of your crew."

Sicily stared at me a long moment, debating if she should take my concerns seriously or not. She finally shook her head dismissively. "Your concerns for my safety are noted. Feel free to unburden yourself of any guilt, should I meet my demise prematurely." She shut the door, putting me back in the dark. I wondered why I had even tried to explain the situation to her. I could talk until my voice gave out, but she would never believe she was the one in danger.

Rescue

S olitude, as I'd suspected, was not my friend. Though my meals were regular and my toilet was sufficiently tended to, I found after a month my mind was betraying me. It was also becoming increasingly more difficult to hide my pregnancy. Even if my skipped cycle went unnoticed by my clean-up crew, they would certainly notice if my belly became a little more bulbous in the next month. I had tried to do the math, but I couldn't know for sure when I had gotten pregnant, and at that point a few weeks would mean the difference between Sicily having leverage or my father's people having a baby lab rat.

I had never wanted that for myself, so I definitely didn't want it for my baby. As aggressive as they were with me, I could only imagine the restrictions they would put on this potentially magical baby. I desperately tried to remember the prophecies my parents had filled my mind with since I was capable of language. My superbaby could be the cure to every disease known to man. Through gene splinting, cloning, and DNA mapping, we could have the answer to all the missing data related to humans and their rainbow of diseases and maladies. Or the child harbors a nearly superhuman brain which could bring us into a new age of enlightenment where telepathy was the norm and telephones were no longer needed because everyone would be psychic.

The second one was highly unlikely, but oh, how the stories dog-piled on the religious rhetoric.

However, sitting alone in near darkness, staring at my four walls, I wondered if maybe that was a more plausible option. Mostly because I wanted my unborn baby to psychically open the door for me so I could escape. I poked at my stomach, trying to activate said superbaby. I looked over at the door, but nothing happened.

Damn.

Just when I thought I was going to plummet off the deep end of bored lunacy, I heard an explosion that rocked the entire ship. Even seated in my uncomfortable ass-flattening position, I still flopped to one side. Aftershocks vibrated the floor beneath me—I suspected from the atmosphere escaping the ship. Within seconds, the ruckus of tremors stopped, replaced by the sounds of bleating alarms.

I naturally hoped my rescue was imminent, but given the circumstances of my abduction, I found it more likely that I was about to be executed. Adding evidence to my suspicions was the sound of muffled gunfire nearby. Whoever had blown a hole in the ship was now on board and prepared to take my body dead or alive.

As helpless as I found myself, I still looked around the room for something to help my escape. As fond as I was of the idea, I didn't think throwing a piss pot at my attackers would lessen the chance of my death.

I heard a heavy *thunk* outside of my cell door. It was quickly followed by a few *clanks* and four successive *screeches*. I scrambled to my feet and moved to the other side of the room in time to avoid a spray of bright orange sparks.

The door's hinges turned to hot molten metal, which dripped onto the floor inside the cell. I coughed on the acrid smoke billowing in from the plasma torch. I ducked down low and covered my mouth with my shirt to save my lungs from some of the toxic air.

The invaders reached the base of the door and pushed it open. It swung in away from the opposing door lock before dropping to the ground with a loud *bang*. The light from the hall—now interspersed with flashes of red—lit the room. Through a veil of smoky haze, I saw two men peer into the room.

"Rayne?" I questioned, seeing the broad-shouldered outline I had been dreaming about since I arrived. Both their heads turned to me and a flashlight blinded my eyes. I raised my hand to shield myself from the light. "Is that you?"

I heard footsteps, but before they could reach me, two pulses from a pistol echoed through the room. Two bodies dropped to the floor in front of me, smoke wafting up from the gunshot burns on their backs. I gasped and crawled toward the men I suspected to be my friends. I pushed over one body and was relieved to see he was a stranger.

A pair of hands looped under my arms and lifted me to my feet. I struggled against my unknown attacker, trying to kick at his legs. "Who are you?" I screamed, even though I didn't really care what the name of my killer was.

"I am a friend," he answered.

I stopped struggling and looked back at his face. Though he was probably classified as humanoid, he didn't look anything like me. In place of what should have been his eyes were two patches of concave flesh. His nose and mouth were nonexistent, but there appeared to be a series of holes, along his jaw. His forehead was the only normal part of him.

"What do you mean, a friend?" I asked, still trying to figure out the face of this unfamiliar species.

He presented his forearm, which was branded with a dot surrounded by a circle, as if that was supposed to mean something to me. To me, it just looked like a cartoon boob. "I have been sent to protect you," he said. While his words were perfectly clear, I still wasn't entirely sure which part of him was the mouth.

He released his grip on me and I turned to face him. "You mean you've been sent to collect me? What would your species do with my DNA?"

"I have no wish to cultivate your DNA. I am only doing as the prophecy commands."

"Oh goody. You know, I really thought what was missing from this entire situation was a few more religious hacks."

His forehead creased. "I am here to rescue you."

"Oh, well, in that case, let's go." I rushed to the door with my rescuer right behind me. As I reached the entrance, a pulse pistol appeared around the frame. It fired right next to my head, making my eardrum hum in protest. I recoiled and watched my savior fall to the floor, dead.

I looked up at Sicily, who was still holding the gun out in case the man got back up. My mouth gaped in furious shock. "Oh, you bitch," I complained.

She lowered her pistol and raised her copper sword. She used it to motion for me to come out of the cell. "The ship is under attack. I need to take you to a more secure location." Even as she finished the statement, another explosion impacted the ship's hull.

A vacuous breeze pulled me forward through the hallway. Sicily grabbed a handful of my hair, holstered her sword, and gripped the handle of an adjacent cell door. For several seconds, I floundered in an almost weightless state. All the while, my hair follicles were screaming in agony.

After a series of shudders and vibrations, the ship compensated for yet another hole in her exterior walls. My feet returned to the ground, and I yanked Sicily's hand from my tortured locks. "I told you, you're walking into a trap," I grumbled as she took my arm and led me down the narrow hall.

"This isn't your father's people," she said.

As we exited the corridor, a group of three men spotted us from across the bay and started shouting at us. They were no doubt eager to kill me, but they didn't move. Their efforts to lift their feet seemed hindered by something. They fired their pulse pistols, but as expected, the energy dissipated before reaching its intended target. Although ultimately safer for space travel, pulse pistols were far less effective in a long-range battle.

"Who is it then?" I asked as Sicily shoved me toward the elevator, which would lead us to the upper decks.

"As near as I can tell, every idiot in the galaxy with a gun," she snarled and shoved me into the lift.

A male gattaw ran up to her before she could get inside. His mouth was cocked open and his tongue nearly hanging out. He had exerted himself enough to require panting. "Captain! There are three more suckerfish attached to the hull. The ship is at maximum containment. We can't fire on them without jeopardizing oxygen levels."

"Shoot them as they enter the ship," she ordered.

"We've lost nearly twenty men. I can't defend three spots at once."

Sicily growled and stepped into the elevator with me. "Then let them in. As soon as they are on board, shut off the gravity and open the bay doors." She pressed her finger into the up arrow and the door shut on him before he could offer another objection to her plan.

The pulley motor hummed as we slowly ascended to the upper deck. "You are becoming far more trouble than you are worth," Sicily said.

"I tried to warn you."

"Yes, I underestimated your value."

"I'm not sure it's about value anymore, so much as a threat."

"And how is that?"

"In the end, it's all about profit. I'm threatening their profit margin, so they will do anything to defend it."

Sicily examined me. "You're saying you're worth more dead than alive?"

"I'm not worth anything to you either way right now. Your ship is being ripped apart. Your crew is being killed. Unless you can get off this ship and get me to a buyer, the argument for my value is moot. And frankly, even if you get me home, I promise you they will kill you right along with me."

"What exactly are you suggesting I do with you, then?"

I took a deep breath. "Hand me a pulse pistol and let me at least try to defend myself. If I'm alive at the end of this and your ship is still intact, then let me go." Sicily scoffed.

"It's your only hope of surviving this entire situation. Trust me, you don't want to be associated with me. Let me and Terrin go and we'll draw the attention away from you."

Sicily's lip perked up. I could only imagine the sarcastic comment she was about to unload on me. Before she could speak, the mechanics of the elevator *clunked* and our ascent stopped. The lights inside the lift flickered and shut off.

I heard a *scrape* from above and reached for Sicily's pistol through the darkness. I yanked it out of her holster and started firing at the ceiling. Each flash of gunfire lit the interior of the elevator. Sicily moved to the doorway in visually interspersed movements. She pried the doors open with her clawed hands, revealing our location midway between two floors.

She crawled out to the upper one and yelled back for me to join her. I reached out to take her hand, but as soon as I stopped firing, a barrage of laser gunfire—far stronger than my pulse pistol—pierced the ceiling of the elevator, potentially decimating anyone inside of it. I bypassed Sicily's hand and opted for the quicker exit.

I leaped out of the elevator to the level below her. I could hear her curse between the scorching laser strikes, but there was nothing I could do to get back to her. With our options limited, I took my floor, and she took hers.

Debts

I shuffled through the ductwork and piping of the ship's maintenance level. I wasn't sure it was a good or bad thing to be in the ship's vital parts. There were certainly plenty of places to hide, but there were also plenty of highly flammable devices around me.

"Mallory!" Sicily's voice echoed through the room. I jumped and looked left to right. "Above you."

I looked up and saw her peering down at me through a small grate in the floor designed for emergency access and airflow for the hot running systems below it.

"Find something to stand on. I'll pull you up," she said as she removed the heavy metal grate.

I holstered my gun and looked around, but everything in the room seemed immobile or extremely heavy. "I don't see anything." I jumped to see how close I could come to the opening, but it was well above my athletic potential.

"How did your species manage to accomplish so much with so little?" she grumbled as she leaned down to lessen the distance.

"Versatility," I answered and jumped up to grab her outstretched hands. She pulled me up, guiding me to link my hands behind her neck. She braced herself on the edge of the vent hole to assist her rise, and me with her like a baby monkey.

As my head came above ground, I saw a man running down the hall towards us. Covered in black soot, he looked like he had just emerged from one of the onboard explosions. He raised a confiscated gattaw sword high over his head, set to plunge it into Sicily's back while she was still distracted. I reached back, drew my confiscated weapon, and shot him in the face twice. He dropped to the ground. His copper sword skidded across the floor until it hit Sicily's leg.

"And luck," I added.

She looked down at the sword and then at me. The look on her face was more grateful than I would have expected. She didn't strike me as the type to be afraid of death, but there was no honor in dying from a sword in the back. Certainly not at the hands of a lesser species.

She pulled me out of the hole, picked up the copper sword, and dragged me down the hall. We veered off into what I had already guessed would be the cockpit—or, in this ship's case, the bridge.

Sicily pushed through the double doors, but slowed to a stop as sparks showered down in front of us, temporarily blocking our progress. She looked her crew over as they frantically pushed buttons, turned dials, and outright prayed to keep the ship afloat. Before she could ask questions, her crew noticed her arrival and battered her with an excess of information, as well as their own questions.

The life-support was hanging from a thread, oxygen reserves were depleted, and the artificial gravity was malfunctioning across the ship. The shields were draining fast, and the weapon systems—although still functional—were no match against the eighteen different ships attacking them. Not to mention they had over a dozen men from invading suckerfish running wild on every deck.

Sicily didn't even bother to instruct her crew on what to do. She knew as well as I did this was a no-win situation. She turned to me, burdening me with the responsibility of destroying her ship and killing her crew. I took a breath and shook my head. "I'm sorry," I said, even though it was technically her fault for taking me.

"How did they even know you were with us?" She snatched the pulse pistol from my hand and returned it to the holster on her hip.

"Either the Coalition told them, or someone intercepted the communication and ran with it."

"There's another ship approaching, Captain," one of the crew members announced. I looked through the view window, but I couldn't pinpoint who the late arrival was.

"What difference would one more ship make?" she snapped at her.

"Because they're calling us," she answered.

"Put them through," she commanded and moved to sit in her designated pilot seat in the center of the room.

An image came up in triplicate on the screens above the observation window. Rayne's handsome face glared back at Sicily. "Well, well, well, how the tables have turned," he drawled.

"So, it would seem." Sicily leaned back in her chair, crossing her long legs. I moved in closer to her, into the path of the camera. As I came into view, Rayne's face momentarily softened and he took in a breath. "What do you want, Captain?"

"What do you think I want?" His eyes deadened again, and he narrowed them on Sicily. "I want my wife back."

"I'm not sure if you've noticed, but I'm under attack. Even if I had time to taxi your little bitch back to you. I doubt she would make it in one piece."

Rayne wavered in his seat as his ship came under fire. Apparently, someone didn't like him conversing with the enemy. The images turned gravelly for a moment, but then he was back. "I can take care of the ships attacking you. You've seen me do it."

"Yes, that is a rather useful piece of technology you have. I was surprised by its capabilities. You will have to let me know who your supplier is." Sicily perked her brow at him.

"Do we have a deal?"

Sicily laughed. "Oh, let's not go that far. You see, my ship is in a rather severe state. We can only do this for so long before everything fails and we all die. Since your beloved is among our passengers, you'll have to do something to save her life either way. Perhaps you might find enough goodwill inside your heart to save us all in the process." Sicily clicked a button on the arm of her chair and Rayne's face disappeared, along with the sneer that had overtaken it.

"I really wish you wouldn't taunt him," I whispered to her.

"Why's that?"

"Because I don't want to watch you die."

Sicily looked me over, examining my face. "You have a lot of confidence in your husband."

"Actually, I lack confidence in him."

"Mmm." Sicily smirked at me. "Sounds like the honeymoon's wearing off. Things not working out for you and the assassin? Shocking."

"Captain, his ship is taking severe weapons fire. He won't hold out much longer," one of her crew members reported.

"That's all right. I've seen this trick before. It's quite impressive."

I watched the screen intently. My beautiful ship was being wracked with massive energy discharges. From this side of things, I could see how the shields shimmered, absorbing the potentially deadly weapons fire. From anyone else's perspective, the static charge radiating through it was a signal that it was about to fail.

"Prepare to shut down the deflector," Sicily mandated.

The crew members at the forward panel looked back at her. "But Captain, we're surrounded."

"Not for long." Sicily smirked. "Do it now!"

Yellow energy swirled around my ship—power that had been absorbed and magnified by Rayne's unusual weapon system. It discharged in all directions, sending a spherical shock wave across the field of ships. As it impacted each one, the shields dissipated, drained away by the energy reversal. To me, it looked as if they had been eaten away.

"Brace for impact!" Sicily yelled. Though the dispersion field was relatively benign with the shields up, Sicily had wisely lowered them to preserve them. Unfortunately, the wave of energy took a toll on her already damaged ship.

I fell back and hit my head on the railing behind Sicily's chair. A blizzard of sparks lit the room before returning it to an even dimmer state than before. Her crew frantically reported further damage to life support, as well as several unauthorized emergency pod ejections.

"Shields up!" Sicily yelled over a new set of alarms and a hissing steam pipe behind us.

"Captain, they're firing on the emergency pods."

I watched on the screen as several small vessels were obliterated with single shots.

"Fire at will!"

Shot after shot spiraled away from the gattaw ship, each and every one colliding with a newly vulnerable vessel. The smaller ships exploded on impact, while the larger ships sustained damage to vital systems. Unlike their adversary, they weren't large enough to stay afloat with damage to multiple areas.

Rayne joined in on the fun, seeding the battlefield with smaller but still effective ammunition. The remaining ships veered away, leaving the battle for another day, or perhaps another bidder altogether.

I breathed a sigh of relief, knowing the ship was not about to blow up or disintegrate around us. However, that didn't stop the attacks from the men already aboard the ship.

The door to the bridge launched across the room, propelled by an explosion on the other side. Smoke added to the already humid air and choked me into a fit of coughs. When I could finally look up, I saw a series of unfamiliar faces. They were all tattooed on every visible surface of skin and possibly beyond—a common trait among the suckerfish pirates.

The one closest to me, presumably the leader, contorted his nose and mouth. I cringed as I waited for him to spit on me, but he sneezed instead.

Sᴎᴇᴇᴢʏ

The man with black hair and diagonal lines striping his face held up his finger once again, allowing everyone to pause while he sneezed twice more. All the while, his men sniffled and held their guns on the room.

"Gesundheit," I said after the third sneeze.

He glanced up at me, suspicious of the nicety, but ultimately mumbled a thank you. "The internal dampeners are malfunctioning," he explained nasally.

"No shit!" Sicily snarled at him. She had already risen from her chair and was close to my back. I wasn't sure she actually intended to defend me, but I was certainly happy to have her nearby. "Maybe if you hadn't put holes in my ship, you could breathe better."

"If you hadn't blown our ships off the hull, you wouldn't have had any problems."

"And if you hadn't dared to board my ship—"

"Dared?" The pirate scoffed. "All of you gattaw are the same. And the women are twice as much as the men."

"And what is that?"

"You think because you're stronger you should automatically win, but the truth is you're only as strong as your biggest weapon." He shifted the bulbous handheld cannon into position. He had probably meant to point it at Sicily, but I was the one standing in front of her, so it was aimed at my chest. Sicily growled behind me; a sound I didn't prefer to have so close to me. "Easy now, gat. I only want my bounty."

"Go ahead. She's turned out to be more of a hassle than I anticipated." Sicily gave me a harsh shove, pushing me into the pirate's chest.

I looked back at her, disappointed she would hand me over to these rejects so quickly. With my body being the only necessary component for full payment, there was no telling what they would do to me before they actually killed me.

"Seriously? That's it?" he asked, looking her over.

"Yeah, that's it?" I asked.

"As long as you leave the rest of my crew alone, I won't hinder your departure."

He tipped his head, analyzing her generosity, but in the end he accepted her word at face value and lowered his cannon. The pirate wrapped his arm around me and raised his wrist to his mouth. "This is Jessex. I got her. We're coming down. Get a ship ready for us."

"Sicily," I pleaded as Jessex dragged me away. "I saved you. Twice! You owe me!"

"I also owe my crew," she responded before they hauled me off the bridge.

I continued to kick and bite at my captor, but Jessex was immune to my forceful temper tantrum. He pulled me through a series of corridors until we reached an emergency ladder. His men climbed down—or rather slid down—ahead of us, shoes squeaking as they scraped down the sidebars of the rungs.

"Your turn," Jessex said.

I took a breath and moved forward. As I took hold of the ladder, the ship shifted suddenly. I held on tight, legs and arms. I couldn't contain a squeal as my center of gravity was almost instantly relocated—very nearly along with the contents of my stomach. The lights blinked out, and I panted in the darkness, trying to figure out why I was upside down.

The hall beside me lit up, and I saw Jessex sprawled on the ceiling, unconscious from his sudden *rise*. Rather than continue to walk around the world upside down, I flipped my legs back and landed next to the pirate.

"That really is a big gun." I pulled the mini bazooka out of his clutches and aimed it down the ladder shaft—or for me, up the shaft.

I fired off a shot, not taking into consideration the power of the weapon. It bucked back, practically forcing me to my knees. I heard screams as a scorching fire blast pummeled the men above me. A plume of flames crawled back through the shaft, forcing me to dive away from impending hair loss.

In the middle of my leap, gravity bellied up again. For a moment, my body hung in midair, but my Peter Pan act soon wore off and I plummeted down. This time, however, down really was the floor.

Jessex fell from the ceiling. Though the fall up had caused his unconscious state, the fall down seemed to revive him. He grunted and groaned as he reached for his gun. When he found it missing, he searched the area. His expression turned furious when he found it aimed mere inches from his face. He tried to snatch it away from me, but I rolled away and jumped to my feet. I held the gun at the ready, but he laughed.

"What's so funny?" I asked.

"You've already fired it."

"Yeah, so?" I glanced at the wafting smoke coming from the end of the gun.

"It needs at least three minutes to cool down. It won't fire."

I pressed the button to test this theory, but just as he said, the cannon wouldn't shoot. All it would do was drone and offer a muted beep, declaring its fatigue.

"Perhaps you should leave the big weapons to the big boys," he said as he stood and swaggered over to me.

"Okay," I agreed and lobbed it at him.

He instinctively caught it, fingers clasping around the hot metal of the muzzle. He yelled and dropped it to the floor. I ran past him, narrowly escaping his reach. I jumped onto the ladder and slid down four decks to the main bay.

Always Room For...

I arrived at the aftermath of my firestorm. Several men lay dead near the ladder and two others wailed in agony from their wounds. Despite my understanding of their ill will toward my survival, as well as other things, I didn't like the idea of causing so much pain.

Even with Rayne's help against our throng of attackers, I could still hear and feel the impact of artillery piercing the shields and challenging the outer hull. The only thing keeping the vacuum of space from sucking the ship's contents and crew out into the cold void was a series of built-in pipes containing a liquid resin matrix. Much as blood forms a clot over a wound, the fibrous material instantly solidified across hull damage, preventing excessive air leakage. Unfortunately, it was only a temporary fix. The oxygen supply was still being depleted faster than the scrubbers could produce it. I had little time before the thinning air reduced my function to sleeping.

I needed to find Terrin and get the hell out of here—if escape was even an option at this point. I snatched a sword off a downed gattaw and quickly located the corridor that led back to my previous containment.

I slid open the peep slot on several cell doors. Almost all of them were empty, except for the last one. "Terrin?"

I asked the sitting figure, barely detectable in the shadows. "Are you hurt?" I asked when he didn't move.

I glanced back down the hall, but so far, no one had discovered my presence. I backed away from the door and stared at the complicated push-button lock system. I glanced at the copper short sword in my hand and shrugged. I stabbed the blade directly into the control panel. For my effort, I received a reprimanding shock from the short-circuiting device. The lock clicked, and the door popped open.

I opened it the rest of the way and stepped inside. "Terrin?" I looked around the room, but I couldn't see the shadowy figure. With the addition of light from the entrance, I could see all four walls clearly. He was gone.

My confusion quickly wore off as I realized I had made a terrible mistake. This was not Terrin's cell. This was not even the cell of a humanoid. Just a creature that pretended to look like one. A creature that had likely earned its place inside of a bounty hunter's cell. I looked to the ceiling in time to see the gelatinous chameleon falling on me.

There was nothing quite like being attacked by a gigantic blob of Jell-O. I struggled and squirmed, trying to free myself from his smothering clutches. He rolled his translucent form over me, recuperating his losses and then some.

I punched him and ripped at the surface tension that barely qualified as his skin. Even stabbing at him had little effect other than to bleed wet, salty goop on me.

He spread his body thin, suctioning me to the floor and cutting off my air supply. I rolled over and pressed against the floor, using the leverage of my arms and legs. The only progress I made was to stretch his indeterminately flexible form.

Through the blur of his layers, I saw the panel I had recently short-circuited. I drew the sword again, plunging it through the creature and into a similar panel on the opposite wall. As before, it gave me a powerful shock.

The creature seized with the introduction of the electrical stimulus, after which he slipped away from me. The tension left his body, and he was reduced to a puddle of water at my feet.

I crawled from the cell, taking in a few grateful breaths to appease my aching lungs. As soon as I was properly oxygenated, my heart took its turn to ache. Terrin wasn't here. If he wasn't here, it meant he was dead.

"There you are," Jessex purred at the entrance to the hall.

I frowned, looking at the bazooka pointing at me. It was surely ready to fire again.

"I hope you don't mind if we skip the kidnapping portion of today's activities. I'm just gonna go straight to the kill." He repositioned the weapon to fire at my crouched body.

I closed my eyes, not wanting to see the blast wave coming. It was bound to be a painful way to die, whether I saw it coming or not.

In my last moment, I thought of Terrin. There was something poetic about us dying together at the end of it all. Not that it didn't suck, but it had a very Romeo and Juliet quality—with or without the sex.

In the microseconds left before my Shakespearean demise, my thoughts turned to Rayne. My brave, handsome—albeit slightly sadistic—husband. He'd survived poison and slept for ten years, only to awaken bloodthirsty for vengeance against his lover's murderer. He was nothing if not a devoted man.

As the heat of the weapon's detonation came barreling towards me, I thought of one last thing.

The cell door next to me was open.

I flung myself through the door and into the cell. The firestorm bloomed, quite literally nipping at my heels as it consumed the hallway and spilled through the threshold behind me.

I landed and rolled to the back wall. Stayed low, I breathed in the last of the untainted air. I listened to the footsteps of Jessex's heavy boots as he plodded down the hall. When he stepped into the light of the doorway, I shook my head and coughed on the smoke. "Don't you people ever give up?" I yelled at him.

"Don't you?" he asked.

"Fine." I reluctantly stood up and raised my blade.

"What exactly do you think you're going to do with that?" he asked, pulling a pulse pistol from behind his back. "Doesn't do much good against this." Jessex raised the weapon, and for the second time in such a brief span, I realized my end was near. There were no more doorways to jump through, no time to think. The best I could do was run around, making myself a difficult target. Then again, at less than ten paces, it still wouldn't be a challenge for him.

A shadow joined him in the doorway, and Jessex stiffened. He let out a small grunt, and his eyes widened with shock. He looked down at his chest. Through the smoky haze, I could barely make out the protrusion bulging under his shirt. I could also see the two razor-sharp horns over his shoulder.

"Doesn't much matter what your weapon is when your attacker is behind you," Sicily whispered into his ear, before ripping the blade out of his chest.

Jessex toppled to the ground and twitched while blood pooled around him.

"That's one." Sicily displayed a finger to me. It took me a moment to realize she was counting this as a repayment on her debt to me. I had saved her life twice since this all began. Now she had saved mine once.

"Come on." She waved for me to follow her.

Payments

"Were you passing by, or did you actually come all this way just to save me?" I asked Sicily as I tried to keep up with her long stride.

"I want to make a deal with your man."

"What deal is that?"

"Your life for mine." Another impact vibrated the floor, causing us to pitch sharply to the left before the ballasts could stabilize us again. "The ship won't hold together much longer. Certainly not long enough to get me to the next planet. My crew has taken the remaining escape pods."

"You need a ride?" I asked.

"In short, yes. Wait!" Sicily jutted out her arm out to stop me. "We'll have to go around."

"Around what?" I asked, not seeing anything in front of us. She pointed up, and I looked at the ceiling. Three men were floating around the open space of the gargantuan bay. The artificial gravity at the far end of the bay was obviously still on the fritz.

We bypassed the gravitational flux and ducked into a small tube that skirted the outer wall of the ship. The tubing was designed to provide airflow to the corrugated walkways used for temporary docking ships. For our purposes, it allowed Sicily and me to stay contained while we passed through the sections of wavering gravity. I half floated, half crawled through the clear plastic tubing ahead of her.

"You know Rayne won't let you live. If you step one foot on that ship, he'll slit your throat."

"You're going to make sure he doesn't."

"I know you and I are running on favor-friendship right now, but what makes you think I would do that for you?"

"Because I know what you want more than my death."

"And what's that?"

"Terrin."

I stopped and looked back at her. I shook my head. "I already know you killed him. And it's taking every last bit of my humanity not to shove this sword down your throat."

"You wouldn't survive that."

"It'd be worth it," I snarled.

Sicily tipped her head. "I didn't kill Terrin. I never had any intention of killing him. I have him tucked away somewhere he won't readily be discovered."

"Where? I'm not leaving without him. We need to go back for him."

Sicily rolled her eyes. "When I am secure inside your ship, I'll tell you where he is. Then and only then."

"Have you hurt him?" I asked.

"Not much hurts Terrin, but yes, I imagine I did."

I scrunched my face at her, unsure of her interpretation of hurt.

"Go." She motioned with her sword and I continued.

We reached an opening for one of the docking walkways. I stood up inside the accordion enclosure, which thankfully was maintaining its artificial gravity. I looked around and saw my ship through the clear plastic conduit. At the other end of the walkway, I saw Rayne step out of the exterior airlock onto the platform.

I stared across the short expanse, taking in his hard features. He was in battle mode and wasn't likely to offer me the sweet run-into-each-other's-arms embrace I really wanted. However, that didn't mean I wouldn't try for it, anyway.

I smiled and moved toward him, but Sicily lassoed a heavy arm around my neck and poked her sword into my back. "What the hell are you doing?" I asked, struggling against her until her blade pressed through my skin.

"Negotiating, remember?"

"Should I drop my weapon?" I waved the copper sword in front of her.

"I thought that was implied." She pressed the point in further.

"Okay, okay." I dropped the sword off to the side of the pathway.

"Let her go!" Rayne yelled through the corridor. His voice promised pain, and his face—well, that promised pain, too.

"I want safe passage to the nearest planet," Sicily yelled back. Rayne shook his head slowly. "Then I'll kill her right now!" She jabbed her sword even deeper, hitting a rib, I suspected. I cried out, unable to maintain a brave face against the excruciating pain.

"No!" Rayne shouted and raised his hand to stop her. He bared his teeth as he panted, staring Sicily down. "You can get on the ship. Just don't hurt her anymore."

Sicily removed the blade from my back and pushed me forward. I walked the short distance with her close behind me. As much as I still wanted to embrace Rayne when I arrived next to him, his eyes were still burning a hole in Sicily, so I moved past him into the ship.

I stepped inside the cargo bay, a small area compared to the gattaw ship. Ayil was inside, ready to greet me. I reached out to embrace him, but a growl from Sicily spun me back around. "No!" I yelled at Rayne as he held a blade at Sicily's throat just inside the door. She, in turn, had her copper sword jammed into his chin. He didn't even flinch at the sharp point digging into his skin and drawing blood.

"I told you your death would not be quick."

"Rayne, stop!" I yelled. "You can't kill her."

"I think you'd better listen to her," Sicily said, tipping her head back as far as she could while still keeping Rayne in view. "Unless you want Terrin to die."

"What are you talking about?" Rayne asked.

"Terrin is still somewhere on that ship. She won't tell us where he is until she is certain she is safe."

"Ayil, get Kit out of here," Rayne said.

I felt a hand rest on my shoulder. I looked back at Ayil as he tried to direct me out of the cargo bay. I shook my head at him. "What are you doing? Didn't you hear me? He is still in there somewhere. We need to go get him."

"It's too late, Kit." Ayil shook his head somberly. "That ship is barely keeping itself together. We need to get you out of here."

I looked between him and Rayne, searching for one of them to have more sympathy for my breaking heart, but all they were seeing was what was right in front of them. They wanted to save me, and the ship, and themselves. It was five lives balanced against one, and they were making a logical choice.

It should have been a simple decision. My fear should have locked in my survival instincts, and pressed my feet firmly onto safe ground. But all I could think about was how Terrin had saved me when my bounty hunters had been traded for hitmen. He had even risked his life to hunt down my runaway lover—a confounding task, considering our history.

"That's not good enough." I slapped Ayil's hand away before he could get a firmer grip on me. I ran past Rayne, barely missing his spinning reach as he tried to keep me on the ship.

"Kit, stop!" His voice broke from the intensity of his words. If I hadn't angered him the first time I sacrificed myself for one of my crew, I had definitely pissed him off this time.

I ran down the corrugated hallway. I could hear the skirmish continue behind me. When I reached the far end, I stopped and looked back. I was disappointed to see Sicily straddling Rayne on the floor of the walkway, her sword pressing vertically against his sternum. Despite the strength in his arms pushing against her thrust, she was barely straining to maintain her position. Ayil had taken up arms behind her, holding a pulse pistol to her head, but she didn't seem concerned about him.

"Let him go!" Ayil drawled fiercely.

"Sicily! Tell me where he is! Let me save him!" I yelled back at her.

She looked up at me and shook her head. She opened her mouth to speak, but her face fell as she stared out through the plastic walkway. I tried to look at whatever had her so alarmed, but the bounty hunter's ship obstructed my view. Sicily turned a scathing glare at me, as if I had done something truly irritating.

She lowered the threat of her sword and leaned down to speak to Rayne. He nodded, and she jumped to her feet, running back down the corridor toward me. I instinctively backed away from her, unsure of what maniacal plot she had in store for me.

"Kit!" Rayne cried out. He rose to his feet, but Ayil tackled him as he entered the walkway. Despite Rayne's struggles, Ayil forcefully dragged him back into our ship. Before he could get to his feet again, Ayil ran to the controls and closed the door. I only caught a glimpse of the sheer agony on his face before the metal barrier came down.

I heard a loud rumble and creaking, shortly before the vibration of a massive impact threw me to the floor. Sicily arrived and yanked me into the walkway. She took my place just inside her ship and held up two fingers to me. Her mouth moved, but the noise behind her swallowed the words up.

She stabbed her sword into the ring surrounding the oversized porthole. A surge of liquid squirted out from several nozzles on the connecting annulus. The material feathered out, immediately crystallizing into a nearly solid semi-transparent candy-like glass.

From the view of the passageway, I saw fire bloom at the front of the ship. An explosion ripped apart the bow of the ship. I looked at Sicily as the compounding explosion reached the aft portion. Her eyes were closed and her chin jutted upward. It wasn't the proud preferred death of the gattaw, but she was leaving this life with her debts paid.

Frozen

A massive cloud of fire plumed and extinguished before me. The ship shattered. Shoved by the force of the explosion, the untethered walkway whipped around like a flag. The debris of the ship battered against it, threatening to puncture it. The artificial gravity gave out, and I volleyed between the hard collapsible metal floor and the flexible walls.

With my face smashed into the clear plastic, I watched the devastation unfold outside. Smaller pieces of the ship zoomed past into the universe beyond. Larger ones bounced against each other, playing a vicious game of bumper cars as they threw more shrapnel into space. I held my breath as two huge chunks floated by, narrowly missing a collision with my temporary safe haven.

Beyond the debris, I could see several of the pirate ships still monitoring the area. Among them was an enormous ship.

A battlerunner.

The sleek black exterior and tapering bow were unmistakable. It was a military vessel that belonged to my father's people. What 18 ships had struggled to do, the Coalition accomplished with one shot.

They had destroyed Sicily's ship attempting to kill me. Unfortunately, far more lives had been eliminated in exchange for mine.

Including Terrin's.

As sad and tormented as I was that Terrin had died because of me, I was furious my father's army had now been recruited to do the dirty work of back-alley deals. The interpretive legacy of generations had translated my childish flee from a cloistered lifestyle into a defection. I had taken away their chance at perfection—and profit—so they were accusing me of treason. I was no longer just a runaway.

I was a renegade.

Renewed by my anger and craving vengeance, I grappled along the passageway, climbing toward the end still attached to my ship. My luck with the scattering shrapnel didn't outlast my efforts, though. Something big hit the tubing, compromising my grip. The impact propelled me back down to the opposite end, away from my target.

I hit the candy glass end cap, which had saved my life up to this point. The fiberglass structure cracked with my impact. The walkway before me collapsed as it wrapped around my ship. The metal floor screeched and groaned as it crumpled into a position beyond its design.

I was trapped between fractured glass and the pinched off section of tubing plastered to the hull of my ship. The last of my air was leaking through the tiny cracks and abrasions around me. My foggy exhales were the only remaining heat source.

I already knew Rayne and Ayil wouldn't be able to reach me. The position of the passageway would prevent them from getting to me, just as it prevented me from getting to them. They wouldn't be able to do a spacewalk with so many ships monitoring the area. Even if they risked revealing my location, I would probably be dead by the time they arrived.

I held my breath and wiped the condensation off of the plastic tubing in front of me. I examined the hull before me. It took me a moment to figure out where I was through the dim light of the ship's running lights, but I quickly calculated the distance between me and the nearest ejection port. It was several meters, and if my calculations were off in the slightest, it would be a tossup which would kill me first, the lack of oxygen or the cold. I may not have had a proud death in mind for myself, as the gattaw did, but it certainly didn't appeal to me to become a space popsicle.

Before I could go anywhere, however, I needed to find a way out of my confinement. I tugged on the clips holding the plastic to the metal annulus, but I quickly realized it would take too much time, and I would lose air before I could free myself.

I remembered my downed sword in the hallway. I looked around, feeling with my hands, hoping the weapon had toppled to the back along with me. I found it jammed along the edge of the floor. I raised it to my lips and kissed it before turning it on the plastic tubing.

I took several quick breaths, then plunged the sword through the thick material, creating a long slit. The remaining air fizzled out of the opening as I did.

I slipped the blade into my back pocket, jamming it through the base of the material, fastening it to my backside. I parted the opening and pulled myself through, expelling myself into space. I kept my movements swift without over exerting myself so I could save the last of the air in my lungs.

I tucked my fingers into the small crevices of the ship's hull and crawled across the exterior. I closed my eyes, trying to protect them against the severe cold, which stung my skin and made my bones instantly ache. Though the ship's hull inevitably emanated some heat from its energy production, it was only the difference between open space and a subarctic climate.

My fingers burned like they were on fire. Another layer of tissue was being peeled away each time I climbed to the next crevice. The moisture beneath my grip added to the pain of each stinging release, but I refuse to give in, no matter how bloody my hands got.

I opened my eyes to check my position. The port wasn't there. I panicked, realizing I had gone the wrong direction. It was a few meters to my left. Not far, but I was running out of air and I still had to open the damn thing up.

I shifted my legs back and torpedoed myself toward it. My fingers barely caught the lip of the depression before I floated out into space. I steadied myself and reached inside to pop it open. It took all of my strength bracing with my legs, but it eventually cracked open, expelling the contents of food waste and other rubbish.

I climbed inside the chamber, which I barely fit into. I repositioned around the sword in my back pocket and pulled the outer door shut behind me. With some further effort, I maneuvered up the tube to open the interior door, but there was no handwheel to spin.

I should have known I wouldn't be able to open it. Trash disposal was a critical concern during space travel. Errant disposal procedures could make unforeseen anti-gravity situations dangerous and downright toxic. Naturally, we didn't want our trash busting back into the ship.

With no air left to breathe, I was sucking on the dead space like a fish out of water. I banged on the hatch. I braced myself on the walls to leverage a more significant exertion on it. I heard a hollow click and an exhaust of rancid air hissed into the compartment.

I took in copious breaths, which sent my already oxygen-deprived dizziness into a nearly euphoric black out. As I panted in the small dark space, I coughed on the excess of fumes which had arrived with my air supply. A hum rumbled on either side of me and I suddenly realized why I had been afforded the privilege of oxygenation.

After all, you can't cremate your over stuffed garbage without a good mix of oxygen and propellant gas.

Burnt

I slammed my fists up against the hatch and screamed at the top of my lungs. I was seconds away from becoming a deep-fried princess. As much as suffocation didn't appeal to me, I was certain it was far less painful than burning to death.

The remaining skin on my fingers tore as they raked against my only acceptable escape route. I searched for a lever or button to secure my freedom.

Anything.

Another influx of gas assaulted my nose. The pilot light clicked, sounding the alarm to my demise. I screamed one last time, but it turned into sobs as I huddled into a trembling ball.

A loud *clunk* vibrated the chute, making me yelp. There was a *creak* above and light illuminated my would-be crematorium. Without a moment's hesitation, I reached up to the rim of the depository and flung myself inside the ship. I flopped onto the cafeteria floor, safely away from death's grip. I blinked the stars from my eyes and turned to look at a pair of pale pink snakeskin boots. The fluffy white rabbit's tails that adorned the laces bobbed with each step Aresties took.

"Oh, Kit, thank God, I thought we had gotten rats again."

I looked up at my friend, shipmate, and savior with tears in my eyes. She looked down at me as I expected her to, somewhat ignorant of her accidental genius, and only beginning to take in my state of injury. "I love you, girl. Don't ever change."

She smiled at me, accepting the compliment with bashful gratitude.

I unfurled from my fetal position, revealing more of my raw skin and bloody hands. Aresties gasped and moved to the first aid kit on the wall. As she sorted through the tiny bandages and iodine sticks, she seemed to realize this was not a boo-boo situation. "Wait right here," she said. "I'll get help." She scrambled out the door in search of supplies more befitting my injuries.

The warmth of the room pressed against me like knives. My skin throbbed as the sensation of a full-body frostbite demanded I ease it back into life more slowly.

My hands shook, traumatized by the injury of climbing the cold metal hull. The skin was bleeding from ragged lesions on the tips of the fingers and the palms. There was nothing to do to make them feel better, other than to not touch them to anything—ever again.

As the pain set in deeper, so did my realization of how close I had come to death. I had once again survived.

But for how long?

The military was involved now. They killed Terrin. How long before they killed someone else I loved? How long before they killed me?

I cried and didn't move until the ship rocked from a nearby detonation. I pulled myself off the floor with great discomfort and began my bow-legged walk to the upper level.

By the time I made it upstairs, Aresties had caught up with me. She was armed with salves and an arsenal of painkillers. She injected me with an air syringe on the way and I instantly felt some relief from the constant burn that was preventing me from breathing too deeply.

We both stepped into the cockpit where Rayne and Ayil were frantically pushing buttons and trying to get a lock on my location.

"Where the fuck *is* she?" Rayne yelled.

"I can't find her," Ayil responded.

"Guys," Aresties tried to interject.

The ship shimmied from another close discharge. The remaining ships were taking their aggression out on anyone and anything. The random weapons' fire wasn't half as much about destroying each other as flexing their muscles, so they didn't lose face.

The warship that had blown up the gattaw ship was now openly broadcasting to the ships in the area. They declared that their attack was sanctioned by the Coalition and any interference would be considered an act of war against their nation. The prerecorded message also demanded all vessels in the vicinity to power down their weapons and vacate the area immediately. Anyone who refused to abandon their position would be terminated in five minutes. Given the strength of their ship's weapons, there wouldn't be much of an argument from any of the marauders.

"She has got to be trapped in that damn tubing," Rayne said. "She could still be alive."

I tried to speak, but my voice had turned raspy. They couldn't hear me over the beeping alarms and the Coalition's announcement.

"Guys," Aresties tried again to draw their attention to my onboard status, but her petite voice wasn't any louder than mine. She gave up on them and proceeded with my much-needed medical attention. With every glob of moisture she added to by skin, a fragment of my remaining pain dissipated.

"I'm going out after her," Ayil insisted. "You just keep those assholes off my back." He stood from the copilot chair, but Rayne pushed him back down.

"No, I'll go. You have a son to worry about."

"But you know the weapons system better than me."

"You'll do fine," Rayne assured him. "If I'm still out there when our deadline runs out, leave without me."

Ayil frowned. "But—"

"Just do it." Rayne gripped his shoulder and stood up. He turned to leave the cockpit and saw me standing at the entrance. His eyes widened, and he rushed to embrace me. I cringed, dreading any contact, and took a step back. Aresties put her arm up to further block his approach and even waved him back.

Rayne's eyes skirted over me, assessing the damage Aresties was trying desperately to soothe with handfuls of antibiotic ointments and burn relief creams. Aside from that, I imagined I looked as sad and tired as I felt.

His myriad of concern and relief came and went. He turned to Ayil and pointed to the control panel. "Get us out of here now."

"What? But aren't you—" Ayil glimpsed me between the back of his chair and Rayne's body. He gasped. "Kit, how the hell—?" Another explosion set off a series of alarms, indicating that it was a good deal closer than the last two.

"Get us out of here now!" Rayne demanded again.

"Right." Ayil pounded on the controls, maneuvering the ship away from the battlefield.

Rayne moved over to me, slower this time. The look of relief on his face barely masked the anger he was harboring. He stopped in front of me, clenching his jaw as he took several deep breaths through his flaring nostrils. "What the hell did you think you were doing?" he asked, almost in a whisper.

"I wanted to save Terrin."

"So first you sacrifice yourself to save me, then you do the same for him. Tell me, what is the point of intentionally risking your life?"

"I couldn't let her kill you. And I couldn't leave him behind to die."

"And where did that get you?"

My lips pinched and tears flooded down my cheeks, stinging the irritated skin. "I had to try."

"And I told you not to," he seethed.

"It's not your decision to make. It's mine."

"Not when you're carrying my child!" he shouted, making me and Aresties flinch. His eyes bore into me, challenging me to deny him the right to protect his offspring.

I, meanwhile, could only drift my gaze to the floor, ashamed to admit that I hadn't thought twice about the life of my child before I'd run back to save Terrin. As guilty as I felt for the death of my friend, it was nothing in comparison to the blame of endangering my unborn child.

I shook my head and let the tears fall to my feet. I mumbled a pathetic apology that was nearly inaudible. After a moment, I heard his breathing slow, and he stepped closer to me. "I'll take it from here, Aresties." He took the bottles of salve from Aresties and directed me out of the cockpit.

Rayne took me to our small medical lab, which was barely the size of a walk-in closet. Beyond my burns, my other immediate concern was about the baby. I appeared to only have superficial injuries, but we needed to be certain.

I lay on the exam table and smirked as I watched Rayne slap the monitor that was supposed to be displaying the baby. He searched along the cords until he found one disconnected from the wide ultrasound belt around my belly. He plugged it back in and the screen exhibited a view of my fetus. It was considerably more developed than I expected—not just a bean anymore.

Rayne stared at the image and even reached his hand to the screen to touch it. His finger glided over the blinking area, which showed our baby's strong heartbeat. He took a breath and looked back at me.

"I'm so mad at you," he said, destroying the tenderness of the moment. "I've never had this before. I don't want to lose it."

"I'm sorry. I didn't mean to endanger the baby."

He shook his head. "I don't just mean the baby."

He grabbed the bottle of cream he had taken from Aresties and squirted a little into his hand. He rubbed it on my red, blistering skin. I hissed, but he quickly adjusted to a softer touch. The ointment did its job, relieving the pain of the freeze burn.

After my limbs were fully treated, he cut away my clothing to access the rest of my injuries. He grimaced as he saw the same marring beneath my shirt and pants. Like a bad sunburn, the only parts of me that didn't hurt on contact were the parts of me covered by my secondary layer of underclothes.

He rubbed the salve over my back and shoulders and down over my chest. Despite my breasts being the least affected, he gave them an extra application. I smirked at his due diligence, and he narrowed his eyes on me. "I'm won't be able to give you a proper welcome home until you heal."

I nodded. "I'm not sure friction would be the best thing for my skin right now."

"I'll be counting the days." He leaned down and kissed my lips gently.

"Ah, guys," Ayil's gentle intrusion brought our attention to the door.

I craned my neck up to see Ayil. He was turned slightly to keep us out of his line of sight. However, Rayne kept his hands over my breasts to conceal them.

"What is it?" Rayne asked.

"We are out of range from the battle, but I got one pirate tailing us pretty close. I'm not sure if he's headed the same direction or if he saw Kit get on board.

I shifted up and Rayne maneuvered to adapt to my new position while maintaining his manual bikini top. "Is the warship following us?"

"No."

"Then that's all that matters."

"Who did that beast belong to anyway?" Rayne asked.

"Short answer? My father."

Bluffing

"What does it mean now that your father's army is involved?" Rayne asked from the far end of the cafeteria table as he evaluated his cards. He grimaced and tossed in his ante.

"My father said they're pressing charges against me," I said and threw in my pebble. "They know I've been donating my eggs, so now I'm considered a traitor to my people. I'm the equivalent of a genetic whistle-blower."

"That's insane," Ayil complained beside me. "They're doing all of this and they still don't even know if your DNA is going to do all the stuff they hope it will."

"You're telling me," I agreed. "The only thing I can think of is that they know more than they are telling anyone."

"You in, Ayil?" Rayne asked, nodding to the cards he had barely looked at.

"No." Ayil shoved his hand away and slumped back in his chair. He had been on edge lately. I had assumed it was because of our recent encounter, but it certainly wasn't the first time we had been in danger. I also wondered if Terrin's death was affecting him more than any of us would've assumed. The two of them hadn't bonded the same way he had with Rayne, but perhaps the loss was causing a general unrest with his own choices in life. After all, he had a son to worry about.

"Like what?" Aresties asked across from me and tossed a pebble into the pot. "What sort of information could your people be keeping from you?"

I shrugged and shook my head. "Oh, I don't know. I've never really suspected any conspiracies before. It's just, I don't understand why they would take it this far. It's one thing for bounty hunters to chase me across the galaxy and another to hire hitmen to kill me, but now they're sending out warships and soldiers. That's an extreme investment for the elimination of one human life."

"From the way you always described them," Ayil said, "the Coalition was more about the science and the empire was more about the prophecy. I'm surprised we haven't seen the Queen's armada chasing the galaxy to save you. I mean, if the empire really thinks you're so damn special, where's the stalkers and fans?"

"Maybe they believe this is part of the prophecy," Aresties interjected diplomatically.

"How is narrowly escaping death every other day part of a prophecy?" I grumbled.

"Maybe it's like hero trials."

"Hero?" I groaned. "That's worse than being a princess."

"Don't tell me you believe in all that fortune, fate crap they've been spinning?" Ayil asked with notable disdain.

Aresties looked uncomfortable for a moment. "No, but you're the one saying her mother doesn't love her enough to save her," she whispered to Ayil—well within audible range of everyone at the table.

"What? I didn't say that!"

"No, no, no," I intervened. "It's never that simple with Mom. Her decisions are based on the betterment of the kingdom. She has made it clear since birth that she is a queen first and a mother second."

"That can't be true." Aresties looked horrified by this revelation. "She's your mother."

I stared blankly at her a moment, an odd, self-sustaining smile on my face. There was a part of me that knew my mother was not what she ought to be, but there was also a part of me that respected her for that. She was a hard woman, and though her love was just as hard, it was not lacking. It was a very confusing dynamic, but one I didn't feel I needed to justify on her behalf or mine.

"It doesn't much matter anymore. I think the empire is content with my sister's DNA potential. But it's funny you should mention religious zealots." I shoved my last few black stones into the center of the table. "I had a strange experience before all hell broke loose on Sicily's ship." Aresties and Rayne matched my bet, and we laid down our cards.

"Dammit," Rayne griped and slapped his cards onto the table.

I shook my head at Aresties's straight flush and she proudly collected her pebbles and stones. "How do you do that?"

Ayil chuckled. "I told you guys, she always wins."

"No one can always win at poker. It's a game of chance," Rayne argued.

"It's not chance. It's about reading people. It's about seeing right through your opponent's bluff." Ayil's gaze turned stoney and Rayne returned the same severe stare.

I shifted myself back, not wanting to be between the two men as they glowered at one another.

"Speaking of money," Aresties happily changed the subject, "I know we are not technically doing any jobs right now, but my allowance has run dry."

I groaned and rubbed my face. "I was afraid of that. Since I'm no longer an egg donor, our nest egg is getting a little low, which means both of you are missing your paychecks."

"I told you I would cover the expenses from now on," Rayne told Aresties.

"You will?" I asked. I knew Rayne had a rather expansive bank account, given the number of upgrades he had put into the ship almost immediately upon waking from his ten-year coma. However, space travel was an expensive lifestyle. The only people who did it independently were usually either pirates or smugglers. Until recently, I might've qualified as a smuggler. Now I was unemployed. "Do you have some income I don't know about?"

"Ten years does wonders for interest-bearing accounts."

"Oh." I frowned at him. "Are you sure that's okay?"

Rayne smiled. "You mean is it okay if I share my money with my wife? Yes, I think that's fine."

"Well, we never really talked about money."

"We never talked about getting married, but here we are." He winked at me and looked at Aresties. "I will cover all the expenses, including whatever you and Ayil need."

"In that case, we should probably stop off at Port Glass on the way by." Ayil stood from the table. "I need to get out of this tin can, anyway." He said it to everyone, but the frustration of containment seemed to be aimed at Rayne. Ayil marched off, leaving Rayne in irritated contemplation.

"Is there something going on between you two I should know about?" I asked.

"No." He shook his head. "He's just disappointed in how I handled things back on the gattaw ship."

"How *you* handled things? I thought I was the one who screwed everything up."

Rayne stood and leaned over to kiss my forehead. I hadn't gotten a lot of kisses on the lips the last few days. He was still treating me with kid gloves even though my skin had healed considerably. "He's angry we couldn't save Terrin."

"It's nobody's fault. There wasn't time," I said, verbalizing the same reassuring mantra I had been using to assuage my guilt.

"I know." He nodded. "I'll go explain that to him... again." Rayne left the cafeteria.

Aresties gathered up her winnings and gave me a sympathetic smile. "How are you dealing with that? I know you must miss him."

"Of course I do, but there's no sense dwelling on it."

She tipped her head and glanced at the door. "It's okay, you can tell me the truth. I know you're trying to hide your grief from Rayne."

I smiled at Aresties even as my eyes watered. I could only assume she had spied me during one of my intermittent breakdowns. I always tried to keep my wailing to myself, but a few of my episodes had involved screaming and punching walls. "I feel like somebody cut a piece out of my heart," I admitted. "I want to move on, but I can't stop thinking about him."

Aresties frowned and touched my hand. "It'll get better... I promise." She slashed her finger over her chest, specifying it was a cross-my-heart promise. She was right, of course. Time eventually made everything better. Although in my case there was an argument for time, making everything worse.

Aresties looked around the room and then back at her pile of stones. "I should check on Edric." She stood and headed to the door. "Oh, what was it you were saying about a strange experience on the bounty ship?"

"Oh, it was nothing. Don't worry about it." I shooed her away to take on her voluntary babysitting duties. I sat back and thought about how my mother might handle my new predicament. As I had told the others, she was a queen first.

So, what would a queen do?

I considered the legitimacy of the crime, the ramifications of disrupting the legal dealings of a foreign planetary union, and the impact on the empire.

After all that, I knew exactly what my mother would do. Nothing.

Regardless of how much she loved me, my defection had effectively taken me out from under her wing. She could not and would not ask the empire's military leaders to go to war purely to save her nuisance daughter.

As I had been from day one, I was on my own.

Port Glass

Port Glass, like most planets we visited, had its own definition of habitable space. The surface was almost exclusively ice, with a temperate climate and a breathable atmosphere. They rarely, if ever, had rainfall or storms, but light snowfall and fog were a daily occurrence. Its beautiful sunsets had made the wintery planet a popular tourist attraction. The reflection of the sun's psychedelic rays over the endless crystalline seas was a spectacular sight.

Unfortunately, getting to and from anywhere on the planet required a set of ice skates and more balance than I could claim to possess.

I stepped out of the pod with a set of razor skates attached to my boots. My skates were an atypical jagged design intended for small children and the elderly so they could control their movements more easily. I technically fell into the category of requiring handicap assistance—i.e. a ski-chair or wheelchair for ice. However, my crewmates insisted I would get the hang of it soon enough.

Ayil slid past me, showing off his skills with a perfect pirouette. I rolled my eyes and shuffled along the ice one step at a time. Edric scooted past me, already better than me, despite his lack of experience. "You can do it, Aunt Kit," he cheered, trying to rally me into motion.

"I'm coming, kiddo. You go ahead without me."

Aresties wobbled up beside me and laughed. "I haven't ice skated for years. This is going to be fun." She moved on, trying to get a feel for the ice beneath her feet. Before long, she was zigzagging along the ice right beside Ayil. They headed out of the parking lot and into the streets of Port Glass in search of their legendary gelato.

"Come on, slowpoke." Rayne pressed his hand on the small of my back, ushering me to move forward.

"I'm just getting a feel for this."

"Are you telling me you didn't have any ice on your home planets? Not even a commercial ice rink?"

I sighed and shook my head. "What part of *sheltered* don't you get? I lived at my father's estate and my mother's mansion. Beyond that, it was just the trip to and from."

He chuckled. "No wonder you wanted to get out of there."

"Yeah." I nodded. "You know, in a way, I have you to thank for that."

"You mean because I left my ship parked in no-man's-land?"

"Yeah, I guess that was the literal reason for my escape."

"What else was there?" He looked at me when I didn't answer. "Don't tell me you ran away because of me."

I cleared my throat and looked away from him. "Maybe a little."

Rayne slid around in front of me, blocking my progress—such as it was. "You did, didn't you?" He laughed. "You really thought I would wake up and fall madly in love with you? That was what motivated you to spurn Terrin and run away. You wanted a love story."

I frowned at the mockery. "It wasn't quite that literal. You exemplified the future I wanted for myself. I was young and stupid. Just forget I mentioned it." I shifted past him, finding a little inspiration to lengthen my strides. Except for the occasional skid, it was almost like walking on dry land.

Rayne skated past me, making a wide circle around me as he smirked at me. "I embarrassed you, didn't I?"

"You don't have to wait for me. I can catch up."

"It bothers you to admit how you feel about me, doesn't it?" He came up alongside of me, skating backwards so he could look at me as we talked. "Admit it. You've wanted me since the day you saw me." He grinned, but it only made me frown more. "Admit it."

"Admit what?" I stopped. "Admit I wanted the fairytale and got an arranged marriage instead?" His smile faded as he looked over my sullen face. "Yes, I wanted you the moment I saw you. And you wanted me since... What, when I stumbled into your room? Or when I guilted you into coming back to protect me?" I hated to acknowledge it, but it was true. On the long list of things we hadn't discussed prior to our wedding, his preferred choice of mate was number one. In the grand scheme of things, his devotion to me could have been summed up as, *"She'll do."* Not exactly the adoration every woman is seeking.

"Wait a minute." He slid forward, pushing into my space. "Please tell me your hormones are talking, because I know you didn't just tell me I don't care about you."

"That's not what I'm saying."

"Then what are you saying?"

"I'm saying I chose you, but you just ended up with me."

His eyes flared with anger and hurt. "How dare you?" He glanced around the parking lot. Aside from a few stragglers futilely trying to find their mini shuttle among the larger ones, we were alone. "Do you think I do anything I don't want to?" he asked in a low, sinister tone. He pushed in close to me and I had to grab his arms to keep from falling backward. "Sooner or later, Kit, you are going to have to trust me."

"I do trust you."

"With your life." He pressed his hand to my chest. "But what about your heart?" He wrapped his arms around me and pressed several soft kisses down my temple until he reached my ear. "You may not have gotten your fairytale," he whispered in my ear, "but I got mine, Princess." He gave my earlobe a bite, which made me jump. He pulled away and looked me over. I swallowed hard and parted my lips, finally ready for the kiss I had been waiting weeks for. Instead, he slid away, putting distance between us.

I smiled at his flirtatious torment. I hadn't enjoyed his bedroom talents in months, and the lack of intimacy made me question our relationship. However, he clearly didn't doubt himself.

"Now where were we, before you questioned my commitment to you?"

"Gelato."

Ice Cream

Normally, I wouldn't have been so keen to eat ice cream scraped from the street, but watching someone mix and fold the cream and sugar right there on the sidewalk felt authentic. The vendor asked if I wanted chocolate or berries. I requested chocolate, and he scattered little umber candies into the batch.

After he had properly distributed it, he scooped the mash into an ice bowl. I slipped on my gloves and took the dessert in hand. Complete with two flat icicles, Rayne and I dug in before our bowl and utensils melted.

We walked down the street and window-shopped while Ayil and Aresties took Edric into a toy store. After a few bites of the most delicious gelato I'd ever had, I laughed. Rayne looked over at me curiously. "What is it?" he asked.

"Something bad is about to happen," I said.

Rayne's head whipped around, searching for the danger. "Where? What do you see?"

"I don't mean right now," I said. "Look at us. We are enjoying a lovely planetary visit. Any moment someone is going to pull a gun and start shooting at us."

"This is a weapon-free area. If anyone wants to pick a fight, they'll have to do it by hand."

"You know what I mean though," I said. "We have barely had a moment's rest since this all started. I'm not sure I know what to do with myself if things go right."

Rayne nodded. "Well, hopefully the explosion convinced the Coalition that you're dead. Until they discover otherwise, we might have a small window of reprieve."

"To do what with?" I grimaced. "Write our wills?"

"What about a honeymoon?" Rayne asked.

I paused and looked at him. "A honeymoon?"

"I recall we never quite finished ours. Something about escaping the planet and your mother's clutches."

I chuckled and walked on. "We've had a honeymoon. It's the courtship we missed."

"It's not the same," Rayne said, almost as a whine. "Making love to you in a cold gray room is hardly the same as a warm sandy beach." He slipped his arm behind me, cupping my rear.

"Easy boy, there aren't any warm sandy beaches around here." I gave him a kiss on the cheek that he pursued further, but I backed away from him. I handed my dessert over to him instead. "Why don't you look into honeymoon packages and I will get my hair done, before more of my roots start showing through this dismal silver gray."

"What is your actual hair color, anyway?" he asked, unable to determine the definition of the dark color at my scalp

"Whatever I want it to be," I said and wandered off to find the nearest hairdresser.

I Scream

I stared at my reflection in the mirror behind the checkout counter. I was quite certain dying my hair had become an addiction, but hardly one worthy of an intervention. I considered it part of my security expenses. By the time my photo made the circuit, I was on to a new color and style.

The voluptuous woman with ringlets of bright red stacked into a bun took my money for the salon service. When I could finally tear my eyes away from the wine-colored locks I had just acquired, I noticed a familiar symbol tattooed on her wrist. "What does that tattoo mean?" I asked.

She flipped over her hand to show off the dot and circle design that I still thought looked like a flat boob. "You're kidding, right?" she asked with a droning accent that elongated every word and made the conversation with her nearly intolerable. "Aren't you a loyalist?" she asked.

"That's a symbol for the empire?" I asked. I should have known my mother's insignia, but the truth was I had been away a long time.

"God save the Queen, right?" She gave me a cockeyed smirk, making me wonder if she was wearing the tattoo ironically.

"Sure." To avoid being traced, I gave her a stack of dosh instead of using my credit stamp. She handed me a packet of extra strength conditioner and a business card in the form of a small compact with the business logo on it. I pocketed them both and headed out to find my friends.

I couldn't help but think about the man who had helped me. Gave his life to save me. Could he really have been working for my mother? My mother's reach certainly didn't stop at the planets under her jurisdiction. She had spies everywhere. It surprised me I hadn't encountered one of them sooner.

Then again, maybe I had and didn't know it. How many narrow escapes had my mother facilitated by mysterious or lucky circumstances? Was my mother helping me all along?

That thought should have been comforting, but it wasn't. It felt like I had been walking with a crutch this whole time, and I was too blind to see it.

As I scooted down the icy paths, store to store, I watched the crowds of shoppers enjoying their gelato and snow cones. I was ultimately searching for the threat I knew was lurking in my near future, but my attention kept shifting to the children. There were dozens of jubilant youngsters skating, laughing, and slurping on fruit *juicicles*.

My thoughts turned to my future of motherhood. I wondered if it would hold the same joys as that of these families, or if it would be more running, more worries, and more losses. I felt scared for the first time since realizing I was pregnant. Scared for my baby and how every decision I made from here on would affect it.

I saw Aresties and Edric coming down the path in front of me. She was laughing at Edric's acrobatic attempts to stay afloat while he experimented with his skating techniques. She caught his arm at the last second and saved him from the bruises of a fall.

If I hadn't known them both, I would have assumed it was just another mother with her son. I hoped Ayil appreciated everything she did to care for his son. As they passed by, I barely got a glance from either of them and I realized they didn't recognize me in my new color.

"Hey, Aresties," I called after them.

She turned back and locked eyes with me. After a beat, her civil smile broadened to a genuine one. "Oh, I like the hair."

"Thanks. Where's Ayil?"

"He went off with Rayne to the hardware store. We're heading back to the shuttle. My ankles aren't used to this."

"Tell me about it." I nodded. "Okay, I'll go find them and meet you back there." I looked around. "And keep an eye out for unfriendly people," I murmured.

Aresties nodded and headed off with Edric. I, meanwhile, went off in search of the men.

When I reached the hardware store, I peeked through the window to see if Rayne and Ayil were still shopping. I could see them inside, meandering the aisles for new tools. I waved at them, but neither took notice of the stranger outside with purple hair. Ayil tossed a tool into their mutual shopping cart, but Rayne took it right back out again. He offered some sort of explanation for not needing it, but Ayil ripped it back out of his hands and threw it into the cart again. The conversation continued with the addition of hard glares.

Rather than stand outside and wonder what the cause of their disagreement was, I went in for a closer inspection.

I slipped into the aisle across from them and explored the astounding array of hammers available for purchase. As if there were so many different ways to bang the crap out of a nail.

"Are you ever going to let this go?" Rayne asked. I could barely see his chest and Ayil's back through the shelves of nails and screws. "I thought you wanted to protect her."

"I *do* want to protect her," Ayil snarled at him, "but I don't want to lie to her."

I grimaced at the thought of lies among my crew, not that I was a pinnacle of honesty while eavesdropping from the neighboring aisle.

"And what do you think telling her the truth is going to do?" Rayne argued. "You and I both know what she'll do."

I gripped one hammer tightly in my hand. I didn't like the direction this conversation was taking.

"Yes, we do, but I have no right to make that decision for her."

"I do," Rayne said.

"That's where you and I disagree."

"What would you do to protect Edric?" Rayne asked.

"That's not fair," Ayil said.

"Why? Because he's a child and not a picture on the screen?"

"The only way I could truly protect Edric from all of this is to leave her behind."

"Doesn't that prove my point?"

"No, because I would never do that to her. Even if there were some extreme circumstances demanding we part ways, I wouldn't lie to her about it. And I certainly wouldn't want her to believe I was dead."

Dead?

"He is as good as dead. I don't want her risking her life and my child's saving Terrin."

The hammer slipped out of my grip. I didn't bother to stop it from clamoring on the floor. The conversation on the other side stopped. Two pairs of eyes peeked down through the display separating us. I stared back at them, my mouth draped open, awaiting further instructions from my brain.

"Kit," Rayne whispered.

Ayil gave me the same guilty, dumbfounded look. He obviously wanted to tell me the truth, but certainly not in this fashion.

"He's still alive?" I asked.

"Kit, you don't understand," Rayne said.

"Is he alive?" I asked again.

"Yes," Ayil answered for him.

"Where is he?" Neither one of them answered. They only exchanged a look, debating their options. Deciding if I could handle the truth. "Tell me."

"He is back on his home world," Rayne said. "Sicily sold him into the dogfights."

I vaguely remembered the stories Rayne had told me about the competitions taking place on the gattaw home planet. It was the equivalent of the gladiator days of ancient humans. Man against man, man against beast, anything and everything they could bet on. Unfortunately, the games were rampant with bribery and underhanded deals, so there was nothing sporting about them. The operations were far from sanctioned by off-worlders since the competitions usually involved the death of one or both of the competitors. For the gattaw, it was a time-honored tradition, but for those involved, it was a brutal death sentence. And I wouldn't stand by and let that happen to my friend.

You Scream

My storm-off was not as regal as I would've hoped. I nearly tripped several times just getting out of the hardware store. Somewhere between the frozen fountains in the main square and the parking lot, I became incensed about my husband's betrayal. By the time his body caught up to his vain shouted pleas for my attention, I was beyond rational conversation or even a civilized screaming match.

He yanked back on my arm and I threw my fist at his face. I nicked his cheek, and he released me. I toppled to the icy sidewalk. For a moment, he stared down at me, sizing up my anger to see if it was even worth an argument.

"I didn't want you to find out like this," he said.

"You didn't want me to find out at all," I said.

"Kit!" Ayil arrived and helped me to my feet again. "I'm so sorry. I wanted to tell you."

"You should have." I turned my anger on him for his part in the betrayal. His brow dipped with shame. "I'll remember in the future that your loyalty to me stops were his begins." I motioned to Rayne.

"Kit, he's just trying to protect you."

"Protect me?" My gaze landed on Rayne, though I was still responding to Ayil. "Is that what he's doing?" Rayne glared back at me. "It seems to me like he's trying to control me. And we all know how well that goes over." Rayne shook his head and brushed past us on his way to the shuttle. "We're going after him. You know that, right?" I hollered at his back.

"No," he said curtly. "We aren't."

"Kit, give him some time," Ayil pleaded. "We can talk about this later."

"Why are you taking his side?" I asked.

"I'm not taking his side," he said.

"If it was you or Aresties, I wouldn't take the time to blink before I went after you."

Ayil nodded. "I know."

"So, because you don't care about Terrin as much as me, I can't depend on you to help me?"

Ayil's eyes widened. "No! I mean—this isn't about my feelings for Terrin. It's about you."

"Then why can't you understand I have to do this?" I wobbled on toward the shuttle, and Ayil followed.

"I do understand. That's why you can't run off guns blazing. You have to think about this."

"There is nothing to think about." I climbed into the shuttle and happily removed my shoe blades. "I am going to go after him whether anyone comes with me or not," I announced for everyone in the shuttle to hear me. Rayne afforded me a scowl from his pilot chair where he was inputting our return flight.

Aresties looked up from the book she was reading to Edric. "Save who?"

"Terrin," Ayil said as he shut the door to the shuttle.

Aresties looked between us guiltily. "Oh." She looked back down at her book.

"You told her?" I asked Ayil.

He shrugged. "I wanted her opinion."

"And what exactly is your opinion, Aresties?"

She looked back up at me and frowned. "I don't think you should go to Miorita. It's too dangerous."

I sighed and shook my head. "That's fine." I sat down and strapped myself into one of the passenger seats. Ayil took up a seat next to Aresties so he could help Edric with his seat belt. "I mean it's not like anyone here owes me anything."

"Kit," Ayil moaned.

"No, I'm serious. All of you have gone above and beyond watching out for me since this all began. Every one of you has paid back my kindnesses ten times over. I have no right to ask anything more of you. I'll figure out a way to do this myself."

Rayne whipped back around, throwing a finger at me. "You are not stepping one foot on Miorita."

"Or what?" I squared my shoulders in defiance. "I appreciate the white knight routine, but I'm not the one who needs a hero right now."

Rayne lowered his brandished finger and stood from his chair. The engines were already kicking in, so I couldn't remove my seat belt to face off with him properly. He took a step toward me and towered over me. He spoke quietly, in a voice that inspired fear and arousal in equal portions. "I am not doing this strictly for you. I am doing it for my child."

I opened my mouth to defend myself, but I couldn't argue that my actions wouldn't equally endanger my unborn child.

"You will not leave the ship. Not while you are responsible for the life of my son or daughter. Do you understand me?" My voice caught in my throat before I could answer. "*Do you understand me?*" he yelled.

"Yes." I gritted my teeth, unhappy with anything resembling submissiveness.

His face dimmed with disappointment and he turned and walked away.

We All Scream

I ducked through the shuttle's port opening into the cargo bay and pushed my hair out of my face. I was still trying to figure out what my next step was. I needed and wanted to rescue Terrin, but everyone was against the idea.

As much as I wanted to heed my friends' advice and not get wrapped up in something I couldn't win, I also couldn't stop thinking about how many times we had all saved each other. Terrin was as important to me as any of them and I couldn't, in good conscience, leave him in the dogfights to be slaughtered. The truth was, losing Terrin at the hands of unfortunate circumstances and bad timing was a turmoil to my heart. Losing him because of inaction would shatter it, right along with my spirit.

"Kit." Ayil touched my shoulder, and I turned around to face him. He gripped my shoulders and gave me a gentle shake. "We aren't giving up yet. But we can't go forward without a really good plan."

I glanced at Rayne as he walked past us. He paused and looked at Ayil. "You know how carefully we had to plan when we were dealing with Gunder? Well, imagine a couple dozen of those assholes. Not to mention an entire stadium of loyal gattaw who won't take kindly to us interfering in their traditions." Rayne looked at me. "I'm sorry, Kit, but the answer is no. Just accept it." He walked on.

"Are you?" I asked.

He stopped and looked back at me. "Am I what?"

"Are you sorry?" I tipped my head, challenging his sincerity. "Or are you a little happy to be rid of him?"

Rayne's face shifted from general irritation to a panting rage, which caused Ayil to tighten his grip on me. I wasn't sure if he was worried Rayne would get violent, or if he knew I would be stupid enough to get in the path of it if he did.

"I do hope I'm interrupting," a woman's voice bellowed from the second-floor catwalk.

We all looked up at the middle-aged redhead leaning over the railing, peering down at us. It only took a second for Ayil and Rayne to jump into action. Planetary restrictions prevented us from carrying weapons onto the planet, but there were plenty stored inside the bay lockers.

I did the same, but our mystery trespasser clicked a few buttons on her wrist device and a network of blue lasers appeared around us. The beams crisscrossed, bouncing off carefully placed mirrors on the walls and floor.

Before I fully understood the purpose of the impromptu laser show, I felt static building with my every movement. I tried to get out of the increasingly powerful field, but the movement caused a stinging pain, which stopped me in my tracks. As soon as I gave up the fight, the pain stopped. I was effectively stuck inside a low-level force field.

I could hear Ayil and Rayne grunting as they discovered and tested the same kinetic roadblock. Luckily, Aresties and Edric were still in the shuttle and spared the discomfort of the containment.

"Now that I have your undivided attention." The short stocky woman in a plaid business suit descended the metal stairs, pausing on the last step to release her heel from the stair tread that had snagged it. She moved across the bay and paused on the other side of the initial threads of bluish hell. Her black eyes stared at me through the veins, evaluating me with a curious disdain. "I thought this would be harder." She glanced at Rayne and smiled at him.

I heard him grunt, and I turned my head, enduring a painful jolt, so I could see him. He was fighting against the field. He was enduring electrocution as he slowly clawed his way through the confining energy streams. Despite his progress, he couldn't move faster than this strange woman.

"I'm almost disappointed," she said as she pulled out a strange-looking pistol. I wasn't sure what it was, but I assumed it was not a pulse pistol, and would be capable of penetrating the force field around me.

I frantically tried to think of something to do to save myself, but our guns were out of reach. Unless I could figure out a way to use extra strength conditioner as a weapon, I was out of options.

Unless...

I dug into my back pocket for the business card the salon gave me. I only had a few more seconds, and the stinging pain kept me from moving too fast. I was once again on the threshold of my death. I should have been used to it by now. Death and I could be golfing buddies.

Although my pride was sorely misplaced, I found some vindication that it was going to be a woman who finally did me in. She wasn't fast, fit, or strong, but she was smart. Apparently, that's what it took to kill me.

The woman raised her pistol and smiled at me. "Better to get it over with, though. I've never been one for the dramatic." Her finger pressed the trigger, but a tiny voice stopped her in her tracks.

"Don't hurt my Auntie Kit!" Edric screamed from inside the shuttle.

She looked back at the shuttle, and her eyes dimmed with confusion. I continued my slow-motion pursuit while Edric was distracting her. Ignoring the pain of my movements, I flipped open the beauty compact and brought it forward, searching for the right beam to reflect.

I found one laser responsible for several branches around Rayne's legs. He saw my accomplishment and dropped to his knees. The woman saw his sudden movement, and turned her weapon on him, but it was too late. I had cleared his path enough to get him out of the static fray.

Rayne dove forward from his crouched position and tackled the woman. She tried to struggle against him, but she wasn't much of a fighter. Her talents were purely technological.

He wrestled her to the ground and took her weapon from her. He aimed it at her face.

"Rayne!" Ayil yelled at him. "Not in front of my son!"

Rayne looked back at the child and nodded. He stood up and motioned for her to stand. She slowly brought her overstuffed body to an upright position.

"Shut off the field," Rayne demanded.

The woman took her time to type a code into her wrist device. The gun in Rayne's hand beeped once in warning before it exploded. He stumbled back to cradle his hand, giving the woman enough time to click more codes into her wrist device.

An increasing jolt of electricity crawled across my body, burning my skin. I howled in pain, and Ayil joined in the lamentation behind me. Rayne growled and charged at the woman.

"Ah-ah!" she corrected and raised her finger over her wrist device. "One click and they both die." Rayne froze his attack and stood up straight again. "That's good. At least you're smart enough to know when you've lost." She pulled a second smaller gun out of her ample bosom. She looked over all of us and then back to the shuttle where Edric's whimpered pleas for his daddy were filtering into the cargo bay. If this woman wanted to kill me and collect her bounty, she would have to kill everyone on board. "And so am I." She turned her gun on Rayne. "Another day, perhaps. Let me return to my ship and I'll release them unharmed."

Rayne nodded, and she backed up to the far edge of the cargo bay. I hadn't even noticed the suckerfish when we arrived, so I could only assume this techno-assassin had invested in a cloaking device. Expensive and highly illegal. I hoped another day didn't come soon, because out of all my would-be assassins, I got the feeling she was my biggest concern.

She reached the opening to her small craft and turned to enter. Before she could disappear through the port, a knife lodged in the back of her neck. She grappled to remove it, even as another hit her back, burying deep into her spine. She fell forward against the hull and a third knife struck her in the head.

I turned slightly and saw the vicious hatred in Rayne's eyes. No remorse for breaking his promise, though I was sure he would claim he made no such promise. He moved to the woman and picked up her downed gun. With impressive accuracy, he shot out each and every device that was contributing to our laser containment.

Ayil immediately returned for his son and demanded he shut his eyes as they exited the cargo bay. Aresties paused beside me to see if I was okay. She only glanced at Rayne before following Ayil out.

I turned to Rayne and watched him tugging his knives out of the woman's back and neck. The last one in her head was stuck deep, and every tug caused her body to flop like a life-sized puppet. All the while, he bore an expression of pure vengeance.

I told myself this was what I wanted. This was what having Rayne back in my life was all about. He was here to protect me. To keep the bad men away. And the only way to do that was to put a worse man beside me.

With some effort, albeit not grace, Rayne dumped the woman's body through the cut porthole in the ship. He made a perfunctory effort to clean up the blood, tossing the towels he used in with the woman. Then he started gathering his supplies to mend his ship. When he finally noticed me still standing there, he stopped and stared at me. His eyes scanned over me as if he was checking for injuries. "What's wrong with you?"

"Why did you kill her? She was leaving."

Rayne dropped the welding torch in his hand. It clattered to the floor, echoing through the bay. He marched over to me and stopped in front of me. He stared down at me, making me wilt beneath him. "Another day?

Do you really think you would have survived an attack from her on another day?" Rayne grabbed the compact from my hand and flipped it over, looking at the label on it. A small smile curved his lips before he looked back at me. "Smart girl." He reached for me, but I stepped away. "What is with you?"

"She was running away. You should have let her go. She was no longer a threat."

"Did you miss what happened when I gave that woman leeway the first time at Ayil's request?" He moved forward to tower over me again. "She got the upper hand again." He narrowed his eyes at me. "That's what happens when you give an assassin the benefit of the doubt. They stick a knife in your back."

"Are we talking about you now or her? Because you were the one throwing knives in here."

"You know what?" he whispered. "I'm not really in the mood to have you challenging every decision I make to protect you. This is what I do. This is what I am good at. If you can't accept that, then maybe you shouldn't have dragged me out of the mud swamps." He turned to walk away.

"In that case, maybe we can make a loop to the swamp after we get done on Miorita."

Rayne stopped and turned back slowly. A smile slowly curved his lips, a warning that his anger had reached its max. "Oh, my lovely wife, I know you think you can stomp your glass slippers and win this fight, but you won't."

I scoffed and turned to leave, but he grabbed my arm and pulled me back. He squeezed me tight against his chest and put his face next to mine. "I tell you what. Because I love you, I will retrieve your beloved gattaw." He kissed my cheek.

"Really?" I asked, not seeing where his temperament had taken the turn.

"Of course." He shifted his hand down to my belly, caressing the supposed superbaby growing inside of me. "In about seven months, I would be happy to do that for you."

I elbowed him to get away, but he wouldn't release me. "Let me go."

"Promise me you won't endanger what we have created." He turned me around, gripping my arms and shaking me. "Kit? Promise me you will protect my child."

The anger was gone from his eyes, replaced by desperation. I never kept my promises, so I didn't know why he was still requesting them, but I could see he needed some proof that I wouldn't take a shuttle off the ship and fly to Miorita on my own.

"I promise I won't endanger our child."

The tension in his arms released, and he looked relieved. He pulled me forward to kiss me, but I turned my face away. He sighed and kissed my temple instead. His hands slowly released, dragging down my arms as if to keep contact as long as possible. At the very end, he tried to raise one of my hands to his lips—a gentlemanly kiss and an apology—but I wanted nothing to do with it. I ripped it free from his grip and stomped away, glass slippers cracking beneath me as I did.

MINE

With the remainder of the day spent in a stalemate, Rayne and I found ourselves just as distant in the bedroom. Though our bed was small, we rolled on our sides, backs facing each other. It was as cold as our bed had ever been.

My thoughts bounced between Terrin and my child. Somehow, no matter what move I made, I was endangering one of them. Terrin could be dead already, killed in the dogfights on Miorita. Going there could put everyone in danger for no reason. And yet I couldn't stop thinking about him.

I spent six years separated from Terrin while traveling the stars. Although my adventures in space had failed to live up to my expectations, I was happy. I was free. I certainly missed him, but I had created a new fantasy to take his place.

Rayne.

While Terrin was my frog prince—a constant companion forever out of my reach—Rayne was my sleeping beauty, always within reach, but never good company.

When he woke, I'd thought I had found the best of both worlds. I was finally complete. A princess with a prince.

Then why was I thinking about a frog?

Thoroughly lost and on the verge of tears, I sat up in bed. I slipped on my slippers and prepared to take my woes to new ears. I felt a hand on my shoulder, pulling me back down to the mattress. As I sat back down, Rayne moved his fingers, tickling them down my spine, until they fell away. "Where are you going?"

I shook my head.

"Kit." He sighed and sat up. "Talk to me," he whispered.

"I have already talked to you," I whispered back. "I know you don't care about him. I know nobody really cares much about him, but..." I blinked away my tears and stared up at the ceiling. "I know you're making the right choice, but if Terrin dies, and I had a chance to save him..." I shook my head, trying to fight the catch in my throat. "I will never forgive you," I blurted out, followed shortly by a sob.

Rayne shifted behind me, and his legs slid up on either side of me. He reached his arms around me and hugged me from behind. His head rested against my neck as he breathed on me. "I know," he whispered. "I don't know what else to do, Kit." He kissed the back of my neck. "If it was only you and me, I would risk it, because I love you."

"If you loved me, you would understand how important he is to me."

Rayne sighed and tightened his grip on me. "I do understand how important he is to you. You just don't seem to understand how important you are to me."

I lowered my head. "This isn't fair. I feel like I'm taking sides. No matter which side I take, someone is going to get hurt."

Rayne pressed his forehead against my shoulder. "I think we can both agree this decision won't be made tonight."

I scoffed. "No."

He moved his hands to my legs and squeezed my thighs. "Can we forget about how angry you are with me for a little while?" He moved one of his hands away from my knee and caressed my stomach, where I noticed a little bulge, a baby bump—or perhaps just bloating. "I've missed you. More than I thought possible." I leaned back against him, letting my head rest against his shoulder. "It's killing me being next to you and not being able to hold you." His hand moved from my stomach to my neck. He brushed his fingers along the soft skin of my throat and back down to my breasts. He squeezed them each in turn, as his breathing hastened against my ear. "Please don't make me feel like a bad guy. Not in here."

Rayne dragged me back into the bed, pressing me down to my back. He lay on top of me, pressing me into the mattress with his weight. He looked me over as if waiting for me to object. As angry as I was with him, I was extremely happy to be back in his arms. Though he was theoretically mine, I still craved his touch as much as the first time a laid my eyes on him.

When I didn't object to our union, he hastily assisted in the removal of my clothes and his. Free of any obstructions, he dove back on top of me, smothering my lips with a hard kiss. He continued to pepper my cheeks and neck with soft kisses as he worked his way down my breasts and to my stomach. He paused there for a moment, examining my body, as if he might see right through me to the child within. A curious smile grew and his face and he looked back up at me.

"That's my baby in there." I nodded. "My baby. My wife." His smile grew a little broader and his eyes narrowed into a hunter's gaze. "All mine." He licked his lips and shifted down to further explore the parts of me he had already staked claim to.

Yours

A resties and I stood on one side of the large metallic device, while Rayne and Ayil stood on the other side. We all examined it respectively with curiosity, fear, concern, and intrigue. The double-sided contraption wasn't much bigger than the one-by-two-foot box it came in, but with the attachments in place, it was nearly five feet long. The metallic heads on the extensions were polished silver phallic tubes. They were the source of Ayil's sideways smirk and my clenched thighs.

I gulped and looked at Rayne. He looked back at me and frowned. "Are you sure this is safe for them?" he asked Ayil.

"Of course it's safe." Ayil once again picked up the instructions for the device and read through them very carefully. "Position machine between females. Insert vaginal probes, select distribution variables, execute operation, wait until cycle is fully completed before removal."

"That didn't say anything about being safe." Rayne glared at him.

"98% accuracy."

"You said it was 99%," I said.

"Oh yeah, well, 98.9."

"Is it going to hurt?" Aresties asked.

"Not on your end." Ayil smirked at her. "At least not this part of it. I can't speak for six months from now."

I turned to Aresties and dipped my brow. "You know you don't have to do this?"

"I want to. You've got too many people trying to hurt you. I want to do something to help."

I sighed and touched her arm. "I know you do, but this is a lot to ask."

"I always wanted to have a baby. This way I'll be the aunt and the mom—kind of."

"All right." Ayil rubbed his hands together. "Let's get your pants off." I glared at Ayil and he shrugged. "Oh, come on, you know what this thing looks like. There's no way I won't find some amusement in this process."

Twenty minutes later, I found myself end-to-end with Aresties. With our two operative tables in position and a stool to hold the frightening transference device between us, we were nearly ready to begin. Rayne tugged on my lap blanket, helping to preserve the last of my dignity. I reached for his hand, and he pulled it up to his lips for a kiss. "Remind me why I'm doing this?"

"Because you have a target on your back, and the only way to protect our child is to disguise the fact that it is our child."

"Oh, right."

"You girls ready?" Ayil asked, eager to press the button.

"You know, you could try to hide the entertainment you are getting from this."

"I could." He nodded and smiled. "But I won't."

Ayil clicked the button and a loud hum reverberated between my legs. I grimaced at Rayne and then peeked over my spread legs to Aresties. She had the same disturbed look on her face as mine.

Cool, vibrating metal slipped inside of me. As suspicious as I was of the slightly pleasurable sensation, I rested my head back and endured the increasing pressure. Ayil whispered something to Aresties on the other side and she giggled. I could only imagine the range of jokes he was getting from this.

"Are you okay?" Rayne asked, squeezing my hand.

"Yeah, it's not really that—" My sentence cut off as a sharp stabbing pain shot through my body. I gasped against the pain that was literally my insides being ripped out.

I crunched my stomach, trying to curl into a ball, but Ayil was immediately at my side, pressing my shoulders down. "Okay, Rayne, our turn." He nodded toward my lower half as if they had discussed this part of the procedure already. As angry as I was about not being included, it was probably best I hadn't been aware of how much it was going to hurt.

I screamed as Rayne pressed down my hips to keep me aligned with the device. Ayil practically laid across my chest to keep me still. Out of spite, I wrapped my hands around his back, piercing him with my fingernails.

He grunted as I dug them in deep. He turned his face, breathing against my cheek. "We have to keep you flat and immobile, or that 98% chance goes down significantly."

I gritted my teeth and released the tension in my muscles. Aside from an increase in breathing and a tremble I couldn't control, I remained still. Ayil released some of his pressure and looked down at me. His eyes curiously inspected my renewed determination. The corners of his lips tipped up slightly. He switched positions, holding me down from behind my head.

Rayne exchanged a look with him before looking at me. A similar smile appeared on his face.

"Kit?" Aresties looked at me over her blanketed knees.

"I'm okay," I whispered. I could feel the sweat pouring down my face, and a warmth in my limbs, signaling that it was time to pass out, but I lied to her, anyway. "It doesn't hurt that bad."

One

I sat across the table from Aresties, watching her gobble down a small chicken and every green vegetable she could find. It should have pleased me that her appetite had increased and that her cravings were steering toward healthier choices, but the vacancy inside of me was from more than my missing child. I hadn't thought a few months was long enough to connect with the life growing inside of me.

Baby? What baby? It was only a blob on a screen. At best, it was an overgrown amoeba. Certainly nothing to get excited about.

And yet as I watched Aresties's belly swell, adapting gracefully to the second trimester of her forced pregnancy, I couldn't help but feel cheated. The decision was logical and the safest option. And yet, the part of me that always got what I wanted was screaming at me, demanding I take back what was mine. It was impossible, of course. The procedure was not reversible. The first transfer was a minimal risk, but the second one would surely kill the fetus. Not to mention we were well past the size requirements for it. And my uterus was still recovering from the damaging robbery.

That made it all the worse, because the remaining scar tissue could leave my womb inhospitable. The baby inside of Aresties might be my only chance to bear a child. I might've given it all up for the sake of saving Terrin.

I couldn't help wondering if it was worth it. I loved Terrin. I would do anything for him. But the hormones inside of me bouncing from extreme highs to extreme lows were telling me otherwise. Somehow, everything happening to me was no longer my fault but everyone else's.

It was my parents for keeping me sheltered to where I had no choice but to escape to gain some kind of independence. It was Terrin for denying our love. And it was Rayne for prioritizing his child over me. It was the whole goddamn galaxy for putting their faith in a religious prophecy backed by mad scientists.

I watched Aresties stuff another spoonful of creamed spinach into her mouth, satisfying a hunger brought on by my offspring now growing inside of her. All at once I stood, tipping over my chair. It clattered against the cafeteria floor. My eyes filled with tears, but I said nothing. I just stared daggers at the poor sweet girl across from me.

Aresties looked up at me from her meal, her eyes filled with concern. Ayil and Edric also stopped eating to gawk at my display, waiting for some kind of explanation. Rayne had long since finished his meal, but had stayed to catch up on the news. His eyes drifted from his reading tablet to me, trying to discern my mood before reacting to my outburst.

They didn't understand. It was just another day for them. In a matter of an hour-long procedure, I had gone from the mother of a genetically perfect child back to me. Plain old, boring me.

Rather than bore them with the rants of my traumatized hormonal mind, I backed away. I nearly tripped on my chair as I found my way to the door. I ran down the corridor, making my way to the cockpit. No one followed me. No one came to check on me. It wasn't my first random outburst of this nature and probably wouldn't be my last. I just needed time to adjust to the hole in my heart.

Miorita

I had been on dozens of different planets throughout the galaxy. I had witnessed every manner of weather inconsistency and anomalous terrain. I had interacted with hundreds of different species: humanoids, sentient invertebrates, pet cephalopods, and even biomechanoids. There wasn't a social structure, political regime, or medium of exchange that surprised me anymore. And yet when I set foot on Miorita, I felt like I had entered the forbidden land. One not intended for me.

I stepped out of the shuttle and took in the familiar markers of an arid climate. Round cacti, ranging in size from baseballs to small houses, dotted the pale sand. Their green color reminded me of Terrin's skin—a perfect camouflage for him.

As we meandered through a maze of the thorny oversized cacti, I noticed the immense structures visible in the distance ahead of us. The city, such as it was, looked more like a series of gigantic termite colonies. The mud and stone buildings looked sloppy. Despite that, though, the tallest one was at least 20 stories high and, doubtless, had been there for a very long time.

It was easy to see how the gattaw had gained the stigma of being uncivilized and unintelligent. And how that determination had ignited a prejudice that encouraged off-worlders to take advantage of their loyal, hard-working nature.

Their lack of assets had left them in a state of simplicity. Without advancements in technology, they were wholly reliant on their natural resources. As such, the customs most people viewed as violent, oppressive behavior—including myself—had become threaded into their culture.

Somewhere ahead of us, I heard the roar of a cheering audience. I stopped and looked back at Rayne. His eyes lit with an almost sinister anticipation. I had thought his memories of the dogfights might sour his mood, but he seemed to be looking forward to seeing them again. "Just follow the sound of carnage." He nodded for Ayil and me to continue."

"Are these poisonous?" Ayil asked, pointing at the sharp barbs protruding from the cacti he was standing next to.

"Not poisonous, but..." Rayne narrowed his eyes at him. "What did you do?"

"Um, well." Ayil turned to reveal a half a dozen orange-tipped needles stuck in his bicep. "I brushed up against it." Rayne groaned, and started yanking the spikes out. "Am I gonna die?"

"No, you idiot." Rayne shook his head. "In high quantities, they have a hallucinatory effect though."

Ayil smiled. "Really?"

"Yes. Just ignore it. It doesn't last long." Rayne rolled his eyes at me before taking the lead.

By the time we reached the Coliseum-style auditorium, Ayil was drunk and singing me a lullaby usually reserved for Edric. He rested his arm across my shoulder, leaning into me to help support his weight as he stumbled along beside me.

The guards standing at the entrance blocked our passage through the heavy doors. I noticed the smears of reddish-brown on the wood and wondered if the rumors were true about the gates into the dogfights being painted with the blood of its victims. I frowned at one particular smear that looked like a bloody hand print sliding down it.

"Who are you?" one guard asked.

"We've come to see the dogfights," I answered, nodding to the door behind them.

They looked at one another and laughed before turning back to me. "Pleasure girls can go to the back entrance." The other guard pointed the way.

I shook my head. "I'm here to watch."

"This is no place for a human girl. Now get on with you." The first guard drew his copper sword and waved me away.

"Gentlemen," Ayil managed to say without slurring. "My wife and I are here to conduct business."

The guards glanced at each other and then looked behind both of us at Rayne. "He won't last long. Are you sure you don't want the back entrance?"

"The front entrance is all we're interested in. Now, do you want my dog or not?" Ayil said. I glanced at him and then back at Rayne. He shook his head at me.

"Yeah, I will take him." The guard shoved between us, nearly toppling Ayil. He grabbed Rayne by the arm and dragged him away, toward the aforementioned back entrance.

"What's going on?" I looked between him and Ayil. "Wait." I went after Rayne, but Ayil grabbed my arm, linking it to his.

"I'll explain later," he murmured to me.

The remaining guard opened the doors to the arena. A loud creak preceded an odorous punch of food, sweat, and death. "Go," the guard demanded, waving us through. Ayil pulled me along beside him. We entered under a wooden structure that skirted the stone arena. It looked like an endless line of rickety scaffolding about to collapse.

A roar from the audience came at us from all directions, but mostly from the open stone steps in front of us. Wood squeaked over our heads, and dust sifted down from between the cracks.

We ascended the stone steps and returned to Miorita's blinding sunlight. I blinked and shielded my eyes as we emerged into the amphitheater. Ayil did the same, pausing on the top step.

After my pupils compensated, I found myself looking straight out at the pit. Just three feet from us was a short stone wall serving as a railing. Beyond that was a two-story drop. Legend claimed that the infamous dogfights took place on a bed of red sand—tinted by the blood of men who had met their death there. However, there wasn't really any sand to speak of. It was just dirt and rock.

I stepped up to the wall to get a better look at the arena below. What I saw wasn't actually the construct of an arena, but rather a deep rent in the ground. The gattaw had simply dug down and exposed a natural cave. The battleground was full of random stalagmite columns, tall and short. They provided cover for the competitors, as well as obstacles—and, judging by the discoloration on some of them, weapons.

I stared down into the hole, watching a male gattaw pummeling another humanoid. His fists were red with blood from the man's peeling face. The rabid enthusiasm of the crowd gave me chills. The fact that this carnage was being enjoyed as lightheartedly as a sporting event made the smell of fried food even more distasteful.

Though the dogfights were a centuries-old tradition on Miorita, it was the humans who monetized it and politicians who corrupted it. As if that wasn't bad enough, long after the influence of colonization ended, the gattaw themselves transformed the competitions into a tourist trap with intermission entertainment, snacks, and souvenirs. As unpleasant as the games were to begin with, they were now a travesty of the gattaw culture.

The humanoid in the pit let out a final war cry and shoved the gattaw off of him. The gattaw jumped up and dove back at him. The man slashed his blade across his attacker's throat. I flinched as something hit my face. I wiped my hand down my cheek and found blood. Apparently, this was an interactive show.

The gattaw doubled over, holding his lacerated throat. Despite his effort to contain it, blood dribbled between his fingers and onto the floor of the arena.

While he was distracted, the humanoid rushed at the gattaw, but that was his undoing. The gattaw twisted clear of his lunge and came full circle, plunging his copper sword into the man's neck. It nearly decapitated him. The humanoid dropped to the ground. His glassy-eyed stare remained on the sky above.

The crowd cheered for the win. Three truncated "*rahs*" filled the stadium, but no applause. Then an eerie silence followed. The chanting stopped and the calls for blood quelled. Even the shuffling of feet from the arena went quiet. I looked around at the intense concentration all around us. The entire audience seemed to be on the edge of their seats.

Anticipation for what? Wasn't the fight over? Hadn't they seen enough bloodshed?

The victorious gattaw stood for a long moment in the center of the arena. His mouth was partially open to assist his breathing and thermoregulation. He tilted his head upward, causing the gash in his neck to open further. A fresh rush of blood dribble down his chest. He mouthed something to himself, or perhaps it was a prayer. I could almost hear the words—not that I could understand them.

The gattaw leaned over and wiped his blade on the fallen man's tunic. He then kissed the clean blade. When he rose again, the crowd rose with him—a silent standing ovation. He looked around at them, bowed slightly, and raised his sword high, blade pointed downward.

This wasn't Terrin. He was a stranger I had never met, but I couldn't help feeling as if I was watching Terrin's fate. Seeing his demise first hand, in person.

The sword plunged down. I called out, "No!" just as the crowd roared with excitement. The copper blade buried into his barrel chest, no doubt into his heart. He fell to his knees and then careened forward. The blade pushed even deeper, poking up through his back.

I made an "*ugh*" sound and nearly gagged as I turned away from the sight. "I hate these games. What a ridiculous waste of—" I stifled my criticism when I saw an elderly gattaw standing behind us next to a food cart. The look of disapproval on his face could have been his general distaste for all lifeforms not native to Miorita, but I got the sense he understood English and did not approve of my condescension for his beloved traditions. I shrank back, clutching Ayil's arm and shoving him onward. "Let's find a seat."

Ayil led the way to some open seats—or rather, the stone block my ass would hate me for later. As I situated myself, I noticed the elderly food vendor pushing his cart past us on the mezzanine below. His eyes were on me, no longer angry, but curious. I pretended not to be bothered by his attention, but I didn't like anyone showing an interest in me, no matter what planet I was on.

"Where did they take Rayne?" I asked, leaning closer to Ayil so he could hear me over the festivities taking place in the pit. I wasn't entirely sure it was possible to have commercials during live performances, but I was pretty sure the song and dance being performed below was advertising for a chafing cream.

"These are the dogfights, Kit. Foreigners don't get in here unless they participate in the carnage somehow." Ayil glanced around at the audience members, who were mostly gattaw. We got more than a few looks, but otherwise no one seemed to care about the humans. Humans were not a threat to them. We might as well be two fluffy kittens in a den of lions.

"You knew about this?" I asked him.

"Is this a porno?" Ayil squinted his eyes at the performance. I glanced over, but my previous assessment of a chafing cream ad still applied, just not for the body parts I would have suspected.

"You knew we would have to give them Rayne. Why didn't you tell me?"

"It's the same play as when we got Edric back. The only difference is Rayne is the bait this time. Or the payment. Whatever. You wanted to save Terrin; this is how we do it."

I stared at Ayil. "Yes, but now we have *two* people to save."

"What's new?" Ayil raised his hand and waved over the guard who had taken Rayne. The gattaw climbed up the steep steps with easy strides and stood before us.

"They will give you 10,000 units for him," he said in a deep bass voice that made my ears tickle.

"10,000!" Ayil stood up in objection. "He is a former fighter. I would have thought to get double that."

The gattaw laughed and shoved Ayil back into his seat. His thick black claws dug into Ayil's shoulder and didn't release until his flinch signaled his yield. "He's still in good shape, but no one thinks that a forty-year-old human to do well here. He'll be an excellent starter fighter for our trainees. It's a good price. Now, do you accept the exchange, or should I show you the door?"

Ayil looked at me as if he needed my permission to sell my husband. However, I didn't understand this game, let alone whether the plan—I hadn't been told about—was going well or not.

Ayil nodded and held out his hand. The guard slapped a small computer tablet into his hand and jogged back down the steps. Ayil immediately started punching on the glass screen.

"Is Rayne really forty?" I murmured, staring after the guard. "Geez, that's weird."

"What's weird?" Ayil asked, not looking up from his device.

"I just never put the word forty and Rayne in the same sentence before."

"He couldn't have aged more than a few years in hypersleep. At most, he's mid-thirties."

"Ten years? That's not a horrible age difference, is it?"

"Why would that matter to you? Terrin is twenty years older, and it didn't stop your full-on crush mode."

"Yeah, but gattaw live to be in their hundreds on average, so he was practically a teenager when we met."

"Tell yourself whatever you want, Kit. You just like older men. I'd say it was a daddy issue, but from what you've told me, your dad is an okay guy."

"Yeah, he is." I grimaced thinking about the last conversation I had with my father. What if that was the last time I would ever see him? One tormented phone call at gunpoint from both sides. I shook away the thought. One dire situation at a time. "So how are we going to get Rayne back?"

"We got some decent credits for him. We'll use it to gamble with. Once we have enough dosh, we buy him back and hopefully have plenty left over to buy Terrin as well.

"So, we are literally gambling with Rayne's and Terrin's lives?"

"Well, don't say it like that. No one knows what Rayne can do. His reputation has long since become rumor." Ayil lifted the screen for me to look at it. "They've already got Rayne penciled in for a match later today. I put 5,000 on it.

His odds are so low we'll make a fortune in the first match alone."

"Alex Turner?" I questioned the name designation at the top of the screen.

"Yeah, pseudonym. Apparently, the name Rayne Baloch doesn't have a pleasant reputation around here. He didn't want to draw any undue attention to himself."

"Does that thing say whether or not Terrin is alive?"

"Yeah, I already checked." Ayil smiled. "He's alive."

Unable to mask my relief, I took a swift breath and leaned my head on Ayil's shoulder. "Thank you for doing this." I looked back up at him.

He shook his head, and all but rolled his eyes. "You know I wouldn't let you do this alone."

"I know." I wanted to tell him he shouldn't help me. He should run as far away from me as he could get, but I knew he never would. The moment I brought him onboard my ship, I had linked our fates.

Ayil patted my back and stood up. "I'm going to go check out the... natives." He pushed his fingers through his hair, straightened his airy white shirt, and winked at me.

"Be good." I grimaced and watched him go.

Familiar

While the crowd cheered for the new contenders, I surveyed the arena. It was fairly typical of an outdoor event center, albeit old and a little substandard in quality. At the very top of the stadium was a line of box seats—technically tents, which sat on the scaffolding we had seen on our way in. The variations in bright and wild fabrics decorated the circumference of the stadium. Though some were closed up, veiling the members inside, others were wide open.

The occupants were just as ornate as their tents. The women wore lavish gowns and draped themselves with gold and jewels. The men donned silky tunics and heavy medallions. Their rings shimmered as they lifted their hands to applaud the games. There was more wealth on the rim of this stadium than in the entire system. These were the real players of the games. These were the men and women who had taken a violent tradition and turned it into a profitable gambling operation.

It was hard to remember a time in my life when I had belonged up in those tents. Dressed to excess, prim and proper, and miserable. I knew my wealth and prestige had made me the envy of others, but I had no interest in the bank accounts that tethered me to the obligations of the

Crown. I was certain my decisions were a different version of selfish—especially as far as my mother was concerned. However, leaving Brahama had not been the whimsy of a spoiled child—it had been a compulsion. One I couldn't resist.

Light shimmered in my face, and I shifted my gaze to see the gaudy jewelry causing the glare. In one tent behind me, I saw a woman dressed in what the distinguishing eye would describe as a fashionable day dress with gold medallions sewn into the collar. To me, it was a garish moo-moo.

She was leaning over the edge of the railing, surveying the people below her, much as I was surveying the people above me. There was nothing particularly special about the woman. A slender build, aging face, with silvery gray hair in a tight bun. She had likely been a debutante in her day, but of course, that was before the plastic surgery stopped working. Before the gray stopped taking the color. Before...

My brow dipped as I took in her features hardened by age and a smile soured by years of political bullshit. I knew her. I couldn't place her, but I had met her.

I had probably met half the people in the tents above me. So many royal and advantageous people had strolled through my life over the years. My father had paraded me through more fund raisers than a picture of an underprivileged child. My mother had also had her fair share of dinner parties, displaying me like a shiny trophy, proof of a miracle in progress.

Some miracle I turned out to be.

The woman caught me looking at her and glared down at me. I was an ant trespassing on her picnic. Her snarl eased as she continued to take in my features. I was certain age and endless hair color changes would keep her from recognizing me, but she was thinking the same thing I was: *I know you from somewhere.*

Before she could connect my face to a political fallout, I turned away. I looked back to the arena where they were removing the bodies of the competitors. I half expected them to shove the dead off to the side and let them dry out in the sun, but that wasn't the case. A cleric arrived to bless the bodies before the guards carried them away on stretchers. They placed the gattaw's copper sword on his chest before removing him. I should have known the gattaw would honor death more than they honored life.

The food vendor I had irritated earlier came back around. He stopped below my section and looked up at me. He filled a paper cone with fresh steaming pellets and climbed the precarious stone steps.

After his first two arduous steps, the old man grasped his weak knee. My every instinct demanded I move to assist the poor man, but I knew pity was never a compliment to a gattaw, no matter how sincere the sentiment. Instead, I kept my eyes forward while he climbed to his destination, which turned out to be me.

The old man grunted as he sat down beside me. I looked at him, bewildered. I swallowed hard and looked over his features. He might have been handsome once, but his once vivid avocado green was now a gray green, caused by perpetual molting. His eyes had once been a beautiful amber brown, but time had fogged them.

He extended his bag of treats to me. I blinked at them and searched the area for Ayil. "Ah, my friend has the credits."

"It's free of charge," the elderly gattaw said. My mouth dropped slightly when I realized he was well versed in my tongue. I took his offering and looked down at the shiny brown nuggets suspiciously. They smelled delicious, but I wasn't entirely sure they would be safe to eat. Rather than dig in, I folded the bag closed and set them off to one side. "You're not hungry?" he asked.

"I think I'll save them for later," I said, not wanting to be impolite.

The elderly gattaw chuckled. The rumble in his chest sounded congested and labored. "You suspect I'm trying to poison you."

I let out a soft laugh and shook my head. "No, of course not." I gave him a tight smile.

"I'll let you in on a little secret." The man leaned closer to me. "Gattaw do not poison their victims. It is considered cowardly and weak." He motioned to the arena. "As you can see, we take great *pride* in the art of physical combat."

"I was afraid I might've offended you with what I said earlier."

The old man looked at me like an errant child. The disciplining gaze, however, had a hint of amusement. "Ignorance does not offend me." I resisted the urge to deny my ignorance. "What has brought you to the games, if not the enjoyments of the battle?"

"A friend of mine is competing in the games. I came here to... to support him."

"He'll need all the support he can get. Humans don't last long in the games."

I grimaced at that thought. "No, I suppose they don't." I reached for the treats he had offered me and opened them up. He smiled as I took one from the bag and popped it in my mouth. The sweet, salty flavor made my mouth water. As I bit down on the crunchy delight, I tasted the nutty, almost spicy interior. "Wow, these are good," I said, covering my mouth.

"I'm glad you enjoy it. Not many prefer the flavor of Miorita's belly beans."

"Belly beans?" I smiled at him, but he didn't see any irony in the name.

"I think most people are turned off by how they are procured."

"Procured?"

"The belly bean is inedible in its natural state. The only creatures on Miorita that eat them are rodents. After they are digested once, the bean's encasement is broken down and can then be digested by humanoids."

I froze, holding my teeth against the belly bean I had just popped into my mouth. "This bean has already been eaten?"

"Yes, we gather them from feces. Then we clean and roast them. Add a little sugar and you have a delicious snack."

I stared at the old man, trying to discern his temperament. At first, I thought he had given me the beans as punishment for my harsh criticism, but as I watched him gauging my response, I sensed his plot was more complex than that. He was testing me. Why? I had no idea, but I wasn't about to fail.

"They don't know what they're missing." I crunched down on the bean in my mouth. "I'm not as finicky as some humanoids. I have an extensive palate."

"Yes, I'm sure your travels have exposed you to a great number of culinary delights."

I nodded, ignoring his assumption about my travel habits. I popped another belly bean into my mouth. I let out a moan of enjoyment, even though the description of its origin had sullied its flavor. "Are you always this generous to newcomers, or are you trying to get rid of your beans?"

"Neither, but there's no harm in sucking up to a princess."

My body froze, mouth poised mid-chew. I hadn't considered the old man a threat. Harmless was not an apt description for any gattaw, but he seemed too feeble to be an assassin. Unless he was faking his maladies.

I slowly reached for my pistol until I remembered it wasn't there. Like on most planets, firearms were illegal on Miorita unless you had a permit or a very hefty budget for bribes.

I considered my options for escape. Where the hell was Ayil!

"There's no need to be afraid. I mean you no harm." The old man rested his hand on my leg. I looked down at his palm encompassing half my thigh.

I glanced at him. "Who are you?" I could hear the tremble in my voice, but I couldn't control it.

"I'm just an old man," he said, but I wasn't convinced. I shifted away from him. He may have been an old man, but he was still strong enough to break my neck with his bare hands. His eyes flitted over my face while I frantically searched for Ayil. "You are as beautiful as they say. With or without that absurd hair."

"Who exactly has been commenting on my beauty?"

He leaned forward to whisper his answer. "Anyone with eyes."

I frowned at his playful smile. "What do you want?"

"Nothing." He scooted to the edge of his seat and, with some effort, got himself upright again.

"How do you know who I am?"

He looked around the arena before speaking. "These games bring a variety of people. Many of them seeking financial gain." He looked back at me. "Be very careful who you speak with and how much attention you draw to yourself."

He reached into his back pocket and pulled out a flat envelope-sized package. He handed it to me and I reluctantly took it. "Who *are* you?" I asked again.

He looked down at me, a cold, calm amusement perched in his eyes. "Enjoy the show." He turned away and shouted out in his native tongue about his many tasty delights. He proceeded down the steps and pushed his food cart on without another glance in my direction.

I unfolded the bundle he had given me, which when fully expanded turned out to be a floppy hat to provide shade from the sun, as well as hide my face.

It was a strange turn of events—someone actually trying to help me instead of kill me. Though I still didn't trust the stranger, I slipped on the hat, popped a few more complimentary nuts in my mouth and watched the battle coming to its finale in the ring.

The two bare-chested gattaw were in such a scuffle it was hard to tell who was winning. Eventually, one of them got the upper hand and straddled the other. His fists moved to the beat of the audience's clapping hands. This fighter must have been a favorite, because everyone was cheering him on.

I looked over to my nearest neighbor, trying to read their tablet. I squinted at the names of the competitors on the game schedule. I blinked at the name and returned my gaze to the man in the pit. I rose to my feet and gravitated back down the steps to get a better view of his face from the railing.

The gattaw loomed over his stilled enemy, his teeth bared in a maniacal grimace. His eyes were ever vigilant of another potential attack. He panted hard, trying to regulate his body temperature from his exertion, as well as from the blistering sun beating down on his exposed back and chest.

My mouth dropped open, and I gripped the wall lining the pit. Even as my eyes concluded the truth, my mind refused to grasp it. His horns were shorter than most gattaw, but longer than I had ever seen them. It occurred to me that though I had been in his arms on more than one occasion. I had never seen the breadth of his muscular chest or his sculpted biceps without a shirt. As exhilarated as I should've been by his masterful physique, my heart twisted with the anguish of his display.

My beautiful Frog Prince was down in the pit, standing over the victim of his heavy fists, no longer the pinnacle of oppressive calm I knew and loved. He was feral. His emotions were unfurled and unchecked. It sickened me to see him this way, reduced to such a savage state. And yet, I was elated to see him alive.

Wishing Well

I watched Terrin leave the arena. I followed along the barrier, trying not to make my interest in him obvious and yet silently begging for him to look up at me. I resisted the urge to call out to him. What I really wanted to do was hurl myself into the pit and run into his arms. Unfortunately, much as the food vendor had warned me, it was unwise to draw attention to myself.

It didn't surprise me to see him marching proudly through the ring despite his circumstances. He had always presented himself assertively to humans and gattaw alike, but it had never been about his ego. It was about theirs. So many people viewed the gattaw as barbarians, including the gattaw. He didn't want anyone to confuse his strength with violence or his mind with ignorance.

Yet, here he was, competing in the very games which had earned the gattaw those descriptions.

And still, he walked proudly.

I watched him disappear under the awning of the cave ceiling. I dodged in and out of groups of spectators until I reached a set of stairs that descended into the pit. The small staircase wasn't much more than a stack of rocks, but it was enough to get me beneath the seats.

Around the corner, I found another set of stairs descending into a grotto. I looked around for someone to object to my presence, but there was no one around to complain. I stepped off the arena floor onto a set of wide, shallow stairs. With every step, the temperature dropped a little more. By the time I reached the bottom, nature's best air conditioning had reduced the sun's beating rays to a comfortable chill.

Though the cavern stretched on, a heavy iron fence with an ornate gate barred my admittance. Guarding that gate was the biggest gattaw I had ever seen. I stopped before him, waiting for him to draw a weapon or grunt his disapproval of my presence, but he didn't move or speak.

I took my life into my hands and stepped forward. When he didn't lob my head off, I took another. Step by slow step, I approached until I was right in front of him. He dropped his head, turning his stoic gaze on the shaking leaf in front of him.

His horns were long and slightly twisted like a bull's. I was quite certain if he applied for the position of Satan, he would be a shoo-in with the exception of his green skin.

I cleared my throat and spoke in the meekest voice I had ever used this side of puberty. "Is this where the champions live?" He tipped his head, not understanding my words. I took another tentative step forward, and he reached for his sword. I raised my hands, surrendering any construed intent. "Easy, big guy," I whispered. "I just want to peek." I pointed to my eyes and then the room he was guarding. After a brief pause, a small smirk tipped his lips, and he stepped to one side, revealing the entrance gates to me.

The detailed design depicted on them was of two male gattaw simultaneously killing each other with their copper swords. Thick twisted iron rods exaggerated their horns. Their faces, morphed in rage and pain, were the epitome of a good gattaw death.

I stepped forward and peered between the lethal swords to the expansive space behind the gates, which branched off into several slender passageways. Much of the cave's interior was dried out, including the stone-built fountain in the center of the room. Copper coins filled the basin instead of water. Each one glimmered in the sunlight from a skylight above them.

I shifted to see a little better and bumped into the beast next to me. I looked up at him and pointed to the fountain. "What are the coins for?" I rubbed my fingers together in the semi-universal symbol for money, which, to be fair, he might understand as some kind of sexual proposition—it was always a toss-up.

He glanced back to where I was pointing and pulled his sword. I took a giant step back, but instead of running me through, he tapped the blade with his claw, making it *ting*. I nodded in understanding and looked back at the fountain. Instead of being filled with wishes, this well was filled with the dead. A handful of coins were all that remained of each gattaw killed in the arena. How deep did the hole go? Or was that only this year's quota?

The men had died valiantly in the games.

It was a great honor to be one of the fallen.

No matter how many times I tried to feed myself that load of bullshit, I still ended up vomiting it back up.

I just couldn't swallow it.

The guard grumbled something and stepped back in front of the door. His latitude for sightseeing had finally run out. I thanked him and headed back to my seat.

Forever Ago

I sat on the long stone steps of the auditorium, inexcusably called seats. Ignoring the prejudicial glares from a group of gattaw several steps below me, I scanned the crowd for Ayil. He had been gone for hours. I knew he was schmoozing for information, but I really didn't enjoy roasting in the sun alone. If not for my hat, I would have been beet red with a blistered nose by now.

I caught the eye of a human behind me. I gave him a slight nod, acknowledging the camaraderie of our similarities. As much as it pleased me to meet new people and explore the elaborate tapestry of species the universe provided, it was always good to see a familiar face.

The human flipped up his sunglasses and smiled at me, no doubt also pleased to see a pale face among a sea of green. I gave him a civil smile and moved my attention up to the box seats above our section.

Finally, I had located Ayil.

He was laughing it up with someone inside. He also had a glass of wine in one hand and a cluster of berries in the other. I narrowed my eyes on him, psychically willing him to choke on the damned things. Here I was dying of thirst and he was getting sauced.

"Son of a bitch," I mumbled. I caught the human's attention behind me again, and he smirked. "Not you, sorry." I turned around and waved my hand as a makeshift fan.

I could feel eyes on me, so I ventured to take another peek at the grinning human. He winked at me, adding to his creep factor. I grimaced, realizing this man had mistaken my social nicety as flirtation.

I didn't bother with the civility of a smile this time. I just turned back around, prepared to ignore him. However, my fears for my safety prevented me from keeping my eyes straight for too long.

I turned to check on him and found him gone. I surveyed the upper area to see if he had changed seats, but I didn't see him.

"You must be lost," the man said from directly beside me.

I gasped and twisted back to face him. "What the hell? You scared the crap out of me."

"Sorry, I thought you heard me." He chuckled. "You looked like you might want some company."

I sighed and rolled my eyes. "I am not a pleasure girl, if that's what you're getting at." I shifted away from the intrusive conversationalist.

"I'm not sure how anyone could confuse you with a pleasure girl. You are far too regal for prostitution, Princess."

Son of a bitch! Was I wearing a damn sign on my back? Was my execution bid now being advertised on galactic billboards?

My heart went into overdrive. I shifted to the edge of my seat, once again prepared to make a quick escape. I turned my head slowly to examine the threat being presented, or at least to spot the knife aimed at my side. The spectators weren't supposed to have any weapons, but they didn't exactly search everyone on the way in.

I looked over the stranger before me. He wasn't a pirate. He wasn't a traditional hitman—although that description was expanding every day. His designer black suit was complete with a red silk tie and streamlined sunglasses. He had a handheld computer tablet similar to the one given to Ayil, only bigger. He was slender—almost skinny—but that didn't guarantee he wasn't strong.

"You don't remember me, do you?" he asked.

I stared at the eyes behind the sunglasses, trying to determine whether the smirk on his face was at my expense or not. His trimmed goatee, sharp features, and coiffed brunet hair made him handsome, but not really my type.

He leaned in a little closer. "I'm disappointed. I thought I might have made an impression on you."

I frowned, trying to remember the many nameless faces that had tried to kidnap me or kill me over the past few years. "Don't take it to heart. I have a lot of men in my past."

"That's a shame. For the last seven years, I've been taking credit for setting you free."

I dipped my brow and narrowed my eyes, trying desperately to place his face and voice. Unlike the plastic surgery victim in the tent above, I remembered this man. "You..." I tipped my head, still questioning my mental calculation. "Mr. Davis?" I asked.

He beamed. "There you go." He clicked his tongue and poked his nose. "I was hoping I hadn't become a spec in your rear-view mirror." I dropped my mouth open, but instead of the usual friendly banter, I wrapped my arms around him in an all-consuming hug. He chuckled and patted my arm. "Well, I wasn't expecting that reaction."

I leaned back and looked at him. Mr. Davis was the man responsible for selling me Rayne's ship. If it hadn't been for his quick wheeling and dealing, I would not have been able to have my space adventures. Granted, my space adventures now included multiple near-death experiences, but I was still grateful for the opportunities Mr. Davis had opened up for me.

"That's a belated thank you." I smiled and he chuckled. "What are you even doing here?"

"I should ask you the same thing." He glanced at the fight going on in the ring and checked his tablet. I had no doubt he was placing bets, winning ample amounts of money, and all from the comfort—such as it was—of his seat.

"Oh, what, me? I come here all the time." He glanced over at me, trying to see if I was kidding or not. "Long story. My friend has gotten himself tangled into the dogfights. We are hoping to buy him out of it."

Mr. Davis hissed. "The prices around here for buybacks are pretty steep. Especially if they know you want them. Most of the people sold into this sport start out with a debt. The head traders usually won't let them go until their debt is paid and they can make a significant profit on them. The buyout would have to be pretty high for them to consider it. What's his name? I'll take a peek at his odds." Mr. Davis poked his tablet to bring up the stats.

"Terrin, 23rd tribe of the Agoff. He was competing earlier."

Davis raised his brow. "That's a pretty well-known name around here." He browsed the tablet, searching for the information he wanted. When he found it he shook his head. "I'm not sure you're going to have any luck with a buyout."

"What do you mean?"

"I mean, your friend is one of the top competitors. In fact, he is *the* top competitor."

"I can't buy him?" I frowned, seeing our plan falling to pieces already.

"Don't get me wrong, you could, but..." He looked me over. "I guess it depends if your credit scan still works."

I rubbed my forehead. "I can't use credit, Mr. Davis. I'm in a situation that requires extreme anonymity."

"Yeah, I figured that, but..." He looked around, as if he getting a sense of my need for paranoia. "I'm not suggesting you endanger yourself, but short of a ringer, I'm not sure you're going to earn enough money to buy him back."

"A ringer, huh?" I scooted a little closer to him. "You're putting a lot of money on bets, aren't you?"

"Yeah, why?" He narrowed his eyes; immediately suspicious I was hitting him up for money.

"Maybe I could give you a tip on a competitor, and maybe you could give me a finder's fee when you win big on him."

"Which one is he?"

I shook my head. "This is business, Mr. Davis. First, we talk money."

"You're sure he will win?"

"As long as they put a blade in his hand, he will win."

"Okay, Princess, because I'm a nice guy, I'll give you 10% of my winnings."

I scoffed. "I'll take 50%, because I'm *not* a nice girl."

Mr. Davis smiled and leaned in a little closer. "Are you aware how much you are worth? It would be much more profitable for me to claim your bounty."

I narrowed my eyes at him, but I was mostly certain he was teasing. "Are you threatening me, Mr. Davis?"

"Not at all. This is business. I'm just reminding you that you don't have crap for leverage with me."

"No, I have something better."

"And what's that?"

"Desperation. You helped me once, when you could have walked away. You could have made more money by keeping that ship. If money is all you really cared about, you wouldn't have sold me that ship."

A sly smile spread across Mr. Davis's face. "That's sweet. You've made me out to be a hero." He bit his lip in contemplation. "Well, we all make mistakes. I tell you what..." Mr. Davis shifted and looked out over the crowd as if someone might be watching us. "If your fighter wins his next match, I'll give you 20% of my winnings."

I lifted my hand to shake on the deal and he gave my hand a squeeze. "He's listed under Alex Turner." He paused, holding my hand a moment longer before going back to peck on his tablet. "How did you go from buying clunkers to betting on dogfights?" I asked.

He chuckled under his breath. "This isn't work, Kit. This is my vacation."

"You're a strange cat, Mr. Davis." I looked out onto the battle below. Two gattaw were beating the crap out of each other, much as the ones before them. I wasn't sure how these games continued to appeal to the non-gambling spectators. "You might be my greatest ally, though."

He chuckled. "Like I said, we all make mistakes." I looked back at his smirk and he lowered his sunglasses so I could see him wink. "A word of advice from a more seasoned negotiator. Don't ever let them know what you really want until it's paid for and in your back pocket. Not everyone can be swayed by a pretty face."

"I'll remember that."

"Now—" Mr. Davis held up the tablet, which displayed a picture of Rayne. "Could you explain to me how a dead man is competing?"

"He was never technically dead."

"He woke up?"

"Yup."

Mr. Davis shook his head. "That's not possible."

"There were some very specific factors contributing to his long sleep."

He looked down at the tablet and frowned. "How interesting. Mr. Turner is alive and well, and about to beat the hell out of a gattaw."

"No, Mr. Davis, if I know my husband, he is going to kill him."

Tбe Plan

Mr. Davis descended the steps as Ayil came down from his party upstairs. He gave the man a weary look before plopping down beside me. "Who the hell is that?"

"Old friend."

"Since when do you have old friends?" He wrinkled his nose at me.

"What did you find out?"

"Damn, it is *hot* out here." He pulled his shirt away from him to fan his chest.

"No shit, I've been sitting here for over an hour while you've been getting red-faced with cocktails. What did you find out?"

"There's a series of caves running under this entire facility, just like in the pit. That's where Terrin and Rayne will be when they aren't competing. You see those guys up there?" Ayil pointed behind me to the box seats he had recently left. I looked at the two bald men, both human, in ornate robes. They were observing the competition from plush chairs while two half-naked gattaw women fanned them—part bodyguard, part playboy bunny. "Those guys are the highest of the high. They pretty much run the games."

"Why am I not surprised they're human?"

"The gattaw don't want to handle the financing. They let the humans deal with that in exchange for keeping the rest of the universe off their backs and out of their business. They do this for the love of the game."

"You mean for the love of the gore," I grumbled. "Speaking of financing. We may not have enough money to buy Terrin back."

"What do you mean?"

"Apparently, he's made a name for himself. He's going to be pretty expensive."

"How expensive?"

"Expensive enough that I tipped Mr. Davis off about Rayne." I nodded to Mr. Davis, who was conversing with a pretty young humanoid in the first row. "He'll pay us a 20% finder's fee when Rayne wins his first match. If I'm right about the flexibility in his bank account, we should be on the right track, but we will still need more. When does Rayne fight?"

"Looks like they're saving him for the end of the afternoon. They like to end the day with a... kill."

I looked at Ayil and frowned. "*When* he wins, his ranking will go up, right? We may not be the only ones betting on him."

"Probably."

"It's going to take us forever to get enough money together."

"Time we have. No one is going to be looking for you on Miorita."

"I hope you're right." I glanced around at the threats skirting me. I didn't want to worry Ayil by explaining the very busy social calendar of my youth, and that it was only a matter of time before somebody recognized me. "And what happens when Rayne wins? He's pretty lethal and the gattaw don't like it when humans win. How long before someone decides to even the playing field and get rid of the nuisance human screwing up their bets?"

"I don't know."

"So, the plan stopped pretty much after "Let's hand Rayne over to the dogfights." How are we—"

Ayil turned and pressed his fingers to my lips, stilling my queries and concerns. He raised his eyebrows and shook his head. "I don't know, Kit, but we're gonna deal. We always get out of this shit, and this time will be no exception."

I nodded, and he released my mouth. "I saw Terrin." Ayil looked at me, gauging how I felt about seeing a man I had until recently thought was dead. "He didn't see me, though. We need to talk to him—let him know we're here and going to get him out. How do we get in to see him?"

Ayil smiled at me. "How do you think?" He winked at me. "Suck up to the bosses." He nodded up to the tent behind us.

Schmoozing

"What did you say your name was again, my dear?" I glanced down at the third refill of spiked fruit juice being poured into my goblet. Liquid truth serum, if there ever was; I was already getting lightheaded from the alcohol content. I looked up at the robust man sitting next to me. His cheeks were rosy, despite the ample shade of his luxury seating.

"Kit," I answered.

"Kit what?" the other man asked. I shifted on the plush chair, which had been graciously placed between the two men.

"Just Kit." I smiled at the taller, lankier bald man. His features were far from rosy, but the berries he was eating had made his lips purple. If I had come in on him lying down, I might have assumed he was choking on his fruit. As it was, I wasn't convinced he didn't have a vitamin deficiency. "I prefer to keep things simple. Not to mention first names are friendlier."

"Oh, I agree," Rosy Cheeks said. "That's why I like to conduct business over drinks."

"And food," Pale Face added.

I was certain their volleying conversation was all to benefit their negotiation process, but between my drink and my head turning to look at the men, I would sooner spill my lunch than the beans. "Oh, my." I placed my hand to my forehead, feigning my feminine weakness to spirits. "I think I need a little air." I stood up, waved my hand in my face and moved to the front of the box to lean on the railing. "Sweetheart, would you mind getting my fan?"

Ayil's eyes bulged at me from the back of the box next to the snack table. There was, of course, no fan, nor anywhere to fetch it from. I blinked my eyes at him coyly, and he tipped his head and pinched his lips in disapproval. Without a socially acceptable way of denying my request, he indulged me and left the tent.

Once he was gone, I lost my disingenuous smile and looked over the men before me. "All right, let's cut to the chase. I am a woman of means and I couldn't care less about your stupid games. However, what intrigues me is the men who play them. Young, strong, virile men." I took a breath and fanned myself again. "Men who could provide certain services, beyond household chores." I raised my brow and looked at them. "Am I being blunt enough, gentlemen?"

"Quite, my dear," Rosy Cheeks said with a hint of displeasure in his voice. "There are a few humans who could provide you with a memorable—"

"I want a gat."

Rosy Cheeks blanched—figuratively—at my suggestion.

"Madam, you do realize that your..." Pale Face wiggled his finger over my lower extremities. "...is not compatible with a gat?"

I laughed. "I only need his mouth."

"What about the man you brought in?" Rosy Cheeks asked. "Wasn't he up to your standards?"

"Oh, definitely, and I'll be happy to buy him back—should he live, I mean. But I'm ready to add to my collection." I turned and looked out at the deathblows being swung inside the pit. Green skin on either side had turned puce. "Something different. Something dangerous." I glanced back at the men. "To be perfectly honest, gentlemen, I've been enamored with the gattaw since I was a child. Something about the horns, I think."

"If..." Pale Face shifted to lean over his knees. "...we were willing to part with one of our gats. It would be up to you to contain him. I can't guarantee the competitor would agree to work for you in any capacity, let alone that specific job role. I'm sure your young companion is quite capable, but as you know, these creatures are not easily manhandled."

I bit my lip, ignoring the word *creatures*. "I am aware of the gattaw strength and I am looking forward to it, but... I do agree I will have to find the right one for my needs. One not just willing, but enthusiastic at the prospect." I shifted to lean against the rail and bowed my head slightly. "Which brings us to a rather awkward conversation." I pinched my lips before continuing. "I was hoping to... sample the men. Get to know their skills and assets, as well as ascertain their loyalties."

The men exchanged a glance, and Rosy Cheeks spoke first. "We rarely allow participants into the caves. It creates a conflict of interest for the betting."

"I understand, but I think we can all agree I'm not a heavy better."

"Not yet, anyway," Rosy Cheeks pointed out.

"And even if you aren't, Mr. Davis is," Pale Face added. "We saw you talking to him earlier."

I raised my brow, impressed at how closely these men were monitoring the social activities of little ole me. Or perhaps it was Mr. Davis they were watching. "He's an old friend."

"Mr. Davis is a very high-stakes player in the game," Rosy Cheeks explained. "He is usually quite profitable."

"Profit..." Pale Face stood and moved to stand beside me. Though he was still only sipping on his beverage, the movement seemed hostile. "...is something we prefer to keep on our end of the dogfights."

I stared at his purple lips, trying to discern whether it was a threat against me or Mr. Davis. "I spoke to him about the games, but only because I'm completely out of my element here. I needed some advice. Naturally, he wasn't willing to give away his trade secrets."

Pale Face chuckled. "No, I imagine not. But that doesn't mean you didn't give him crucial information about your competitor. Information he might use to increase his profit."

I took a breath and blinked at him. "Truthfully, I don't know if I did or didn't. It never occurred to me I might have information he could use." I feigned ignorance. "May I ask? If he's a problem for you, why do you let him participate?"

Rosy Cheeks snorted. "Apparently, you don't know his employer."

"His employer? No, I'm afraid my knowledge of Mr. Davis is limited."

"Let's just say we prefer to keep Mr. Davis happy," Pale Face said. "However, that doesn't mean we want to make his time here any more lucrative than it already is."

"I'll be sure to limit my conversations with Mr. Davis to the weather and cosmic phenomena. Now what about my request to… interview some slaves?"

"I'm afraid that's out of the question," Pale Face said.

I sighed and looked between them. "Are you really telling me no?" I dipped my brow at them. "I must say, I don't think I've ever encountered a situation that wasn't negotiable. Is it the numbers? How much?"

Rosy Cheeks snorted, nearly choking on one of his grapes. "As you've said, madam, you aren't much of a gambler. I doubt you could afford to buy your way into the caves." I was certain I could. My credit stamp was still active. However, I didn't want to risk bringing a warship to Miorita. Knowing my luck, they would bomb the entire planet from space.

An interstellar war caused by one act of teenage rebellion. Yeah, that sounded about right.

"Frankly," Pale Face continued, "even if you could, we don't trust you," he said flatly, leveling a stare at me that told me there would be no negotiating with him.

"Then I am sorry to have wasted your time." I lowered my goblet to the railing and bowed to each of them.

"Not at all," Pale Face said, once again congenial. "We always enjoy company, especially as distinguished and refined as you." I heard a slight snort from Rosy Cheeks, and though Pale Face was deigning to kiss my hand, I got the distinct impression they considered me to be a bit of a yokel. They had no reason to assume otherwise—I wasn't exactly dressed like royalty. However, the spoiled part of me, which always demanded to have my way, reared its ugly head and I had to keep myself from flaunting how valuable I really was. Never mind the threat to my life, I just wanted to see the looks on their faces when I told them I was the carrier of the most revered DNA strand since the birth of civilization.

"I'll do my shopping from a distance." I resisted my baser, over-privileged instincts and moved to exit the tent.

"In the meantime," Rosy Cheeks said, making me stop to listen, "you should really reconsider your choice of a gat slave." He swirled his wine absentmindedly, as if contemplating his own words. "They really are a stubborn sort. They don't train well. And believe you me, you can't discipline them. By God, it's a good thing they come house broken, or you'd have to keep them outside." The men laughed at his joke.

My mind reeled with a dozen snappish comments to correct their blatant prejudice, but I remembered what Mr. Davis had said about not revealing what I really wanted. Rather than give a hint about my sympathy to the gattaw—and ultimately my inclination toward one specific one—I laughed at his joke and promised to take his recommendation into consideration.

Horns

"What do we do now?" I asked again.

"We'll figure something out," Ayil said as he blocked the setting sun from his eyes. "Regardless if we can get in to see him, we still have to make enough money to buy him back. And since we have a ringer, it will only be a matter of time."

The games were almost done for the day, and Rayne was the next up to compete. Our money was down for a steep bet and we were hoping to triple it.

"Speaking of our ringer." I pointed into the arena where Rayne was being placed for his battle. Despite my confidence in his abilities, I was excessively pleased to see he was fighting a rather slender gattaw. I shifted to the edge of my seat and endured a stuttered translation of the introductions over the loudspeakers.

I saw Rayne scanning the crowd and when his gaze landed on us, I resisted the urge to wave or holler out his name like an obsessed fan. He held my gaze a moment before looking around at the remainder of the audience, as if he was evaluating each and every one of them.

Ayil leaned into my ear and whispered, "Where's the knife?"

I searched him with my eyes, but I couldn't see anything resembling a weapon on him. I looked over at the gattaw and saw no copper sword to speak of. This was going to be hand-to-hand combat only. "Shit."

The drums sounded and the men immediately crouched, preparing for a match of muscle to muscle. Never mind that Rayne was biologically lacking in that department.

The gattaw lunged at him, barreling into him at full speed. Rayne easily avoided the impact and even helped direct his opponent's head into a nearby stalagmite. The crowd booed at his success, but they quieted to a din as the gattaw pulled away from the layered rock. He reached up and tugged on the broken tip of his horn.

"Oh, hell, that's not a good way to start, is it?" Ayil asked.

"No, they are rather fond of their horns."

I could see Rayne cuss under his breath. He knew he had pissed off this guy a little too early in the game. The fight had just gotten personal.

The gattaw came at him again, but this time Rayne couldn't avoid him. He was shoved to the ground and punched repeatedly. I grimaced and shifted uncomfortably in my seat. I wanted more than anything to jump down into the pit and help him, but aside from being a completely inadequate fighter, I knew we still had to play our parts until the very end.

Rayne got his feet up under the man's chest and used all of his leg strength to shove him off. He rolled over and jumped back to his feet. The gattaw tried to use his head as a punching bag, but Rayne dodged every hit.

He slipped behind his attacker and looped his arm around his neck. It wasn't the best strategy against the gattaw, since their necks were difficult to strangle, but he was running out of options. He needed to wear this man out before he got worn out himself.

The crowd cheered and laughed as the gattaw flailed with Rayne on his back. He finally got a grip on Rayne's leg and yanked him off. Looking out at the crowd, he pointed down at his prey. He dragged Rayne around, letting his head hit the rough ridges on the cave floor. The crowd laughed at Rayne's expense.

When he'd sapped the last of the laughter from them, he spun in a circle and launched Rayne across the ring. He landed and rolled behind one of the rocky outcrops. The gattaw raised his arms, milking the crowd's enthusiastic cheers.

"This must be his first competition," Ayil said. "He's showboating more than an ugly prostitute."

Rayne came out from behind his column and marched toward the gattaw. The crowd shouted in warning, but the gattaw was far too smitten with his own grandeur to be distracted.

I breathed a sigh of relief when I noticed the rock Rayne was carrying. It certainly wasn't a knife, but it was undoubtedly a bigger punch than he could inflict on his own.

The crowd's uproar finally alerted the gattaw to Rayne's presence, and he turned to defend himself. With the assistance of his rock, Rayne slammed a hard punch into the gattaw's face. He growled and Rayne punched him again. The second time, the gattaw tried to duck, putting his remaining horn right in the path of the impact.

A second horn tip rattled against the rocky floor of the cave pit.

Ayil groaned. "Another one bites the dust."

Rayne all but rolled his eyes at his luck. Meanwhile, his opponent roared to the skies, demanding vengeance for what was the equivalent of a bad haircut. However, symbolically, it was as if Rayne had castrated him.

"These guys must associate their horns with masculinity," Ayil said, coming to the same conclusion about the warrior's irrational anger.

"Yup, and Rayne just turned him into a eunuch."

The gattaw grabbed Rayne's wrist and ripped the rock out of his hand. He thankfully threw it away and punched him with a bare fist only.

Unfortunately, this time the gattaw didn't let up to get his kudos from the crowd. He punched him again and again until he dropped to the ground. He straddled him and kept hitting him.

I bit the inside of my cheek as I watched his face turn puce and bleed. Ayil grabbed my hand and squeezed it hard.

The loudspeakers prematurely announced a win, and the gattaw looked up from his attack. The crowd cheered again, and rather than continue to pummel Rayne, the gattaw stood and raised his fists in triumph. I was more than happy to see him walk away before killing my husband, but it still left me with one minor problem.

Rayne had just lost.

Consequently, Ayil and I had lost too. I looked over at him and frowned. He frowned back at me. "We just lost 5000 units," I said.

"Yup."

"We don't even have enough to buy Rayne back."

"Nope."

I looked down into the pit where Rayne was being dragged away. He was technically conscious, but pretty loopy. As I looked away, I caught sight of Mr. Davis. He was sitting a few steps below us glaring at me.

"Oh shit," I mumbled and moved down the steps to speak with him.

Rather than listen to my rambled apology, he walked away. I persisted and followed him, but the crowd was already disbanding for the evening and I got caught up by several tall gattaw who were not interested in allowing me past them.

"Mr. Davis!" I shouted and hopped up and down, trying to get him to stop. I bobbed left and right, but I couldn't even see him anymore. I looked back to see if I could return to Ayil, but I was stuck in the herd. All I could do was follow them out and meet Ayil outside.

As the crowd ambled down the steps, I shifted off to one side between the end of the stone bleachers and the wood scaffolding that supported the box seating. I ignored the occasional translatable slurs about weak, pathetic humans and waited for everyone to clear out through the outer wooden gates.

"Thanks for the tip," Mr. Davis said right beside me.

I jumped and whipped around to face him. "How the hell do you do that?" He shifted against the stone wall behind him, notably monitoring the people behind me. "Mr. Davis, I'm so sorry. I didn't mean for you to lose any money. I really thought he was going to win, but—"

"—they didn't give him a knife," he finished for me.

"Exactly."

"They didn't give him a knife because I told them not to."

"You what?" Ayil said before I had the chance to. I looked back and saw him coming around the corner.

"You wanted him to lose?" I asked.

"Of course," Mr. Davis said.

"You son of a bitch!" Ayil jumped at his throat, pressing him harder against the wall. "You could have gotten him killed!"

"Quiet!" Mr. Davis shoved his hands away. "Don't draw attention to us."

"He's right, Rayne nearly died out there."

"I made sure they called the win before the gat finished him. He's an attention whore. I knew his anger wouldn't outlive his ego."

"You'd better have a good reason for this," I said.

"There are always people who bet on a beginner, just in case they win. Rayne will play again tomorrow, but his odds will be as low as they could be. However, tomorrow he *will* be armed. Put your money on his next fight and you'll win, even bigger than you would have won today."

"You might have told us this before we spent half of it on this one," I said.

"I lost too. We can't dismiss him today and then suddenly start betting on him tomorrow. The brothers don't like cheaters unless *they* are on the winning side. We lose today and we win tomorrow."

"And we're supposed to trust that he'll be armed tomorrow?" Ayil asked.

Mr. Davis nodded. "Feel free to check my bets." He leaned a little closer to Ayil. "I never willingly lose money—unless I can win it back." He moved to leave, but I grabbed his arm.

"Does our agreement still stand? 20%?"

Mr. Davis smiled and shook his head. "The agreement was for the first match."

"Which you intentionally threw," I argued

"Yeah. Thanks for the tip." He gave me a dismissive shrug and pushed his way into the exiting crowd.

"Who the hell is that guy?" Ayil asked.

I stared after my former savior, reconsidering my sentiments regarding his past actions. "Honestly? I have no idea."

TRAMPS

Rather than fight shoulder to shoulder with crowds of gattaw, Ayil and I waited for the stadium to clear out before we made our way out the exit. As we passed the wooden gates with the bloody handprint, I noticed a cluster of women and some men gathered at the far end of the coliseum. They were being allowed entrance through a separate door. Ayil noted the side entrance as well. We glanced at each other and meandered over to see what was going on.

Before being admitted through the small door, the people ahead of us were searched thoroughly. However, they weren't being asked for any credentials.

"Kit," Ayil whispered to me as we got near the front of the line. "We need to get out of here. I think this is the prostitute's entrance." I frowned and glanced at the gattaw women in front of me. I noted their provocative attire and pungent perfume, which I assumed allured male gattaw.

"This might be our only chance to talk to Terrin. Plus, I think we should check on Rayne."

"Kit, there is no pretending in sex. They will expect you to do something while you are in there. Either you open your legs or your mouth."

"Do you have a better way to get in?"

"I'll go in and find him. Just step out of line."

My heart pounded as I watched the women before us being vigorously searched, practically molested, to check for weapons. I swallowed hard and nodded to Ayil. I hated sending him in to do the dirty work I wasn't willing to do myself. He could tell himself he enjoyed his sexuality until he was blue in the face, but I knew he wanted a choice. He wanted the freedom to choose his partners as much as I did.

I stepped to the side behind him to duck out of the path to the door, but a hand grabbed my wrist and pulled me back. I stared into the face of a gattaw as he looked me over. "No, I changed my mind." I shook my head, but he searched me anyway, pressing his hands under my armpits and around my breasts.

"She's in the wrong line." Ayil tried to pull me away, but he got caught up in his own search from another gattaw.

"No, I don't want to go in." I tried to press away his hands as he infiltrated my pants. I gasped as his fingers probed me, checking each cavity for contraband. "Holy crap!" I looked at Ayil wide-eyed, but he was receiving his own cavity check. His jaw was tensed and I could see he was resisting the urge to fight by clenching his hands into tight fists. It reminded me of how he'd reacted to Gunder kissing him the first time we met. I hated to see it again.

The gattaw barked a foreign word at me and shoved me toward the door. I turned back to explain I had made a mistake, but he didn't understand my language. Since the only gattaw words I knew were the cuss words Terrin threw at me when he was angry with me, I could hardly translate my objections well enough to get out of the predicament.

They shoved Ayil inside right after me, and the door slammed behind us. We turned to each other, and both said, "Are you okay?"

He chuckled at me and shook his head. "Next time, move a little faster, okay?"

"Next time? How many times do you think we'll be hooking together?"

"You never know."

A gattaw standing farther down the narrow descending passageway barked an order at us. The rest of the group was well ahead of us and he was waiting for us.

Ayil grabbed my hand and led the way past the interior guard. I was pleased to see he didn't follow us. I supposed we were meant to go cell to cell peddling our bodies to whomever was willing to spend their winnings on us.

As we proceeded down the cave trails, I heard animalistic moans and groans. My hand squeezed tight around Ayil's and he pulled me a little closer.

We rounded a turn in the path and came upon a wider section, where the cells were built into rock cavities. The first cell was small, containing two male gattaw. One man was pressed up to the bars, pants down, receiving an oral favor from the female gattaw kneeling on the other side of the cell. I couldn't help but notice the technique she was using to avoid cutting her mouth on his spurs.

The other man was lying on a bench in the back of the cell. He looked thoroughly content, having already received his services.

We slipped by, careful not to disturb the woman at our feet. After a wide pillar of rock, we reached a second cell. This one contained multiple male humanoids. Three human women were already at the bars, two performing orally for the mewling men inside, and one bruising her ass on the bars while her partner yanked her back against them to get as much access to her as possible.

Two other men jumped forward and started shouting for us to come on over. I grimaced at their bruised and bloody faces before cowering behind Ayil's shoulder.

"This is our cell!" the woman with an empty mouth yelled at us. "Get on with ya!" She motioned for us to leave and we did, without delay.

We passed several more single cells; all being serviced or already serviced. Thankfully, there were lots of prostitutes to go around, or Ayil and I would be in a troublesome situation. Not to mention very sore.

As we rounded another bend, the passage narrowed, and we were right up against several of the cells. A gattaw came up to the bars, but scoffed at us and turned back. I wondered if it was just as disappointing to them to be limited to a certain species for their sexual pleasure, or if they considered other races beneath them—unworthy of their genitalia.

We reached another cell filled with two human men. I bit my lip as the men came to the bars and started undoing the snaps on their flies. There was no question what we were offering or the cost. They just slung themselves through the bars and waited.

Ayil stepped forward and shoved me back. "These two are mine."

"I want the girl," one of them objected and stepped away from Ayil.

"Tough shit, she's got a standing appointment for first dibs. Either take me, or take sloppy seconds."

The man grimaced. "I can't get hard for a guy; at least let me touch her." I shook my head and moved away. "Hey, bitch! I got money to spend. I won two fights today. Get your ass over here."

"She's got an appointment, I said." Ayil grabbed at the man to distract him. The man pulled away and moved down the bars to look at me. "What kind of prostitute are you?" He narrowed his eyes at me. "Guards!" he called.

"Easy, bud." Ayil moved over to me and kissed my cheek. "She's new, okay. She's shy."

"Holy shit," the man whispered. "Is she... a virgin?"

Ayil chuckled. "In all the ways that count."

"I've never had a virgin before." The man continued to salivate over the prospect of having me. "What's that cost, anyway?"

"More than you could afford after twenty fights. Now, do you want your blow or not?"

"Yeah, but like I said, I need her, too. Just let me touch her."

"What do you say, girl?" Ayil nuzzled up close to my ear to whisper. "If they find out we aren't prostitutes, they will either beat us to a bloody pulp or throw us in a cell overnight to teach us a lesson." I nodded, agreeing to the only option I had. "Just think about what we are trying to accomplish."

Ayil moved back to the bars and kneeled down before the man. I moved up beside him, not hindering his access, but giving the man something to grab while Ayil worked his magic. I cringed as the man pinched at my buttocks and breasts. He harshly manhandled any part of me he could get to.

For a moment, I thought about Rayne and how angry he would be with me for allowing myself to be in this situation. Was this cheating? I certainly wasn't enjoying it. I wasn't even participating, technically.

After a few minutes, Ayil finished off the man. To my relief, the other man seemed content with Ayil for entertainment. Unfortunately, he wanted more than Ayil's mouth. I grimaced as Ayil lowered his drawers and backed into the bars. Rather than watch my friend being defiled, I moved on without him.

I rushed past several cells as if I were in a hurry and late for an appointment. The humanoid men inside whistled and hollered after me, trying to get my attention, but I held up a finger as if I would be right back to attend to them.

My outstretched finger was still up when I rounded the corner to the next set of cells. A hand reached out from the bars and pulled me forward, pressing me to the bars. "Oh, yes, human," the man rejoiced from behind the bars. He was not quite human, but rather a half-breed between gattaw and human. It was a rare thing, since human males couldn't usually impregnate gattaw women, and for obvious reasons, it didn't work well the other way around either. Regardless, there were a few of them running around—defying the laws of reproduction like mules.

"I am so sick of hard knobby skin," he said and pulled me forward into a sloppy kiss. "Oh God, your lips are so soft."

"Don't!" I tried to wrench away. "I have an appointment."

"Yeah, with me." He pinched my ass. I yelped, and he moved his hand to my breast and squeezed it to a painful level too. "Take your shirt off and jump up and down. I want to see your tits bounce." He released me and then released himself. I stared at his large member as I backed away from the cell. "Don't worry, the spines aren't very long. They won't hurt that much. I'm told it's no worse than period cramps."

I frowned and ran away from his cell.

"Hey!" he yelled after me. "Come back. I'll pay extra!"

I made it down several more cells, ducking through a round of low-hanging stalactites to get past without being molested by the occupants. Finally, I reached a fork in the road.

There were two choices and both of them involved passing a gattaw guard sleeping against a rock. I headed down the passageway, but he put out his foot to stop me. "Wrong way, human?" he asked, barely lifting his eyelids to identify me.

I was beyond pleased the man could speak my language, but that also left more room for error. Grunting and pointing were easy to mistake for ignorance. "What do you mean?"

"This is the winner's circle. The humanoids are back the way you came."

I looked back at the passageway I had recently left. The moans and groans I had left behind were getting closer. The harem was making their way down to me. They were making quick work of their duties. For a moment, I wondered how much they were making in a night. It was a demeaning occupation and beyond repugnant, but what a racket.

"I'm here for the gattaw. The winners pay better."

"Oh, yeah?" The guard's lidded eyes opened, and he looked me over. He reached forward, tugging on my pants. "You got an insert?"

My mouth gaped as I tried to remember the many devices invented to protect women from gattaw intercourse. According to my research, they weren't really enjoyable for either party, but it was nice to know someone out there was determined to get laid by whomever they wanted to, no matter the risk.

"I excel in oral, actually."

"Is that so?" The guard didn't sound convinced.

"Just like milking a cow," I said confidently, even though I wasn't familiar with milking cows or gattaw. "Only sideways," I added.

The guard perked his brow and leaned forward. "Why don't you show me?"

I shrugged and pointed toward my preferred destination. "The big money is that way, if I'm not mistaken."

The guard grimaced. "Suit yourself. They never pay as much for humans, though. Especially in the winner's circle. They wear out too easy." He slapped my butt and leaned back in his chair to sleep. "He might be occupied. Just wait in line."

I nodded and headed down the path to the winner's circle, as he called it. As I made my way through the passageway, I met up with two young female gattaw. Their ornate dresses looked a little disheveled, and they were whispering to one another. When they reached me, they took one look at me and broke into a fit of giggles.

I bit back my general annoyance at being the butt of their jokes and continued on. A short distance later, I emerged into a wide cavern with three large cells. The first two appeared empty, but I could see a familiar face lounging in the third one, straight ahead of me.

Guided by the dim firelight, I approached the cell. Terrin was lying on a wooden bench in the center of the cell, barefoot and bare-chested. A heavy layer of hay filled the back of the room. I tried not to be offended by the animalistic bed. Long grasses were a common bedding material for the gattaw. Add an animal hide and it was no worse than the hard beds my ship came equipped with.

Terrin's arm draped over his face, shielding his eyes. I could see the bruises and cuts on his fists. His torso also bore the marks of his fights. He looked tired, dirty, and a little broken. All I wanted to do was take him out of this wretched place.

Unlike the other cells I had passed, his wasn't locked. A privilege, perhaps, for being a high-level competitor. I pushed open the door, which let out a soft squeak. I approached Terrin and sat down next to him on the bench—as best I could with his wide body taking up most of it. I reached up below his draping arm and caressed his cheek.

A soft chuckle shook his chest as I did. "Do they mean to kill me? I'm only just recovered."

Before I could reveal my identity, he sat up, looped his arms under mine, and threw me off the bench. I yelped as I landed in the pile of hay behind the bench. A second later, his heavy body followed, landing on top of me.

Terrin kissed me forcefully as he maneuvered his hips into position to press against me. I pushed against him, trying to break the connection, but it was useless. His hand roamed up my shirt, squeezing my breast. I feared another battering of my fragile skin, but he was gentle. He massaged his thumb over my budding nipple rather than pinch it.

I whimpered, partially from the unsolicited pleasure I was receiving from his erection pressing against me and partly because the strength he possessed frightened me.

There was no question of resistance. It was all up to him. If he wanted me, I would be his. And sadly, there was still a part of me that wanted him to take me. A sick, masochistic little girl who didn't understand the word no, despite hearing it so many times.

All at once, Terrin's lips stopped, his hand freezing on my breast. He drew back and stared at me. I panted in a few desperate breaths to regain my depleted oxygen.

"Mallory," he whispered and kissed me again. The fervency in his second kiss differed from the first one. Slower, yet deeper. As if his intention of having sex with me had changed to making love to me. His lips trailed down my neck, suckling the soft flesh with his hot lips. I was always surprised how warm he was. "Mallory, I thought you were dead," he whispered before raising his head to look at me. He stroked my hair and looked me over as if I had been reborn before his very eyes.

"I thought the same of you. I wanted to save you, but I couldn't get to you," I said, apologetic for my inadequacies as a heroine.

"Shh!" He pressed his forehead against mine. His unsteady breaths poured onto my lips. My breaths came a little deeper as I tried to get a grip on the moment and the emotions that had inundated it. His hand shifted slightly under my shirt, where he was still holding my breast. Our eyes met and his thumb shifted ever so slightly across the attentive flesh, which begged to be suckled. I swallowed hard and wet my lips.

There was an unspoken question between us. Do we finish what we started? Indulge in external pleasure of friction and pretend it's enough? Or do we stop and continue, as we have for some time, as... *friends*?

Terrin let out an exasperated exhale and yanked his hand from under my shirt. "Foolish girl. You shouldn't be here. Miorita is no place for you."

"I've trudged through the mud for Rayne. I bore the ineptitude of Gunder for Ayil. I think I can handle a few cacti for you."

Terrin let out a breathy chuckle and brushed his finger over my cheek. He hadn't moved an inch since he'd initially pinned me into his haystack bed, but the pressure against me had changed from a demanding desire to simply a heavy body weighing me down. I didn't bother mentioning that I couldn't feel my legs. "You should go, Mallory. You should leave here before you get hurt."

"The only thing that will hurt me would be to leave here without you."

Terrin shook his head. "I appreciate what you're trying to do, but nothing is predictable here. Everyone is corrupt. Everyone is trying to win."

"I am going to save you," I said firmly. Terrin stared down at me, his face revealing nothing. "You want to be saved, don't you?"

His eyes flitted over mine. He leaned in and kissed me again. As he released my lips, he pushed himself up. He extended his hand and helped me out of the haystack. I dusted off the excess straw while he watched me intently.

"I can't help but notice that you haven't answered my question," I said. "Are you content here, with your glory... and your harem?" I glanced away as I said it.

He crossed his arms and leaned against the wall behind him. "Do I detect a note of jealousy in your voice? You can't guilt me for every woman who isn't you."

I pursed my lips. "No, I'm pretty sure I can." I smiled to let him know I was kidding. "I'm not sure if it matters to you, but I should probably tell you Sicily is dead."

I noted a small shift in his features, but for the most part he seemed unaffected by the news. "She was a noble woman. I hope she died well."

"She did. She died debt-free."

He nodded. "That's all any of us can hope for. A good life and a respectable death." He looked me over and frowned. He moved toward me and pressed his hand to my belly, where I should've had a round bulge by now. "Oh, Mallory, no."

I placed my hand over his. "It's okay. Aresties is carrying her." His eyes narrowed with confusion. "She's going to be my surrogate, so we can keep the baby safe through the pregnancy."

"That was a wise choice." He frowned. "I hope you didn't do it so you could come here and save me."

"It was my primary motivation, but it's best to disguise her identity as much as we can."

Terrin dropped his arms and shook his head. "I thought motherhood would stop you from running headlong into danger."

"I'm not here to satisfy some teenage rebellion. I came here to get you away from this dangerous place."

Terrin's face lit with anger and he closed the distance between us. "I am in far more danger with you here," he scolded me in a low tone. "Do you know what they could ask of me if they had you as leverage? You are my only weakness, Mallory. My risks are my own, but the closer you are to me, the more they become your risks as well."

"That's why I'm here. To remove you from the risk. To get you—"

Terrin raised his hands to my face, making me flinch at the sudden pressure on my cheeks.

"Do you trust me, Mallory?"

"Of course," I said.

"Do you love me?" I licked my lips and nodded. I loved him more than I could I ever admit. More than I could ever admit and still be happy in my life. He leaned in and kissed me. This time his kiss was gentle, unassuming, and yet I felt the connection between us even stronger than with our heated kisses. He drew back and looked into my eyes. "I need you to leave."

I shook my head and gripped his arms. "I won't leave without you."

"Yes, you will," he whispered. His reddish eyes glistening with moisture, almost tearing over but not quite. "Because for once in your damned life you are going to do what I say."

I swallowed hard and fought back the stinging in my own eyes. "You know I'm not good at that."

"I know." He stroked my hair, examining the burgundy color. "Tell me you will obey me. Please. Just this once."

I touched his face the same as he was touching mine. "Are you telling me you really don't want to be saved? That you would rather stay in this hole in the ground rather than come home?"

He took in a breath and clenched his jaw before he spoke. "Mallory, this is my home. These are my people. This is where I belong." He pulled away from me, breaking all contact. "No, I don't want you to save me."

I stared at him, looking for some sign of deception, but his sympathetic features had returned to the stone cold gattaw I knew all too well.

"I don't believe you."

"You need to leave here. Get off of this planet and get out of the solar system."

"You can't seriously want this." I felt anger rise up in place of my heartbreak. "You are above this, Terrin. You are the most civilized man I know, human and gattaw alike. This barbarism is beneath you!"

"Get out!" Terrin's hand whipped across my face, sending me to the floor. My hip landed on the remnants of a stalagmite stump, adding further injury to insult. I rolled off it and grabbed my stinging cheek. Tears poured from my eyes over more than the pain. I looked back at Terrin's panting chest and bared teeth. He showed no sign of remorse.

Titters sounded from the cavern opening. I looked over and saw three gattaw women entering. After a good snicker, they proceeded to the cell and entered. One of them pointed an accusing finger at me and kicked dirt at me on the way by. I recognized a few of the words in her rant, none of them polite.

I stood and dusted myself off. Terrin kept his eyes locked on me, even as the women disrobed around him. One woman—the same who had kicked dirt on me—grabbed

Terrin's crotch aggressively and then pointed at herself. Another murmured something in her language and then made a choking noise while grasping her throat. I could only imagine the scenario she was acting out.

I rolled my eyes and stepped out of the cell. I wiped away the tears at the edge of my eye, noting the soreness in my cheek. He hadn't held back as much as he could have. I supposed some of the anger he had directed at me was real.

I limped across the cavern, my ego as bruised as my hip. Never mind that his whores had hastened me away, or that Terrin had belittled me in front of them. I just didn't like it when I couldn't get my way.

I paused at the passageway leading away from the cavern and looked back. Terrin's women were all over him, kissing him, caressing him, but his eyes were still on me. "I'm glad you're home again, but in case you didn't know, you were the only thing I had left of mine."

Trollop

I was relieved to see the remaining prostitutes had finally made it down to the end of the passageway. I was now only passing contented men or soon to be contented men. Ayil came down the passage toward me and I gave him a nod. He mouthed something I assumed was, "Are you okay?" I could only imagine the look of disappointment I had in my face—tears streaming down my cheeks and a thoroughly dejected posture. Or perhaps it was my limp that had him more concerned.

I mouthed back, "I'm okay," lest he think I had been beaten and raped since he last saw me. Despite my efforts to calm him, his frown deepened. He picked up his pace, veering around kneeling women left and right to get to me.

Before I could determine the reason for his concern, a hand grabbed my shoulder. A beefy gattaw guard yanked me around to face him. I blinked at him as he looked me over carefully. "You've been requested," he grumbled and pushed me forward.

Ayil met up with us as we started moving again. "Hey, big guy. You looking for someone in particular?"

"Yeah, her."

"Oh, you don't want her. She's a newbie. You want somebody with experience." Ayil touched the man's shoulder.

The gattaw stopped and looked down at the provocation. "It's not for me, you idiot. She passed up a customer a few cells back."

"I am sure one of these ladies can handle it. Look, she's already pretty beaten up."

Ayil tried to retrieve me and the gattaw grabbed his throat, lifting him slightly from the ground. "You must be new, too. Our warriors need to be entertained. Keeps the fight in them fresh. Food, water, and a piece of ass."

The gattaw pushed on my shoulder, forcing me forward even as he shoved Ayil into the nearest wall. I heard his head *thunk*, and I knew he would be down for at least a minute. Not that he could rescue me when he was upright, anyway. I was only beginning to figure this world out—a world where promises were everything, and money bought you promises.

We rounded another bend, and I remembered where I was. The cells I had passed on my way to Terrin. The half-breed must've been insistent on getting me back, bribing the guard to find me. I wasn't fond of the idea of being abused for the sake of covering my true intent, but I was even less keen on the idea of a painful encounter with a half-gattaw.

The guard stopped in front of the cell and pushed me close to the bars. "Is this the one?" he asked.

There was no response from inside, only a slight movement from the shadows within. When the guard unlocked the door, I realized the halfling had paid for more than my retrieval. I took what little opportunity I had while he was turning the key in the lock. I twisted out of his grip and slipped behind him.

I was nearly three steps away when I was yanked back by my hair. The gattaw kept hold of all my purple locks and dragged me back to my *John*. I pleaded with him to keep me outside of the cell, but there was no hope of getting his sympathy now, even if there had been an opportunity for it before.

I landed on the floor inside the cell. Before I could get back to the door, it clanked shut, and the lock clicked into place. I reached through the bars and clawed at the guard, pleading for my release. He brushed off my hands and walked away, unconcerned by the terror in my pleas.

A hand gripped my shoulder and pulled me back. I raised my elbow and hit the man's throat. As he choked, I kicked backward. I intended to hit his crotch, but I only reached his shin. Nonetheless, he retreated, coughing and groaning. I searched the floor and walls for a weapon—a rock or something pointy, anything.

"Kit!" Ayil's voice echoed down the passage.

"Ayil!" I screamed back at him, reaching my hands through the bars to wave at him.

"Kit!" Ayil reached me and stopped outside the cell door. "Oh, thank God." I grabbed him and pulled him to the bars, clanking his head to them as I did. "Ouch."

"Quick, find something to pick the lock!"

"What? Why?" Ayil rubbed his head.

"What do you mean why?" I screeched.

"You'll be safer in there, than out here."

"With him?" I turned an accusing finger at my bunkmate, who just so happened to be my husband. "Rayne?"

"Hi, honey," Rayne rasped as he rubbed his throat.

"Oh, crap, I'm sorry." I ran to him and hugged him, but he flinched at my contact. I shrank back and grimaced. He was still freshly bruised from his first battle—not to mention the new bruises I had given him. "Are you okay?"

He glowered at me, and I threw my hands up. "I didn't know it was you. I couldn't see you back there in the shadows."

"You gonna be able to fight tomorrow, Cap?" Ayil asked him.

Rayne limped to the bars. "The doctor has already been around. Nothing is broken, though my face would disagree." Rayne raised his hand to his forehead and rubbed it.

"Here, take this." Ayil pulled a clear plastic bag from his pocket filled with little white pills and handed them to Rayne. "Those will speed your healing and numb the pain. Just one per day, though. Too much and you're liable to walk on a broken leg and not know it."

"Where did you get those?" I asked.

Ayil winked at me, but didn't answer. "Were you able to get to Terrin?"

"Yes."

Ayil reached through the bars and turned my chin to see my cheek. "Where did you get this?" Rayne leaned over to see what he was looking at. He frowned, shifting his eyes down. The muscles in his jaw tightened and he looked away.

"Terrin refuses to leave," I said, almost as if I were tattling on him. "He won't let us save him. What's worse, I think he *wants* to be here. Like he owes it to his people to slaughter himself for sport."

"There are a lot of obligations instilled in the gattaw from birth," Rayne said. "I'm not surprised he wants to stay."

"It's ridiculous," I sniped.

"It's a different culture, Kit," Ayil defended him.

"That's all well and good for politics and fashion, but where does that leave us?"

"It doesn't leave *us* anywhere," Rayne said. "It leaves him here."

"To die or spend the rest of his days fighting for his life."

"Yes, if that's what he chooses."

"You knew this would happen, didn't you? You *knew* he wouldn't come back with us."

"I suspected, but no, I didn't know for sure. I thought his loyalty to you might be enough to sway him."

"I guess we were both wrong." I crossed my arms and moved back to the bench where Rayne had been sitting.

Rayne conversed with Ayil for a few minutes about the games and the betting, where we stood on our finances. We had already lost too much to buy Rayne back and walk away. We would have to wager on a few more games to boost our funds. However, with our conscience clear of Terrin's fate, we wouldn't have to earn quite as much.

"You'll be all right in here until morning," Ayil assured me.

"You're leaving?" I asked, slightly panicked at being left behind, even though I was perfectly safe.

"See you on the walk of shame." Ayil winked at me and headed back down the passage.

Rayne moved to lean on the cave wall beside me. "You look angry."

"I hate this place."

"Coming here was your idea. Don't be sour just because it didn't turn out the way you wanted."

"The way I wanted?" I raised my brow. "Are you kidding me? You act like I had any say in the planning of this little snatch-and-grab."

"I knew you wouldn't like the idea of me competing again."

"So instead of telling me, you surprised me with it when it's too late for me to argue about it."

"Pretty much."

"Aargh! This is exactly like when you planned to save Edric with me as bait!"

"What does that have to do with this?"

"It has to do with you and Ayil making choices that affect my life!"

"Oh, you mean like rescuing you when you got yourself kidnapped."

"You know what I mean."

"Why is this all coming up now? Are you really mad at me? Or are you mad at him?"

I stared at him a moment, tears forming in my eyes. I looked away, shaking my head. "He didn't even consider leaving. He has always been so determined to protect me, and now he's abandoning me."

"Maybe being here has changed his thinking. Maybe he feels I will be enough protection for you." Rayne sat down beside me and leaned over his knees. "You have to be okay with this, Kit."

"Okay with what?"

"Leaving him behind. Losing him."

I looked over at him and shook my head. "Leaving him I can handle. It's him leaving me I can't handle."

Rayne sighed and stood back up. He moved to the bars and gripped them tightly. "And where does that leave us?"

"What do you mean?"

"I mean, are those hickies on your neck a hello or a goodbye?"

I instinctively reached up to touch my neck, revealing my knowledge of them as well as my guilt over them. There was no point in denying who gave them to me. I opened my mouth to explain the circumstances and confusion resulting in Terrin's uncontrolled greeting, but Rayne found his words before I could find mine.

"Do you think I'm stupid, Kit?" His voice was quiet and angry, but a little hurt. "I see the way you look at him."

"He's my friend."

Rayne turned around and looked at me. "He's your fairy tale." I stared blankly at him, not finding the words to deny the accusation. "But of course, that didn't work out very well for you, did it?"

"It's just a childhood crush, Rayne. It's not the same as what you and I have."

"I know you have to tell me that. I know you have to tell yourself that. But the truth is, if you and Terrin could be together, you would be."

I shook my head slightly, but I wondered if that was true. There was no denying that I was attracted to Rayne, but our relationship thus far had been sex and arguments. What I had with Terrin was a much deeper connection. My draw to him was more about comfort and familiarity than it was about pure lust.

The reality of my situation was that I was married to a man I barely knew, but was almost viscerally attracted to—a one-night stand turned into an arranged marriage.

I remembered my first night with Rayne. The experience, though pleasurable, had felt empty. It was Ayil I'd turned to that night for my comfort. He had gently dispelled the ludicrous idea of romance, love, and sex being found in the same place.

"Say something," Rayne said, snapping me out of my concentration.

"I don't know what I'm supposed to say. I don't know what I'm supposed to do." I looked down at my hands as my fingers nervously twiddled. "What do you want me to say?"

"Nothing." Rayne slammed his hand against a bar, making it reverberate. "Don't say a goddamn thing." He moved over to the patch of hay meant to be his bedding and shuffled it around, elongating it for his body. When it was to his liking, he plopped down into it, linked his hands behind his head, and closed his eyes.

For several minutes I sat there slightly angry, but mostly embarrassed. This was probably one of the many moments where I should apologize, but for once I didn't really feel like there was any need for me to apologize. How was I supposed to change how I feel? Rayne could point it out all he wanted, but that certainly wouldn't make it go away. I probably should've explained once again that Terrin and I had come to terms with our friendship, but obviously, we hadn't come to terms with our attraction toward one another. I was confident one day Terrin and I would reach a point where our bond would overreach our attraction. Unfortunately, we had not yet reached that point, as evident by my hickies.

It wasn't surprising to me that Terrin still held such an allure for me. There had been so few men in my life growing up, I'd been bound to fall head over heels in love with the first one I spent more than two minutes with. Despite our lack of sexual compatibility, we had a history together that made me feel safe and comfortable.

On the other hand, the man I chose to link my life with was dangerous and erratic. His particular skill set had made him an essential element in my security, and his other skills made him a very appreciated participant in the bedroom. But was that love? I had thought it was. I had claimed it was. Perhaps it was just lust.

When all the philosophies had drained from my mind, all that was left was an icy shiver from the cave air. I slipped off the edge of the bench and crawled over to Rayne's pile of hay. I moved carefully beside him; fearful he might kick me out to make me sleep on the cold, dank floor of the cave.

I slid my body in beside his and pushed my chest up against his rib cage. I gently rested my head on his shoulder. I felt him take in a dissatisfied breath, but he didn't move, not to kick me out nor to embrace me.

Even that small rejection made my heart ache. It wasn't lust. It had to be love.

I tipped my chin and kissed his cheek along the jaw. He still didn't move. I moved my hand along his chest and belly, feeling the toned muscles beneath the thin fabric. When there was still no reaction, I dipped my hand below his waistline. He sucked in a quick breath and let out and exasperated exhale.

I refused to let him win. I pushed a little closer to him, making sure he felt my breasts pushing into his side. I leaned in to kiss his lips and he turned his head away.

His denial made me furious and even more determined. Instead of a kiss, I bit him on the jaw.

"Ouch!" He hissed and finally opened his eyes to look at me. "What the hell do you think you're doing?" There was nothing new about him glaring at me. Nothing new about his disapproval of my behavior. However, with his assets growing in my hands, I was emboldened to stare right back at him.

"You paid for the entire night."

His eyelids fluttered slightly, and he shook his head. "I did that to protect you."

"I know." I squeezed him a little harder, finding a firm but gentle rhythm. "And I want to repay you for your kindness."

"I..." He finally brought his arms down from behind his head, putting one hand on my shoulder and one on the arm of my probing hand. "Kit, I'm actually quite sore."

"This part seems to be working just fine."

"Yes... But I can't..." He squeezed my arm but didn't quite push me away. "Why are you doing this?"

"Because I don't know what else to do. I don't know how else to express myself to you." He blinked at me, panting slightly. "I don't know how to win this argument."

"So, you're going to seduce me to get me to shut up."

"Yeah, pretty much," I admitted, feeling a little stupid.

"Well, don't stop now." He nodded to where my hand had stopped moving. "I'll let you win just this once." He pulled me forward and gave me a long, hard kiss. I was pleased to have won the argument, but since it was only more sex, I wasn't sure it was progress

Walk of Shame

I blinked into the glaring Miorita sun as I emerged from the caves. Ayil whistled at me from his resting spot against the outer wall of the arena. I meandered over to him, stretching out the crick in my neck, which had developed overnight. "Why do you look so chipper?" I asked when his devilish smile didn't subside.

"I had a fun night." He used his tongue to waggle the stick hanging out of his mouth.

I narrowed my eyes on the cactus needle before ripping it away. "Ayil," I groaned.

"What?" He shrugged and laughed at me.

I tossed the needle onto the sand. "You'd better hope those aren't addictive."

"Not that it matters. We'll be off this planet in no time."

"That's assuming Rayne wins his match today."

"If he loses again today, his ranking will be so low I can buy him back with a handshake and a blowjob." Ayil looped his arm over my shoulder. Judging by the amount of weight he put on me, I suspected he wasn't able to stand without support. "Speaking of oral pleasures, how did you and Rayne get along last night?" Ayil rubbed his finger along my neck, pointing out my hickies.

"Those aren't from Rayne," I confessed as I looked out over the rising orange globe that made the copper deposits in the sand sparkle.

I could feel Ayil looking at me—not quite judging me, but evaluating where he had gone wrong in raising me. "Kit, you didn't..." Ayil trailed off as three humanoid women passed by us. The two were helping the third between them walk. She was whimpering and limping as if every step was painful.

Once they were past us, I noticed the trails of dried and fresh blood on the back of her legs. Ayil stared after the woman with an empathy few could relate to. When he finally looked back at me, he looked furious. "I thought this thing with Terrin was over."

"It was—it is. He was confused, and I was... happy to see him."

"Mm-hmm." Ayil tugged me along as he staggered toward the hustle and bustle of the local vendors. "Well, I suppose that will be another addiction distance will solve."

I frowned at the thought of putting distance between me and Terrin. Despite making his desire to stay on his home planet very clear to me, I was still trying to figure out a way to break him out. It would have qualified as a kidnapping, but I didn't care. I wasn't ready to give him up.

Ayil and I wobbled through the outside lane of food vendors in search of breakfast. We found two roasted tubers that tasted like greasy potatoes and chowed down while we browsed displays of jewelry and scarves.

Since I had lost my hat somewhere in the caves, I purchased a long orange scarf that would pop against my hair.

I put the scarf over my head and wrapped it loosely around my neck. When I turned to Ayil to check for his approval, he was gone. I spun around and even checked under the table, just in case he had passed out, but he was nowhere to be seen.

"Ayil," I called out.

"Over here," he called back.

I followed the sound of his voice around the corner of the next tent, but still didn't see him. "Ayil?" My movements slowed as I entered a back alley of tents. The aisles of beige went left, right, and forward.

"Kit!"

I saw Ayil as someone yanked him behind a vendor tent several yards to my right.

"Ayil!" I ran down the narrow passageway, jumping over wooden stakes and tension lines as I went. I rounded the corner and found Ayil standing by himself in a cul-de-sac of canvas and sand.

I moved toward him, but he held up his hands to stop me. I searched the area for the danger and found the perpetrator right behind him. A slender leg stepped out from behind Ayil. The torso and head of a short woman bobbed out to look at me.

"Tell her to come closer," she rasped.

Ayil rolled his eyes and motioned for me to come forward. I did so cautiously. "Who are you?" I leaned out to see around Ayil, but the woman ducked back further to hide herself.

"My name doesn't matter, but yours does." She spoke in a hoarse voice that was no doubt intended to disguise her real one. "I know who you are."

I took in a breath and rubbed my face. "Why don't you let Ayil go? He doesn't have any value."

"She doesn't even have a gun, Kit. It's just a pocket knife," Ayil tattled. He hissed in pain.

"It still hurts, doesn't it?" the woman asked.

"Okay, okay." I raised my hands. "No need to get pokey."

"Oh, screw this," Ayil grumbled. He whipped around and punched the woman in the face. She went down to the ground with a screech. She reached out her little knife, prepared to slash Ayil's leg, but he kicked her hand away. She yelped and held her wrist.

As I looked over the young woman's short-cropped dark hair and petite features, a sense of familiarity overwhelmed me. After a moment, the puzzle pieces clicked into place. "Cousin Elder?" I asked with astonishment. The woman blanched and looked as if she had been caught stealing. She shook her head, even though she had already revealed my accuracy. "What are you doing here?"

She pursed her lips. "Traveling for Mother's job."

I snapped my fingers. "Aunt Scarlet. I knew I recognized her."

"Your family is here?" Ayil asked.

I shrugged. "Just from my mother's side."

"Is that good or bad?"

"I don't know." I crossed my arms and glared at Elder. "Are you seriously trying to collect a bounty on your blood relation?"

"What?" Elder squawked and stood up. She dusted herself off. I noted her expensive silk pants and fashionable threadbare top that showed off her black bra. "I would never kill you. I just want a little something for my silence."

"Your silence?" I asked.

"Yeah, haven't you heard? The Coalition has declared you an enemy of the Crown. They say you are letting foreign nations have samples of your DNA."

"What is my mother's opinion of that accusation?" I asked out of curiosity.

"She's put a reward out for you herself."

"She *what*?"

"She said she doesn't condone the murder of her daughter, and she has offered double the pay of the Coalition to any bounty hunter who will bring you home alive. She even sent out a battalion to find you."

I smiled. My mother rarely did anything that would put her at odds with the Coalition. Her duty to the Crown demanded she keep peace at all costs. I'd never dared to hope I could be an exception to her rules. However, with the Coalition making public threats against a member of the royal family, she probably felt she had the leeway to intervene.

"So, you're here to collect the reward."

"No, I don't want the reward. I want a bribe," Elder declared.

"I don't understand."

"Of course you don't," she said snidely. "You know, you aren't the only one in the family to have obligations to the Crown. Do you know how many backwater planets I have visited this month? All in the name of bureaucratic mingling. I haven't slept on a mattress in three weeks. I have more hay up my ass than a scarecrow!"

Ayil snorted, but contained the bulk of his laughter.

"I'm sorry to hear that, Elder, but what can I do about that?"

"I want to do what you did. I want to run away." Elder's eyes gleamed with sinister excitement.

I glanced at Ayil. "I'm not sure you will enjoy the lifestyle that comes with being a runaway."

"I would if I had access to your credit stamp."

I frowned and shook my head. "I haven't used my credit in years. I doubt it still works."

"Bullshit! I heard you used it at a mall. That's how your bodyguard finally found you." Elder shook her head at me. "Stupid," she whispered to herself.

"You know if she uses her credit stamp here, the Coalition will locate her," Ayil said.

"So? You can outrun the bounty hunters. You've been doing it for years."

"I can't leave Miorita yet. I have business to finish here."

Elder took in a deep breath. "I don't care. I refuse to be an emissary for the rest of my life. And since I have no intention of living like a pauper, I want you to transfer twenty million to my private credit stamp."

"Twenty million! Are you zonked!" Ayil yelled at her. "She doesn't have that kind of money!"

Elder's lips peeled back over her bright white teeth and she shook with laughter. "You can't be serious. That's a drop in the bucket. The Crown has trillions at its disposal."

Ayil glanced at me, but I refused to get into the money conversation with him. He knew I was rich, I just never clarified that I was *stinking* rich. Besides that, I didn't technically have access to the trillions. I only had a stipend of about a half billion. However, since we had traveled the galaxy on a shoestring budget while I'd sat on so much money made me feel excessively guilty.

"I want twenty million or I call in an anonymous tip with your location."

"That would be the same as killing her," Ayil said.

Elder shrugged. "Not if she surrenders."

"You little bitch." Ayil moved toward her, but I put my hand on his chest.

"Okay, Elder. I'll give you what you want."

"What?" Ayil frowned at me.

"But not yet. Let me get my affairs together, then I'll pay you right before I leave the planet."

Elder narrowed her eyes on me. "I don't trust you."

"Clearly that is a mutual feeling but I assure you, you have me over a barrel. If I can choose my exit, then I will gladly pay you. But you have to keep this a secret. No one else can know I'm here."

Elder looked around as if she might find a better offer with another wanted fugitive. "Fine, but if you leave without paying me, I will call General Sanders personally."

I blinked, wondering if she actually had direct access to any military leaders. But given her mother's position in the sociopolitical world, it may not have been an exaggeration. I nodded.

"I'll give you two days." Elder picked up her knife and stormed out of the area. I turned to Ayil. He looked a little stunned at the turn of our morning. I grimaced at him. "Are you okay?"

"Your cousin's a dick."

I laughed. "Yeah, she is. Come on." I looped my arm around him. "Let's buy you something pretty."

Toad

Though most of the day had passed without further incident, I still felt like I was being watched by everyone in the stadium. I tugged at my scarf, trying to make my disguise look like a desert fashionista instead of a bank robber.

"Quit messing with it," Ayil scolded. "Your fidgeting is drawing more attention than your face."

"I should be happy my fame has finally brought me into the realm of bloodline blackmail. That's a proud moment, right?"

"We'll get through this."

"If Rayne wins this match, we should have enough to buy him back tonight, right?"

"Yeah, easy," Ayil assured me.

"That leaves us one more day to figure out a way to get Terrin."

"Kit, he doesn't want to leave. You know that."

"I know he doesn't want to leave *now*, but once he is off this planet and I've talked some sense into him, he will realize what an idiot he is being."

"You can't make him leave, and even if you could convince him to, we can't just run away with their greatest warrior. He's like a celebrity here. Kit, look at me." Ayil pulled my chin to face him. "Don't do anything stupid."

"Why change our tactics now?"

"I'm serious. There is a reason Rayne didn't want you coming here. This place still operates under an eye-for-an-eye legal system. You don't want to know what they will do to an outsider that interferes with their games." Ayil sat up straight. "Speaking of outsiders."

Rayne marched into the ring below. Ayil and I rose from our seats. I grabbed his arm and squeezed tight. "One more fight, one more fight," I chanted to myself.

Ayil patted my fingers gently. "He's gonna do f—fuuuck. What the hell is *that*?"

On the far side of the arena, several gattaw pulled in a rolling platform. What looked to be an enormous toad sat atop it. The brown, scaly creature was as big as an elephant and, given the exertion required by the gattaw, it was as heavy as one as well. They came to a stop and quickly unchained the beast, carefully pulling off the plastic netting around the animal's mouth.

With the muzzle out of the way, the toad yawned and touched the bridge of his mouth with his grayish blue tongue. His eyes blinked and his head turned side to side as if he was taking in his surroundings. He noticed Rayne in the center of the arena and his eyes perked up. He looked to be excited by the gift before him.

"Holy hell, is that thing smiling?" Ayil asked.

"Is it going to eat him?"

"This isn't on the schedule." Ayil pounded his fingers into his electronic schedule book. "What is the point of a schedule if they don't actually stick to it?" he grumbled.

Rayne's eyes dimmed as he took in the blubbery beast. He shook his head slowly. I wasn't sure if this was an insult to his abilities or a challenge. I mean, after all, how do you slit the throat of your enemy when you have to go through three layers of fat to get at it?

"Okay, okay, here we go." Ayil scrolled up on his screen. "Known simply as the *Bufo*, it is Miorita's second-deadliest animal. Occasionally called the buffalo toad by off-worlders, this slow-moving creature is deceptively strong and iron-willed. Besides being a threat to small warm-blooded animals, the Bufo has been known to kill prey as large as a man during periods of starvation. For the purposes of the competition, they withhold the Bufo's food for three weeks prior to being put into the ring. If successful, it will eat its prey whole and begin digesting it before it's dead."

"Everything in this place is rigged. Please tell me it has a weakness."

"Hard skin... Fatty tissues..." Ayil scanned the document. "Competitors are rarely successful, but those who have survived have done so through endurance and strength."

"Crap! They gave him a short sword instead of the knife."

"That's close enough," Ayil said. "It's sharp and pointy."

"What is it doing?" I stared, horrified, at the creature's ebullient rocking motion.

"I think the fat stack is going to move."

"I think he's... pooping." Morbid curiosity forced me to shift my position to get a better view of the turd birthing from the creature's rear end. The gooey, garbled mess slopped onto the sand behind the cart. The audience let out a unanimous groan. It was always reassuring to know bodily functions were universally disgusting. One last piece of defecation fell from the bufo's backside. "Wait a minute..." I stared at the rounded addition with squinted eyes, trying to decipher the odd shape. It took me a moment to realize the last segment excreted was a skull.

"Uh-oh, I think he just made room for lunch." Ayil frowned at me.

"Down in front!" someone yelled behind us.

I sat and watched the buffalo toad stand up on his haunches and walk off his cart bipedally. "This is officially the weirdest thing I've ever seen," I said. Just when I thought things couldn't get any worse, the awkwardly balanced bufo squatted down and leaped forward.

Despite his enormous size, the toad landed 20 feet away, a short distance from his targeted meal. Rayne ducked and rolled away from the creature's whip-lashing tongue. "Oh my God, he's going to get eaten by a gigantic toad. Widowed by a flippin' amphibian."

"I'm sure he can handle..." Ayil trailed off as the toad ejected his tongue again, looping it around Rayne's foot. The flexible appendage dragged Rayne toward the creature's open mouth.

I gripped onto Ayil's hand as if that would stop the carnage from unfolding before me.

Rayne grabbed a nearby stalagmite as he passed. He drew his copper sword and slashed at the beast's tongue. Gattaw swords were sharp, but this one only bounced off the creature's rubbery tongue. Rayne changed tactics and used the tip of it to pry the extremity off his boot.

The tongue finally released. Rayne sprinted across the floor of the open cavern, weaving in and out of stone columns to avoid the pink tendril. He stopped and wedged himself between three rock formations and waited.

Apparently exhausted by his first and only jump, the mammoth toad hobbled over on four feet to get to Rayne—a sight as odd as his bipedal motion. The toad extended his tongue and probed the spaces between the rocks. He found Rayne and grabbed him around the waist this time. The muscular appendage yanked on him, trying to dislodge his potential meal. Fortunately, Rayne had positioned himself well enough that nothing short of breaking him in half would remove him. However, given the size of the creature, it was still a possibility.

Rayne's lack of offensive action in this battle surprised me, but I was pretty sure he was biding his time. He either wanted to wear the creature out, or give himself enough time to come up with a better plan.

The audience booed and hissed at his inactivity. They wanted blood. I wasn't sure at this point if it even mattered whose.

One of the rock formations concealing Rayne crumbled. He jolted forward, smacking his shoulder into the adjacent column. Like a human pinball, he toppled back out of his protective rock prison.

The audience cheered, but just as Rayne was about to be swallowed alive, he launched the copper sword into the toad's eye. Instead of receiving any cheers for his efforts, the audience laughed.

"Why are they laughing?" I asked Ayil.

"I'd guess it has something to do with that." Ayil pointed to Rayne as he flew across the arena. Inspired by the eighteen inches of sharp metal puncturing its eye, the toad had thrown him off like a wild bull. The landing certainly left much to be desired in the way of comfort, but Rayne at least could stand up.

With Rayne's less than perfect weapon now acting as a placeholder in the toad's eye socket, he was unarmed. I expected him to be disheartened by his loss of weaponry, but the look on his face told me he was furious. As much as I preferred him to have the confidence of a warrior; I was afraid his ego would get him into trouble.

The audience hooted and hollered as he marched across the arena. With every step, he increased his speed until he was outright running at his enemy.

The bufo saw him coming, but Rayne easily avoided his striking tongue because of the animal's compromised depth perception.

Rayne leaped onto the creature. He grabbed his sword before it bucked him off again. The toad circled to attack, but Rayne stayed outside of its view on the side with the bad eye. Quick, concise movements were all it took to sneak past its defenses. He stabbed the copper sword into its soft underbelly and yanked it back out again just as quick. The creature reeled and bellowed a trumpeting croak.

Rayne repeated his procedure over and over, peppering the toad's belly with bloody incisions. Before long, the bufo's belly had broken open. Its innards spilled out onto the arena floor, adding to the stains that already marred it.

Of course, that wasn't enough to put the damn thing down. Even without a stomach to put Rayne into, it was still trying to swallow him.

Rayne's deft movements were no match for the slippery grizzly mess that had developed beneath him. He slipped on the slimy innards and fell to the ground. The toad was more than eager to take advantage of this mishap. He ratcheted his mouth open and dove in for his meal.

As the creature descended on him, Rayne thrust the copper sword up into its throat. It pushed through the soft tissue of the lower jaw before jamming into the creature's upper palate.

The blade must have struck the bufo's brain, because its limbs went limp. The wet glisten in its good eye faded to a cloudy stare.

The crowd erupted around me. Belatedly, I added my applause to their cheers. Rayne stood over his kill, panting. I expected the pride that was written all over his face—beating a buffalo toad was obviously an incredible achievement. However, the gratification on his face bothered me.

"Wow!" Ayil nudged me with his elbow. "What's wrong with you? Why aren't you jumping for joy? He won."

"I know." I nodded and clapped a little harder. Ayil continued to glance at me, but I ignored his curiosity.

Rayne pulled his sword from the toppled toad and raised his hands in triumph for his victory. He drank in the cheers from the audience. The leering grin on his face looked almost sadistic to me. The bufo was just an animal. Killing it was the same as a hunter killing for food.

I told myself it was only the exhilaration of the games that fed his warrior side, but deep down I knew it wasn't the battle he loved; it was the kill.

The combat was just the foreplay.

Cost

"What do you mean the price went up?" Ayil stared at the pale skinny man before him. Despite recuperating our losses, we were being told we still didn't have enough to buy Rayne back.

"I mean your contestant's value has increased, therefore so has his price."

"He won a match, so you quadrupled his cost?" Ayil grimaced.

"The bufo is a very challenging opponent," the rosy fat man said from the corner of the tent, where he rested on a plush settee. He was nibbling on fruits—he never seemed to stop eating.

"I'm not sure you understand how these games work." The pale man narrowed his eyes at Ayil. "Your man was at the bottom and we expected him to stay there. Since he didn't, we lost money. Now, we either need to receive enough remuneration to compensate for our losses, or we need to retain him long enough to win it back. We don't have a preference, so if you have the credits, you can have your man."

"We don't have that kind of money," Ayil snarled.

"But we can get it," I added.

"What?" Ayil looked at me.

The lanky man turned his attention to me. He was practically salivating over the prospect of my payment. "Is that so?"

"No." Ayil shook his head and glared at me.

"Let the woman talk." Pale Face practically floated over to me in one agile movement. I half expected his jaw to unhinge and reveal vampiric fangs.

"If I can get the money, how soon can I get my man?"

"All exchanges are completed after the last battle of the day. Bring me the credits after the finale and I will have the guards bring him up through the pleasure entrance to be collected."

"Okay," I agreed and turned to leave, but he grabbed my shoulder.

"I hope you understand if you can't get the money today, then tomorrow the price could go up again."

I stared into his eyes, seeing the trap being set. I had revealed too much of my hand. Mr. Davis had warned me not to let anyone know what I really wanted. Pale Face now knew I wanted Rayne back, and he would squeeze every last dime out of me before he would release him.

"Don't worry, I've never been one to mourn the loss of money." I glanced around the extravagant space. "I find wealth to be caustic to one's personality."

Pale Face's mouth tipped up into a crooked smirk. "What was your name again?" His eyes glinted with knowledge, though I was certain it was only suspicion at this point.

"Come along, dear. Let's go count our credits." Ayil growled and yanked me out of the tent. "What the hell are you thinking?" he scolded me as he continued to pull me down the steps out of earshot of the bigwigs. "There is no way in hell I am going to let you reveal your identity to those assholes. They will eat you alive, and I'm not entirely sure that's a metaphor."

"I won't use my credit. Come on." It was my turn to tug him along. I walked us along the mezzanine level, dodging patrons left and right. We came across the old man who was selling belly beans. I gave him a wary look as we passed. His gaze followed me—monitoring my behavior with interest.

When we reached our destination, I started searching my pockets, then Ayil's. "What do you want?" he asked, batting my hands from his pants pockets.

"A coin—something metal." Ayil reached under his shirt and pulled out a coin-sized pendant he was wearing around a chain on his neck. I frowned at it until I realized it was a laser cut *locket*. Edric's image was in relief on one side and on the other was an infinity sign. I smiled at the silver trinket.

"It was a gift," he said shyly.

"It's beautiful—and helpful." I grabbed the pendant and shifted it in the sunlight. I aimed the glaring refraction into the crowd. The blinding light pissed off a few locals before I reached my intended target. Elder batted away the light like a nuisance fly. When it was obviously not going to leave her alone, she searched for the cause. Her glower landed on me, and her eyes widened.

Elder shifted into a stretch and cracked her neck before getting up. She said something to her mother before leaving the tent. Aunt Scarlet stared after her daughter and eyed the audience before resuming her observations of the arena battle.

Elder tromped down the steps of the stadium like a pompous teenager—which, apart from her age, she was. "What?" she asked, pursing her lips out for the extra emphasis on the W.

"I need your help," I said. Elder rolled her eyes and turned on her heel to leave. "I can get you your money by the end of the day if you do."

Elder froze. Her shoulders rose and fell with her breath before she turned around. She was excited by the prospect of getting her payoff, but she was still suspicious. "What do I have to do?"

I took a breath and ushered her a little farther down the path. We ducked into a stairwell which appeared to be an obsolete emergency exit. However, judging by the smell, it had become an emergency bathroom for the male patrons.

Elder grimaced at the smell and crossed her arms tight around her body lest they touch the railing by accident. "What's this about?"

"The business I told you about—I ran into a snag. We don't have enough money to buy my..." I trailed off, realizing my marriage wasn't common knowledge. I was certain my mother hadn't announced the clerical caveat. "My partner is competing in the tournaments and his price just went up to 40,000 credits. I have the money, of course, but I can't let these assholes know that. I need you to use your credit stamp to buy him back for me."

"What?" Elder grimaced. "You want *me* to pay *you* 40,000?"

"It's only a loan. I'll add it back to the total."

"I want money from you, not the other way around."

"I can't leave until I get him. I can't use my credit until I'm about to leave. You have to spend money to make money."

Elder scoffed and turned to leave. I grabbed her arm. "Please, Elder. I don't have anyone else I can trust. I need your help." I begged as I squeezed her arm.

Elder frowned and looked to Ayil. "It's not that I won't. It's that I can't."

"What do you mean?" Ayil asked.

Elder stepped back down to her original position and gritted her teeth. "I don't have the money," she mumbled.

"What? I can't understand you." I leaned in closer.

"I don't have 40,000 credits."

"Okay, well, we have almost 20,000." I looked at Ayil, and he nodded. "We'll add it together. How much do you have?"

"18," she answered.

"18,000," I said to myself. "Maybe Mr. Davis will lend—"

She let out an insolent huff and propped her hands on her hips. "Not 18,000. Just 18."

I furrowed my brow and shook my head. "Only 18 credits? But your mother... How did...?"

"I'm only allowed 40 credits a day. My mother has me on an allowance. Apparently, I spend too much. It takes me *weeks* to save up enough for a decent outfit. I haven't purchased jewelry in over a year."

"Oh, you poor thing," Ayil mocked.

Elder glared at him. "Now you see why I need your money. I can't fix your money problems until you fix mine. Give me the money and I'll buy your partner back."

"You know she can't," Ayil said.

"I need to have one foot off the planet before a transaction like that."

Elder looked at me. "I sympathize with your situation, Kit."

"Yeah, right," Ayil grumbled.

Elder threw him a scathing glance. "But I can't change your life. All I can do is change mine. So, you can help me and I can help your friend. Or you can turn me into the bad guy." Elder held up a finger to Ayil's opening mouth. "Shut it!" She jogged up the steps and disappeared.

I stared down at the steps, formulating my next move. With Rayne's price going up by the day, Ayil and I were in quicksand.

"Don't worry about it." Ayil wrapped his arm around me and guided me out of the stairwell. "We'll just have to spend another night and bet on tomorrow's games."

"Yeah." I debated if I should ask Mr. Davis for help. Surely, he had enough money to cover Rayne's price and then some. I could pay him back the same as I would have Elder. Unfortunately, my previous deal with him had left me wary of conducting business with him. I wasn't entirely sure if I could trust him.

"Were you ever like that?" Ayil asked, nodding to Elder. She had returned to her tent and was primly sipping on champagne.

"Maybe, when I was young."

"It's a damn good thing you got out of there then. That's a sad future."

I shook my head. "No, I was over the majority of my vanity before then."

"Oh yeah? What changed?"

I intended to deny my knowledge of what had caused the change, but I noticed the battle in the arena. Terrin was closing out the day's festivities with a three-on-one hand-to-hand combat, which he was naturally winning. "Terrin," I answered before I even realized how accurate it was.

I could barely remember the long list of rules Terrin had thrown at me on day one. The specifics didn't matter. It was simply the idea of any rules. He was the first person to create boundaries in my life.

Ayil waved his hand in front of me, but it did nothing to end my trance. "What are you thinking?"

"I was thinking I need to get out of here," I said, dragging my eyes away from the battle. I hated seeing Terrin this way. He was savage in this place. He reminded me of Rayne in this place.

Definitions

P bbbbssslppppattttt!

The fart sound Ayil made on his arm put Edric into a fit of giggles that shook his image on the viewscreen. Even I couldn't help but laugh at the ridiculously immature obscenity.

"You're funny, Daddy!" the boy added, in case his laughter wasn't complimentary enough. I smiled as he brought his face so close to the camera that his nostrils were visible.

Since we didn't want to waste the fuel going back and forth to the ship, we had opted to camp out in our shuttle for the night. I had snuggled into one of the passenger chairs, but since Ayil had spent much of the evening conversing with Edric on a video call, I wasn't quite managing the sleep part. It surprised me that Ayil could find so much to talk to a seven-year-old about, but he was apparently well-practiced in relaying the details of his day in child-sized portions.

In truth, I liked his version of our day better. No one ever died in his versions. And no one ever got their heart stomped on. Yup, sign me up for the G-rated version of my life from now on.

"Okay, bud, I've got to get some rest. Give me a kiss and put Auntie R back on." Edric blew him the biggest kiss ever, and the camera shifted over to Aresties. She looked a little overwrought. I felt bad leaving a pregnant woman to care for a hyperactive boy by herself, but she was safer on the ship than down here. "There's my pretty girl. How are you doing?"

Aresties shrugged. "I'm okay. Just a little tired. Hi, Kit." She waved to me on the screen and I waved back. Ayil glanced back at me as if he had forgotten I was there. "Readings are all good up here and no visitors."

"Good, at least something's going right. Remind me to give you a raise, sweetie. Just as soon as I'm not buying our crew members back." Aresties snickered at my humor. "I think you should get a raise from Ayil, too." I winked at her.

Ayil cleared his throat and shifted closer to the console. "You know how much I appreciate you watching over him, don't you?" he whispered.

Aresties smiled. "I like taking care of him."

There was a long silence, and Ayil cleared his throat. "You know how important you are to me too, right?" he whispered.

Aresties smiled and nodded. "Yeah. You should get some sleep. You look like you got too much sun today."

Ayil agreed and they said their goodbyes. I waved at Aresties and the screen clicked off. Ayil exhaled and sat back in his chair. I let several seconds of silence tick by before I asked the question I had been waiting years to ask. "What's the deal with you two?"

Ayil swung his chair around to face me. He never quite looked right in the captain's chair, but then again, I suppose neither did I. "What do you mean?"

"What do mean what do I mean? Are you a couple? Are you friends with benefits?"

"Seriously?" Ayil stood and removed his shirt and kicked off his shoes. "You, of all people, are asking for a definition of relationships."

I scoffed. "What does that mean?"

"You know damn well what it means." He slipped off his pants, revealing a pair of bright pink boxers. "Tell me what your relationship with Terrin is?"

"We are as we have always been. Just friends."

"Same here." He moved to me and motioned for me to get up. "Move, I want to fold these down." I shifted out of my chair and watched him fold down several of the seats along the wall.

"That is so not the same thing. Terrin and I aren't sleeping together."

"Only because you can't." He pulled out a thermal blanket from our emergency pack and tossed it to me. "Or because both of you are too stubborn to settle for a less than perfect sex life."

"We aren't sleeping together because I love Rayne."

"You've loved Terrin since you were fifteen. Just because you fall in love with someone new doesn't mean your love for him evaporates into thin air." Ayil jumped onto the makeshift bed and cuddled up against the wall to give me room to join. "You can't tell me you didn't enjoy getting those hickies from him."

I scowled at him. "This isn't about me. And even if it was, you and I have made out on more than one occasion and we are still friends." I crawled into bed beside him, wrapping the thermal blanket around me.

"That's different. I'm your number one."

"Number one what?"

"Your favorite."

I frowned at him. "You're my favorite?"

"Yeah. If you had to choose to spend the rest of your life with one of us—sex or no sex, it doesn't matter. Who would you choose? Rayne, Terrin, or me?"

"I don't know."

"Yeah, you do. It's totally me."

"Really?" I asked.

"Yup."

"Why?" I asked, legitimately curious about the reason.

"Because I'm the only one you can be completely yourself with. Rayne makes you nervous and self-conscious. And Terrin makes you feel inadequate—on a number of levels."

I stared at Ayil while I considered his statement. He wasn't wrong. "What about you? Is Aresties your number one?"

"Nah." Ayil poked my nose. "You are."

"Aww, that's sweet. We're stuck with each other because we're both shit with relationships." Ayil chuckled. "But you love her, right?" I asked after a moment.

"Aresties? Yeah."

"Not enough to commit to her?"

He swallowed hard. "Too much to commit to her."

I propped myself on my elbow to look down at him. "What do you mean by that?"

He took a breath. "You know my past. You know what I come from."

"So? That doesn't define you."

"Yes, it does." Ayil propped his head on his elbow to meet me face to face. "I'm always going to be confused about where to draw the line with people. I know when I slip into bed with you, we are friends. I know when I slip into bed with Aresties, we are lovers. Everything else is blurry. And I won't commit to her knowing I could break her heart someday."

"I'm sorry. I didn't know you were still struggling with… all that."

"I'm not," he said sternly. "I know who I am. That's why I don't and won't define my relationship with Aresties as anything more than *friend.*"

I smiled and kissed his forehead. "That's a good enough definition for me." I settled in beside him and closed my eyes. "You're lucky."

"Why is that?" he mumbled.

"Cause, you get to call her a friend. I have to call her my *baby momma.*"

Early-Riser

I groaned as Ayil dropped on top of me, pressing my back into our makeshift bed. I was barely conscious, but I could feel a distinct pressure that made my mind snap to attention. "What the hell are you doing?" I complained.

"Sorry, I gotta take a whiz," he mumbled and rolled off me. His body hit the metal floor with a *thud*. "I was trying not to wake you." He jumped to his feet and moved to the shuttle door. "Avert your eyes. I'm about to break several laws."

"Avert my eyes?" I groaned. "I haven't even opened them yet."

The metal door popped open with a squawk and I felt the cool morning breeze wafting in, refreshing our otherwise stuffy accommodations. "Whoa, watch out! I about pissed on you," Ayil said to someone outside. I blinked open my eyes, but the bright daylight was masking our visitor's identity. "In or out, bud. Either way, I gotta take care of business here."

"I'll step inside, if you don't mind." Mr. Davis shifted past Ayil as he lowered his drawers to relieve himself. "Good morning, Princess."

"Eck, don't call me that—especially in the morning." I sat up on the edge of the bed and looked over Mr. Davis's perfectly pressed suit and purple tie. "Don't you get hot in that thing?"

He looked down at it and shook his head. "It's designed for a hot climate." Ayil let out an exuberant groan of satisfaction. I shook my head at his vacillating maturity.

"What do you want, Mr. Davis?" I asked, unable to restrain my snippy tone.

"I came to talk. I noticed you didn't buy Mr. Turner back. I assume he is no longer in your price range."

"Rayne? Yeah—no, the assholes jacked up the price because they lost money on their bets."

"Yeah, I probably should have warned you about that. I didn't realize they had bet so high against him. He must not have impressed them much."

"They know we want him now, so the price is going to keep going up. I don't suppose you would consider a short-term loan."

Mr. Davis's eyes widened, but then he seemed to take an interest in the idea, as if he remembered how much I was worth. "It's not entirely out of the realm of possibilities, but my interest rates are pretty high."

"We don't need your money," Ayil yelled at us from the door. His all-inclusive glare told me that dealing with this loan shark was off the table for now.

"Down, boy. I didn't come here to squabble about money, anyway. I thought you should know your gattaw friend has applied for a working position."

I shrugged. "I'm sorry. I don't know what that is."

"The men who fight in the pits have to be guarded by someone. The best people for the job are the men from the winner's circle. Since your friend is still under the status of a slave, the only way to earn his freedom is to become part of the group containing him."

"Wait, so if they hire him, then he's employed instead of enslaved."

"There's not much difference, I assure you, but yes. He could leave the dungeons, and he would have a wage. Certainly not enough to buy his way off the planet, though."

I looked at Ayil, who was already stowing his equipment and joining the conversation. "What's the catch?" he asked.

"The catch is, he has to compete against a guard to get the position." Mr. Davis glanced at us. "It's a battle to the death. Only one of them can have the job."

Despite the disillusionment on Mr. Davis's face, I still didn't see a problem. It certainly wasn't the best route, but I had every confidence in Terrin's fighting abilities. He had obviously earned his place in the winner's circle. Why should I doubt him now?

"Who does he have to fight?" Ayil asked.

"He has requested to fight Dagon, the gattaw responsible for guarding the dungeon gates."

I frowned and narrowed my eyes. "Why the hell would he ask to fight that guy?"

"Who's Dagon?" Ayil asked.

"A seven-foot gattaw carved out of rock," I said.

"Dagon is a legend among the gattaw," Mr. Davis explained further. "He has never lost a fight. Fighting him has become as much about winning as it has about losing. Winning would be the ultimate honor, but since Dagon is such a formidable opponent, losing to him is just as honorable."

"Son of a bitch." I moved away from the men and paced in front of the shuttle's console. "What am I supposed to do with this information? Can I stop it?"

"No," Mr. Davis said. "I didn't come here so you could stop him. I just wanted you to know that now no amount of money will buy him back. Terrin can't make them any more money in the pit. The bad thing about being in the winner's circle is you're a guaranteed win. Terrin's only value to them is as an icon. He's a walking billboard for new recruits."

"Is there any way into the dungeons—besides the service entrance?" I asked. "There's got to be a way to sneak in so I can talk some sense into him."

"Not that I know of."

"Maybe the locals would know," Ayil suggested.

"Possibly, but the locals aren't likely to help you. They aren't fond of foreigners to begin with, let alone when they trifle with their proudest traditions," Mr. Davis said. "Even if you could find your way in and get him out, you would never get him off the planet."

Ayil glanced at me. "We aren't the type of people to leave our friends behind."

Mr. Davis smiled. "Don't confuse stupidity with morality. Miorita is not bound by common law. If they catch you, they will either kill you on the spot or put you in the pit. There is no penal system here." Mr. Davis turned to me and perked his brow. "Your title won't save you, Princess."

Rivals

Throughout the day, my thoughts crowded with plots and plans to untangle the mess I had made. With Rayne financially out of reach and Terrin physically out of reach, my attempt at rescuing one man was putting a second in harm's way. That was always a risk with hero work, but I also had the clock to factor in.

Ever since I had offered to pay for Rayne in full, the game masters were watching me. I knew they suspected I was someone important. And judging by the craning looks my Aunt Scarlett was throwing at me, my visit with Elder had not gone unnoticed. If she hadn't put two and two together by now, she soon would. All it would take is one intercepted tattle to my mother to send a fleet of ships to my location.

Yes, the clock was definitely ticking.

"This can't be right." Ayil looked between his electronic pad and the arena. He clicked through a few more screens before shaking his head. "This wasn't on the schedule last night."

"What wasn't on the schedule last night?" I asked, trying to peer over his shoulder at the device.

"*That* wasn't on the schedule." Ayil pointed at the arena floor.

I looked out at Terrin's arrival in the arena. He stopped in the center and bowed as the audience applauded him. I still didn't understand Ayil's concern. They had scheduled Terrin to fight again, so there was no reason to be surprised by his presence. However, it was a surprise to see him fighting a human opponent.

I frowned at the second familiar face marching into the arena. Rayne looked around at the crowd. He was searching for something or someone. When he reached the center of the arena, he turned to greet his opponent for the day.

A moment of shock transpired between the men. Then Rayne's jaw clenched; he was no doubt still angry about the evidence Terrin had left on my neck with his wandering lips.

To my surprise, Terrin's mouth curved in a somewhat sadistic smile. Something about this impromptu battle amused him. I hoped he wasn't discounting Rayne as an opponent—especially if he was holding a grudge.

"This must be their idea of incentive," Ayil nodded behind us.

I glanced back at the tent above us. Pale Face was standing at the window, looking down at me. He shrugged and rubbed his fingers in that universal sign. Apparently, if I didn't pay up, Rayne was going to continue to get stomped on. I wondered how much he would charge me to stop this fight before it started. Enough that I would have to reveal myself.

I wasn't sure what soundless thoughts Rayne and Terrin exchanged, but at once, they approached each other.

The horn had not sounded the beginning of the match, nor had they announced the match. This was the pre-match time, which offered opponents time for smack talk.

Rayne and Terrin stopped with only inches to spare. I leaned forward, straining my ears to hear their conversation, but they were much too far away and the din of the audience was too encompassing.

Rayne pointed to his neck and shook his head. As I suspected, he was still mad about my interlude with Terrrin. Rayne pointed to himself.

Terrin turned his attention from Rayne and looked directly at me in the audience. I was a little surprised he knew right where I was since he had never looked up at me before. However, I assumed he had been making an effort to hide our association.

Terrin shook his head and returned his gaze to Rayne, although it would have been more aptly described as a glare. Something about the conversation was making his smirk disappear.

"This isn't good," I murmured.

"Eh," Ayil said and shrugged. "They'll just have to take it easy on each other."

"Assuming they *want* to take it easy on each other."

Terrin said something to Rayne and Rayne put a finger in his face. He pulled his lips back taut as he threw his words at Terrin.

Terrin's head tipped back and I could see he was laughing at whatever Rayne had said. However, judging by the menace in my husband's eyes, he hadn't meant what he was saying as a joke. Terrin continued to mock him, gesturing to Rayne's body and his own. He even pointed back up at me again.

"Oh, God, this isn't good." I grimaced and dared to glance back at Pale Face in the tent. He narrowed his eyes at the activities in the pit. When he turned his attention to me, a certain delight played across his features. I had officially revealed everything. He now not only knew I wanted Rayne, but that the gattaw I had been seeking was Terrin.

"What are they arguing about?" Ayil asked.

"I think me." I pinched my eyes shut, willing it not to be true, but when I opened them, Rayne was glaring at me. Punishing me for whatever Terrin was saying.

"Why?"

"The hickies, remember?"

"Oh shit, that's right." Ayil grimaced. "This isn't good."

"I know.

"They're going to kill each other," Ayil said, joining me on my level of worry.

"I know!"

The announcement came for the match and the horn blew. I looked up, but nothing had changed. Terrin and Rayne were still staring at each other. A question had formed on their faces—a question that apparently my wavering devotion had put there. Or perhaps it had nothing to do with me anymore.

The game masters had put two animals in a cage, each of them as lethal as the other. If they had designs to prove their strength, whether for the sake of ego or conquest, it would only take a spark of anger to motivate them.

I could see the bloodlust in Rayne's eyes as he shifted away from Terrin. It was the same as when he faced anyone he intended to kill. I had stupidly assumed his time with Terrin might have changed his prejudice toward the gattaw, or that their bond over this blood-sport had created a friendship, but I had been wrong.

I had been so very wrong.

As if that wasn't bad enough, I saw the same bloodlust on Terrin's face. I expected virulent condescension, but this was something different.

I was certain Terrin had no desire to actually kill Rayne. However, he abhorred the ego in him. Had their worlds collided under different circumstances, I was certain Terrin would have wasted no time in enlightening Rayne about his human inadequacies.

Neither of them had any intention of throwing the fight. A loss to a human would disgrace Terrin. Not only could he kiss the winner's circle goodbye, he would lose his honor as a gattaw.

And Rayne, of course, had something to prove. I wasn't sure if he was proving it to himself, to Terrin, or to me, but I suspected he had every intention of winning this match. And since his way of winning always involved a blade puncturing his opponent's vital organs, I couldn't imagine a life or death scenario where Terrin wouldn't break him in two.

When the dance had gone on long enough, Rayne reached behind his back and pulled out his tried-and-true weapon. The dagger glinted against the sun before he lunged at Terrin.

No, this definitely wasn't good.

My mind wandered as I stared out at the reality of Terrin's fists pummeling Rayne's face. While some gattaw were slow and bumbling, Terrin was fast enough to avoid Rayne's slashing blade. He was also clever enough to predict his attacks.

However, Rayne's training had not ended with his days in the pit. He had spent most of his life as an assassin. And every good assassin, in my experience, knows how to adapt.

Rayne pulled out a second knife seemingly from nowhere and stabbed Terrin in the wrist as he threw another punch. It didn't stop the impact, but he had hurt him. Both men stumbled back, bloodied and in pain. Terrin looked at his wrist and let out an awful war cry.

He stomped forward, batting away Rayne's stabbing hands. He picked him up by the chin and threw him. Rayne landed and rolled, but he was up and running before the audience had even finished their cheer.

Terrin only took a moment to assess his injury, but it was enough time for Rayne to get the drop on him. He vaulted off the remnants of a stalagmite and buried his two blades into Terrin's shoulders. I gasped and covered my mouth lest I scream for Rayne to stop.

Terrin roared in agony, but instead of dropping to his knees, he dipped down into a forward flip. Rayne landed beneath him, body-slammed by Terrin's weight. The gattaw pulled himself away from the blades in his back. Rayne tried to get up also, but Terrin pinned him down, straddling his hips with his own.

Terrin's fists beat on his face and chest. The endless barrage didn't let up, even when Rayne stabbed his knives into his arms. I clasped my hands and silently begged Terrin to show the mercy Rayne wouldn't. There was no choosing a winner or loser in this match. No matter who hurt whom, I was still going to be the one bleeding in the end.

At the last second, when I thought Rayne could take no more and Terrin could give no less, he stopped. Terrin rose to his feet, panting from his exertion and his overheated body. The audience's cheers turned into a mixture of demands. They were confused. They wanted him to finish the human.

Terrin turned his attention up to the crowd and, once again, his eyes landed on mine. I could see the debate in his eyes—the raw anger and the visceral instinct that demanded that he finish what he had started. Remove the threat against him and claim his prize. But what would his prize be? What would he receive for killing my lover? Would it win my love or destroy it? Would it give him pride or guilt?

As his debate continued, I saw Rayne shift behind him. There was no debate in his eyes. There was no question of the consequences in his mind. He sat up, flipped his blade up in his hand, and caught it between his fingertips. He raised it and drew it back.

My eyes widened, and my mouth gaped. There wasn't time to warn Terrin about the backstabbing attack. Rayne's arm came forward, and the knife released.

I gasped and stood up. I wasn't the only one. The arena went silent. The crowd froze as we all waited for Terrin to pitch forward.

A rumble of chuckles carried over the air from Terrin. Seemingly unharmed, he turned and bent down. He retrieved the knife Rayne had intended to bury in his back. The hilt must have hit instead of the blade. Given his proficiency with sharp objects, it was hard to believe Rayne would accidentally miss his target.

Terrin examined it, then looked back at Rayne. He was flipping his remaining knife between his fingers, as if he were debating whether he should throw it as well. I wasn't sure it was the same debate Terrin was having, but I was certain there were even fewer rewards for him in a lethal win.

After a long moment, Terrin stalked over to Rayne and threw his fist across his jaw. Rayne did nothing to defend himself and once struck, fell to the side unconscious.

Terrin marched out of the arena. He didn't afford me a glance, nor did he stick around for the accolades of his fans, few though there would be today. The crowd was not happy with his mercy. Nor, I think, was Terrin.

Debt

"It's for the best," Ayil said as we meandered through the local market in search of a dinner that didn't involve plastic wrap or reconstitution.

"They almost killed each other," I responded, glancing back at the sun setting behind the stadium. I didn't particularly like the idea of being out in the city after dark, but I was also getting sick of pulverized nutritionally enhanced grain particulate... aka gruel.

"Yeah, but they've been wanting to do that for a while now. This way, at least they got it out of their systems."

"Did they? Or did they just open up a whole new can of worms?" I dragged my hands over the various melons available for purchase. I didn't know much about the food on Miorita, but I was pretty sure I couldn't go wrong with fruit. "What does that say about me? That two of the men I love want to kill each other?"

"That you're a good kisser."

"I'm serious." I sniffed the melon and determined it was not to my liking.

"So am I. You *are* a good kisser."

"I just hate the idea that my love is indirectly or otherwise inspiring them to fight to the death."

"You love me and *I* haven't tried to kill anybody today."

"No, but that's only because your weapon of choice is your penis."

"Say what you will about my penis, but it gets results." He winked at me.

"Well, I can't argue with that." I frowned at the spiked fruit the vendor was trying to sell me as an alternative to the melon. "That's not food," I told her, declaring the one thing I actually knew about gattaw food. The woman frowned and slammed the spiky, orange, cucumber-like fruit back on its pile.

"What is it?" Ayil asked.

"Do you think Rayne missed on purpose?" I asked as I continued through the market in an obsessive daze.

"No, I mean the orange thing. What was it?"

"I mean, he obviously wouldn't have killed him, because ultimately he's a good guy, right?"

"Of course," Ayil said, linking his arm through mine and pulling me in a different direction. "Why are you asking?"

"Because I... I think... I don't..."

"Geez, Kit what's wrong with you?"

"Nothing. I just don't know if inviting an assassin into my life was the wisest choice."

"*Now* you question that?"

"I know why I did it. I just... I don't think I understand my relationship with Rayne."

"What's to understand? You love him, don't you?"

"Yes, but that's just it. I don't know him that well. Our relationship feels like an arranged marriage sometimes. Necessary and fun, but otherwise awkward."

"What exactly do you want to know? He has pretty much been an open book about his past since the mud hut."

"Yeah, but not counting travel time when I've been in a sleep pod. We have only known each other a matter of weeks."

"So?"

"So, I don't know if that's enough time to figure someone out. To commit to a marriage. To have children together."

Ayil laughed and pulled me down a different lane of vendors. This one didn't even have food. It was mostly clothing and accessories. "I don't think you have a choice about that, but you do have a choice about the other."

"What do you mean?"

"Just break up." Ayil stopped at one vendor and pointed to a copper short sword in among the used crap. It looked to be dinged up, and the tip was a little crooked. My guess was it had gotten caught up in some kind of machinery and no one wanted it anymore. "How much?" The vendor held up two fingers. A good deal, even for the pathetic condition of the blade.

"Are you talking about getting a divorce?"

Ayil handed the man two coins and took the sword before ushering me on. "Kit, the only place you're actually married is on a piece of paper on Brahama. And I'm sure your mother has long since ripped it up. Quit putting so much pressure on the relationship. If your happily ever after with Rayne is over, then find a new one. Preferably with someone who is biologically compatible."

I stared at him, trying to wrap my mind around the simplicity of his statement. It *was* that simple, of course.

Technically, no one universally acknowledged marriage documents. And on many planets, the contractual obligation between two beings in any form, consensual or otherwise, was illegal. The only ones clinging to it were Rayne and I. All I had to do to get out of my relationship was break up with Rayne. Why then was there a lump in my throat at the mere thought of it?

I looked around at the empty stands around us. This section of the market had either closed up early, or had contained no vendors. "Ayil, where the hell are you taking us? I thought you wanted to get food."

"I did, but we have three gattaw following us."

"What?" I glanced back and noticed the three burly gattaw meandering behind us in a short line, blockading our path. Their eyes unmistakably set on us. Waiting for an opportunity to rob us, kill us, or was this something else? "Shit." I hissed and turned back around.

"I noticed them a few minutes ago. I was hoping it was just a coincidence." Ayil raised the short sword he had recently purchased and looked it over. "I'll create a distraction. Then you get the hell out of here."

"No way, I'm not leaving you here with three gattaw."

"We don't have a lot of options. You're gonna have to suck it up and play the damsel."

"If I leave, then *you* will be the damsel."

"If you stay, then we will *both* be the damsel."

Rather than give in to anything resembling weakness, I spun around to face the three men, who were slowly closing the distance between us. "Who are you?" I asked boldly. "Who sent you? What do you want from us?"

Notably shocked by my audacity, the men stopped and glanced at each other. The middle one pointed to me. "Co-llect." He formed the word carefully, not quite comfortable with the language on his tongue.

I frowned. Someone had figured out who I was. "Who sent you?"

The gattaw shrugged. "Debt," he answered.

I swallowed and took a step back as the men advanced. Apparently someone owed someone something, and I was the payment. Why did it have to be that? Why couldn't it be a good old-fashioned group of thugs wanting to take our money? What was wrong with the universe these days?

"Go!" Ayil jumped in front of me, waving the copper short sword. He knew well enough how to use one, but he wouldn't last long against three attackers.

"You should be the one running. They only want me." I reached around to take the sword from him, but he ripped it away.

We both shuffled back as the men drew their own swords and advanced, trying to surround us. My opportunity to run was there and gone in an instant as one man circled around behind us. I turned my back to Ayil and pressed against him. I had no weapons. No pulse pistol either, since they were illegal on Miorita. A cowardly weapon by their standards, however I was quite certain I could bear the stigma for the sake of self-defense.

"Let him go and I will come willingly," I said to the gattaw in front of me. All three of them laughed.

"Kit, would you stop trying to sacrifice yourself?"

"You were doing the exact same thing."

"Yes, and you didn't leave, so why do you think I would?"

I looked around the area once more, searching for an exit. Anywhere we could make a proper stand-off or get our backs to a wall. Cornered wasn't the best solution, but it was better than splitting our attention. All I could see was a series of long column cacti, as if we had walked into a desert forest. Unfortunately, there wouldn't be enough room to run between them without puncturing ourselves with the incapacitating barbs.

Without thinking about the ramifications, I dove forward, barreling my shoulder into the gut of the gattaw before me. Though he was far stronger, he let out an "*umph*" before stumbling back. He naturally flailed to keep his balance, which threw his arms and back into a cluster of towering cacti. The pink spines latched onto his skin like a furious porcupine. Almost immediately, his eyes glazed, and he faltered. He swiped at either side of me as if he was seeing two of me instead of the usual one.

I heard the clank of swords. Ayil was taking on the other two gattaw. He parried their attacks skillfully, but I could tell the men were only playing with him. I launched myself at one of the other gattaw to duplicate my previous genius. Unfortunately, he saw me coming and dodged my shoulder. He intercepted me, scooping me up around my waist and pinning my right arm between our bodies. He used his free hand to clamp my left wrist with a tight grip. All I could do was flounder and buck—to no avail.

Meanwhile, Ayil was barely keeping a grip on his copper sword as the gattaw swung harder and harder blows at him. Even with two hands, the blade whipped left and right until finally the gattaw let out a roar and slammed metal to metal. The jarring hit knocked the sword from Ayil's grip. There was nothing more for him to do beyond staring at his murderer with angry defiance. With his last bit of strength, Ayil charged the man. However, the gattaw easily avoided Ayil and seized him in an inescapable grasp.

My captor moved my hand, pressing it against something cold, flat, and hard. I looked down and nearly screamed as the familiar screen flashed its approval of my credit stamp. I was as good as dead—possibly soon, if these thugs had any say in my life span.

Ayil grunted, and I looked back at his predicament. The gattaw had wrapped the crook of his elbow around Ayil's neck. He was holding him tight despite Ayil's scraping fingers and pounding fists. The gattaw raised his sword and, without ceremony, plunged it toward Ayil's belly. I gasped, sucking in a breath for the horrific scream that would follow my friend's death, a new pain that might trump all the pain I had felt so far in my life.

"*STOP!*"

It was, of course, not "stop" but instead a gattaw word. However, to my ears, there was no other interpretation for it. The sword plummeting into Ayil's belly stopped just short of a paper cut. His would-be murderer looked up to see who had interrupted his execution. The gattaw holding me swung around, allowing me a view of the old gattaw approaching us from the vacant side of the market.

The familiar food vendor had no weapons and was limping as much, if not more, than when I saw him the first time. My hope of a savior diminished as I looked over the frail gattaw. My eyes met his for a moment before my head sagged in disappointment. I would now be responsible for a second death. I was tired of being the damsel, but I was far more tired of causing so much violence and murder. My friends had escaped death so far, but it was only a matter of time before their sacrifices became fatal.

"Just walk away." I shook my head and pleaded for the old man to find safety. He looked at me with narrowed eyes, examining me. "Save yourself! Get out of here!" I yelled at him.

The gattaw holding me said something in his foreign language. It didn't take a translator to tell me he was making the same request of him, albeit with a little more flourish.

The vendor looked at the scene before him. Ayil was bent over backward, attempting to crab-walk away from his captor. However, the gattaw still had his neck in a vice-like grip. The awkward position ultimately left his body open for the sword still perched in his enemy's hand.

"*Let him go.*" Again, I wasn't sure what the vendor had actually said. The gattaw language was still very fresh to my ears, but everything in his tone and mannerisms dictated he was asking for our freedom.

It would be fair to say neither of the gattaw were interested in abiding by the vendor's request. It could have been the tone of their response that convinced me of this, or maybe it was the spittle that landed on the vendor's face thanks to my captor.

Both gattaw rumbled with laughter. The vendor took great care, wiping the saliva from his cheek. He looked over his wet hand before lowering it and bidding my gattaw forward. His laughter stopped as he looked at the old man more carefully. It was a quick assessment, one which left him scoffing.

In one dizzying movement, he threw me into the chest of the third intoxicated gattaw. His arms clumsily clasped around me, barely directing themselves correctly enough to contain me. I struggled to get my face away from his hand, but at some point he decided pinching my nose was an appropriate way to contain me, so I bit him. He finally released my face and grabbed my throat. Not quite an improvement for my breathing, but at least I could see the battle unfolding before me. My struggling ceased as my curiosity won out and tipped me into the territory of stupefied gawking.

The vendor had drawn his sword and was holding steady while my former captor shuffled around him, taunting him and pointing at his obvious maladies. The vendor retorted calmly and waved him forward again.

The enemy gattaw said something else to taunt him. The vendor's lips peeled back, revealing a harsh, angry grimace. He repeated his statement in a gritty tone and waved the man forward with his entire arm.

The younger gattaw rushed him. I grimaced at the carnage about to unfold. I hoped it would be quick, so the old man didn't suffer.

And it was.

So quick, in fact, that I wasn't entirely sure what I had just witnessed.

Not quite a deception and yet not quite a fair fight. The vendor had dived low, deflecting his enemy's copper sword with his wrist. I hadn't noticed the gauntlet beneath the sleeve of his tunic. Nor had anyone else. It was enough to save his hand from being severed, though I could see some blood seeping into the cloth.

The old man's copper sword thrust upward into the belly of his enemy. It buried deep, no doubt piercing the man's lungs and heart. It was a noble death to be sure, but not one his grandchildren would retell in the future. There was very little pride in dying at the hands of an old man, especially one with such a handicap.

The old man withdrew his sword, and the gattaw dropped to the ground. There was no life left in his eyes, but plenty of blood still poured from his wound. The old man stood upright, pressing against his knee for the leverage to raise his aging body.

I looked to the second gattaw, waiting for him to drop Ayil and attack the vendor outright, but he didn't make a move. After a moment of staring at the elderly gattaw, no doubt in as much shock as I was, he dropped Ayil to the ground and sheathed his sword. The gattaw holding me did the same, dropping me to the sand. He nearly tripped over me as he moved to his downed comrade. They each took an arm and dragged the dead man away.

The vendor approached me with an unsteady gait—further evidence of his miraculous triumph. He held out his hand to me. Though I knew I was in reasonable enough condition to stand on my own, I didn't dare refuse the generous offer, especially after he had saved my life.

I put my hand in his and my first thought, as usual, was of the heat it produced. He hoisted me up with ease. My eyes met his and for a moment, I stared back at him. My fingers gently squeezed the flaking skin on the back of his hand. "Thank you," I mumbled.

"I told you to be careful," he said and released my hand. "Come with me." He turned his attention to Ayil. "Both of you."

Guests

Ayil and I followed the elderly gattaw through a myriad of cacti across the sandy, rocky terrain. I had no idea where he was taking us, but it was clear we were leaving the commerce of the city center and heading into the village to the east, farther away from our shuttle. I wasn't sure that was a good thing, but I could hardly refuse his request after he had saved our lives. Surely, his intentions would remain heroic.

My concerns continued to rise as we entered a section of the desert forest with gigantic cacti being used as huts. More than a few wary-eyed strangers looked up at us as we passed by their homes.

Ayil glanced at me, no doubt concerned about the same thing. If I was wrong about this man's intentions and he meant to harm us, there was nothing to stop him, since we were hopelessly lost among the bulbous ball cacti.

As we passed one hut, a child came bounding out to us—beyond exuberant for the opportunity to see a real live Earth-origin human. The little girl stopped in front of me and pulled on my hand. She couldn't have been more than five or six, but her strength was already enough to force me to kneel before her. She spoke frantically in her native language as she pressed her hands to my face and stroked my hair.

She turned to Ayil next and yanked him down with almost as much ease. He chuckled and glanced at me. "She's strong."

I smiled. "Yes, she is."

"Hi there," he mumbled as her fingers probed his lips. She even went so far as to pry his mouth open to examine his teeth and tongue.

Before the examination could continue, a screeching female gattaw exited her hut and yelled at the child. The little girl ran back inside while the mother continued her tirade on our guide.

She screamed at the vendor, but he didn't flinch. When she finished her scolding, he calmly made a statement and pointed back to her home. She made what I assumed to be a snide comment before retreating to her hut.

"Have we done something wrong?" I stood and brushed off my knees. Ayil did the same.

"Not at all. She doesn't like humans."

"Her daughter doesn't seem to agree," Ayil pointed out.

"No, but parents rarely learn from their children. Come along, the sun is down to a sliver." He moved on and we followed him deeper into the neighborhood. After another dozen huts, he slipped through the darkened cut-out doorway of one of them.

I looked between it and the other three identical huts in view. I could hardly see any distinction between them, no sign or insignia to keep track of who lived where.

"Who wants to go into the stranger's van first?" Ayil murmured behind me.

I glanced at him and sighed. I was running on instinct at this point. Unfortunately, my instincts were telling me two different things about this gattaw. The part of me that saw him as an old man offering sweet treats wanted to go with him. However, the part of me that had seen him defeat a gattaw half his age with surprising speed and little to no mercy wanted to run like hell.

I took a leap of faith and stepped inside the darkened hut. Ayil came in right after me, pressing tight against my back. As my eyes adjusted, I could see red coals in the center of the room and movement around them. After a moment, the coals bore new flames and firelight bloomed, illuminating the room. The old man was crouched down beside the fire, poking and prodding it back into life with new wood—or in this case, dead dried out cactus.

I looked around at the hollowed-out cacti. Much like any other desert plant, the construction was based on a thick fibrous network designed to absorb water and hold it for the duration of long droughts. It wouldn't have taken much effort to bore out the excess cellulose and create a home. Though the core of the plant was gone, the outer walls were technically still living. I touched the white stringy mesh and felt the moisture contained within.

"You can take a sip if you like," the old man said.

"What?" I asked.

"You may drink from the walls. That's how we get our water during the summer." He opened a pot hanging over the fire. Steam rose from it, joining the smoke that traveled up to a metal tube which served as a chimney.

Except for a few plush stacks of hay, a shelf for tools, and a trunk, there wasn't much for furnishings. It was simple to the point of being impoverished and yet there was something cozy and inviting about the space.

There was no sign of a trap being laid for us. We were simply guests in this stranger's home. For the first time in days, I felt safe. Ayil must have felt the same because he flopped onto one stack of hay and made himself at home.

"I never got your name." I moved to the center of the room and squatted on the opposite side of the fire across from our host. He paused from his pot-stirring to look at me.

"My name is Genaro," he answered, peering through the smoky haze at me.

"Nice to meet you, Genaro. This is Ayil." I nodded to Ayil, and he gave the man an upward salute as he suckled a drink of water from the wall. I was a little concerned Ayil might annoy Genaro for injecting himself into the man's home like a long-lost, needy relative, but he seemed amused by my partner. "And I am Kit Mallory. Or Mallory Kit if you prefer."

Genaro's eyes turned back to me, the smirk meant for Ayil still tipping his lips. For a moment, he gazed at me introspectively. I forced myself to keep eye contact with him in case the intimidation he was imparting was intentional. "And what do you prefer? Kit?" After a pause, he finished. "Or Mallory?"

I took in a deep breath and chuckled. "Depends what planet I am on, but most people off-planet call me Kit."

"Very well." He bowed his head at me. "Are you hungry, Kit?" He motioned for me to sit on the floor near the fire, where a bubbling pot of stew was filling the air with a wholesome fragrance. I nodded at him and situated myself on the grass rug surrounding the fire.

"I am starving." Ayil jumped away from his water fountain and plopped down beside me. Genaro scooped up a bowl and handed it to him. Ayil raised the bowl to his lips, but I reached over and pressed his arms down before he could take a mouthful. He glanced at me, but I kept my eyes on our host.

"Why are you being so nice to us?" I tried to ask casually, but there was suspicion bleeding into my voice. The tension in Ayil's arm released as he gleaned my purpose in elongating his hunger.

Genaro smiled as he handed me a bowl of his stew. "You still think I'm trying to poison you? I told you, gattaw don't use poison. We consider it cowardly. Besides, if I wanted you dead, I would have left you in the hands of those brutes."

"Unless your plan only requires me to be incapacitated." I glanced down at the stew in my bowl. Genaro narrowed his eyes at me and ripped the bowl back from me. He dug the spoon in and took a generous bite. After swallowing, he handed the bowl back to me and motioned for Ayil to hand over his bowl. Ayil did so, and Genaro took a heaping scoop from him as well. He returned Ayil's bowl and looked at me for my conclusion. I nodded to Ayil, and he dove into his meal with zeal. I did the same while Genaro scooped up a bowl for himself.

"I'm sorry," I mumbled before swallowing my bite. "I'm a little suspicious of generosity, especially since I don't know how you came to know my identity."

Genaro nodded. "You don't believe a gattaw keeps up with local gossip?"

"Local, yes, but my planets aren't exactly in the neighborhood."

"Ah, but you have forgotten what my job is. As a lowly old man, no one suspects I might be listening in on the conversations around me. I have overheard enough gossip in my life to overthrow governments."

"Or get someone assassinated."

"Is that what you think? That I invited you into my home so I could kill you and collect your bounty?" My feigned amusement at our conversation died, along with my phony smile. "Oh, yes, Princess, I know about the bounty. Half the galaxy is paying very close attention to the outcome of that drama." What little remained of Genaro's friendly smile drained away as well. "You're lucky you haven't been identified yet. Miorita isn't a governed planet, but our games bring more politicians and royalty to the table than a charity ball. It's only a matter of time before one of them sees past that ridiculous purple mop and tries to kill you. The sooner you leave this planet, the better."

I stared at Genaro. Was he for real? Was he actually scolding me? Who the hell was he to be telling me what to do? And did he just insult my hair?

"I'll take your warning into consideration, but I am not leaving this planet until I have Terrin at my side."

"Terrin?" Genaro shook his head. "He is in the winner's circle. His destiny lies in the arms of death."

"Yeah, well, I never was one for following one's destiny."

"Destiny doesn't guide you. It pushes you. It steers every step you take."

"I don't believe Terrin is destined to die on this planet."

"Why? Because it's not what you want?"

"Because it's not what he deserves."

"Deserves...?" Genaro dropped his bowl and, despite the creaking in his elderly joints, stood with ease. He paced the length of the room behind the fire. "You come here to save a gattaw, and yet you don't understand the games or the culture that created them."

"I respect the gattaw, more than most, but you're right, I don't understand the games. And I don't give a damn about what deviance created them."

"Deviance!" Genaro broke his stride and pointed at me. "Hold your tongue, girl. I will tolerate many things in my home, but condescension is not one of them." His eyes bore into me and my head sank as if my mother had reprimanded me.

Oh, he was good.

"I'm not trying to insult your heritage—"

"No, of course not." Genaro grunted as he returned to the grass mat around the fire. "You're merely trying to bypass it as one does an unsavory grape on a platter. You rationalize your choices over another's because your culture deems theirs less civilized. You say you respect the gattaw, and yet in the same sentence you demean their history."

I glanced at Ayil, wondering if it was my birthright to piss off the gattaw men I associated with. "I have been unforgivably rude, sir, and I apologize for upsetting you." I spoke quickly before he could interrupt me again. "However, if you think your reproof will convince me I'm in the wrong to free my friend, then I assure you it is useless. I have never abided by the rules of my culture's traditions nor its mandates on how I should live my life. My dismissal of Terrin's culture is not an insult to his culture, but proof of my regard for him. I have never, nor will I ever, be steered by anything other than my heart. Not money, not politics, and certainly not a culturally-guilted death-sentence!"

I panted, recovering from the long-winded tirade. I stared across the fire at Genaro's eyes, glowing even redder in the firelight. I was certain he was debating how to cut me up and add me to his pot.

"Would you disgrace him for love?" The question rang with judgment, but he was calm, and so far he hadn't started sharpening his butcher knives. "Would you shame his name and his family for love?"

"Yes," I answered quickly, not allowing any interpretation of dithering in my answer. "For love, I would do anything."

Genaro's brow dipped and his eyes narrowed on me. "Then you are a selfish girl."

I could hear the tension in his voice. My selfishness irritated him. And yet it didn't feel like selfishness to me. It felt right. I may not have been a hero with a cape and a glinting smile, but was I really the villain? Where was the line to be drawn between ego and altruism?

Oh, that's right. When it involved a DEATH SENTENCE.

"Yes, I am selfish," I said resolutely. "I am a spoiled little narcissistic princess who refuses to watch her friend die. And as long as there is a sliver of hope to save him and breath in my body, I will not give up trying!"

Genaro exhaled and looked down at his lap. "Then I suppose I have no choice."

"No choice?" I glanced at Ayil and he also tensed, prepared to jump up at the first sign of a weapon or bad guy catchphrase.

Genaro looked at me and shook his head slightly. He looked sad. The anger I had spurred in him was gone. "No choice but to take you to him."

Cave

I followed Genaro's bobbing lantern down into a deep crevice hidden among a cluster of rocks and dying cacti. Ayil squeezed into the narrow fissure behind me and grabbed my hand. I had hoped the space would get wider as we progressed, but we never had more than a few inches on either side of us. In the tightest sections, I had to climb to align my body to match the wider spots, lest my ass get jammed between the rocks. I wasn't specifically claustrophobic, but I got the sense I shouldn't sign up for spelunking on my next vacation.

As I caught up to the halo of light Genaro's lantern provided, I saw a pair of shoes peeking out from one of the many divergent passageways ahead of us. "Who is that?" I pulled back on Genaro's shoulder.

He glanced back at me and shrugged. "He got lost." Genaro moved on. I followed behind him. As I crossed the shoes, the remaining lantern light revealed the skeletal remains of a gattaw. The copper sword, which normally hung at his side, had been plunged through his rib-cage. I could only presume the man had been the victim of a merciful suicide.

Evisceration over starvation? If you say so.

Ayil grabbed my arms and pulled me back against his chest. "You realize he could blow out that lantern and we would be lost in these tunnels forever," he whispered in my ears.

"Keep up, you two, or we'll be in here all night," Genaro called back to us.

I patted Ayil's hand and moved on to catch up with our guide. I knew what Ayil was worried about. He suspected my desire to see Terrin again was clouding my judgment of this man. However, if his plan was to murder us, he could have done it the moment we stepped into his home. Poison, sword, or even just clunking our fragile skulls together. Whether I should or not, I trusted this gattaw enough to follow him into a dark, confined space.

We traveled slowly through the underground passages. It seemed like it took hours to reach the dungeons. The tunnel's nonsensical path elongated our journey from what would have been less than a mile above ground to possibly three or four. The dizzying weaving made me lose all sense of direction. I was beyond lost and at the mercy of this gattaw's instruction.

Genaro finally stopped and set down his lantern ahead of me. He raised his hand to stop us, though I wasn't sure I would have breathed without his permission by that point. I froze in place, with Ayil right behind me. We waited patiently as footsteps neared the crossroads ahead of us. A guard passed by our narrow hiding spot without glancing our way. I was certain from his perspective, this was just a crack, not big enough for anyone to escape through—let alone enter through.

The light from the guard's torch came and went. Genaro signaled for us to move and we followed him to the exit—or entrance. One by one, we birthed ourselves from the crack. Genaro maneuvered through the opening with ease, contorting his body as if he knew exactly what angulation was required to get through.

I was next, but the lower end of the crevice was wider than the top. I couldn't climb any higher, so instead, I had to squeeze my upper half through. On the way out, the outcropped rocks snagged on my shirt and I found myself jammed. I tried to pull myself through, but I had compressed my breasts as much as possible. I tried to go down, but the back wall was preventing me from lowering myself any further. My heart raced, and I tried to breathe, but the rocks were in my way.

I let out some weak sound of complaint as I hyperventilated. Ayil tried to pull me backward, but that only caused pain. I groaned and pushed my hand on his chest to stop him.

Genaro returned to me and pressed his hand to my lips. I widened my eyes at him and motioned to my corset from hell. He shushed me with pursed lips, but didn't make a noise.

He raised his hand up and down, allowing his breath to be heard. I again motioned to my chest. I couldn't breathe with rocks pressing my rib cage in.

His eyes dimmed as if I had disappointed him. He moved closer and put his hand on my belly. I hadn't realized how far my shirt had ridden up until I felt his warm—almost hot—touch on my skin. I looked at him, trying to determine what he was doing. He took another breath and patted my tummy.

I took his cue and breathed in, concentrating on expanding my belly rather than my rib cage. It was a challenge for me since my mother had taught me since birth to keep my stomach pressed tightly to my spine at all times. After a moment of this, he guided me to a slower breathing pace, and finally he directed me to exhale long and slow into my lungs, which were aching in their negative capacity.

A quick shove from Ayil and a tug from Genaro released me from the confines of my captivity. Relieved and breathless, I fell into the old man's arms and mouthed a "thank you."

With a little help, Ayil made it through the crevice unscathed and we were on our way down the dungeon passageway to the winner's circle. As we moved away from our only light source, I grappled for Genaro's shoulder. He found my hand and moved it into his firm grip. I reached back and grabbed Ayil's shirt, dragging him along with me so I didn't lose him either.

We bounced against the cave walls, in and out of tunnels, until we finally emerged into an open space. The muffled sound of our scuffing feet expanded into an echo. The air felt a little more humid. We stopped and Genaro released my hand. I waited for further instructions.

"What are they doing here?" I heard Terrin's voice.

I opened my mouth to speak, but Genaro spoke first. "They wanted to see you."

"Terrin?" I asked.

I heard him take a breath before he spoke. "Mallory, why didn't you leave?"

"I would have, but—"

"Will you never do as I say? Must you always wait until the situation is dire before you attempt to save yourself?"

"I'm sorry," I said, for once without extraneous effort. "But I can't let you do this. I know about the fight with... what's his name. And I also know it's suicidal."

"It's not suicide when you're fighting to live to the very end."

"I'm not here to argue the semantics with you. I am here to help you escape."

Terrin chuckled. "I feel like we've had this conversation before."

"I wasn't completely satisfied with the ending of that conversation."

"No, I'm sure you weren't, but this isn't your decision. You're talking about my life."

"No, we are talking about your death."

"What we're talking about is something you simply cannot understand."

"I'm trying to understand this nobility, Terrin. I'm trying to see it from your perspective, but I can't."

"No," he whispered. "You never could understand my obligations or the impact my failures had on me."

"Yes, yes, Terrin. You lost your job. You broke your promise. But why use my slippery, dishonest nature as an excuse to beat the hell out of yourself?"

"You really don't know, do you? Perhaps I never told you that part."

"What part?"

"The promise I made to your people was a blood oath."

"What?" I shook my head. I had heard of blood oaths, but it had never occurred to me that Terrin would have entered such a contract with anyone outside of his own race.

"I swore on my life to protect you and contain you. When you escaped my grasp, the only honorable thing I could do was retrieve you or kill myself for the failure."

"You did eventually catch me. You redeemed yourself."

"I redeemed nothing, Mallory. With every passing day you were gone, I trashed the name of my family. Every time you conveniently slipped through my fingers was another level of disgrace to my brethren."

I moved closer to his voice and bumped into the bars separating us. I reached through them to touch him, but he was staying out of reach. "I can see how you would want to restore your family name, but there has to be another way."

"The games are the ultimate symbol of a gattaw warrior. Nothing could be more honorable than dying in the competition. Even more honorable than winning."

"Okay, okay." I rubbed my forehead and nodded. "I get it. I totally get it. And if you were a criminal or something, this would be a great option for you. But Terrin, you are a free man, not a slave. Sicily was wrong to sell you into the games."

"She didn't sell me to the games."

"What?"

"She didn't sell me. She gave me a choice. I chose the games. I'm a free man, Mallory."

"But you're in here." After a brief pause, I heard the door to his cell screech open beside me, hitting me in the shoulder.

"I can leave whenever I want... always could."

I stood in front of the cell, staring into the darkness. My breathing turned raspy and my eyes watered. "Please don't do this," I whispered, but I heard nothing in response. "I beg you. I watched you die once—or so I thought. Please don't make me do it again." Silence. "Do you hear me, Terrin?"

"I can't be who you want me to be right now."

"Damn you, Terrin!" I smacked the bars in front of me, causing the metal to warble.

"Quiet," Genaro scolded me. I glanced back, though I couldn't see him any more than the bars right in front of my face.

I pressed my forehead against the bars and whispered as quietly as I could. "Please, come with me. I'll do as you ask for the rest of my life, if you will only leave with me now."

"And what of my namesake?"

"And what of me?" I momentarily raised my voice, but corrected myself before Genaro cautioned me. "I need you." I reached out for him again, but my hand only swiped air. I wanted to go into the cell and beat my fists against his chest, but I restrained myself.

"Not anymore." I opened my mouth to spell out a thousand ways I still needed him. "Leave, Mallory. Leave Miorita before you get hurt."

I threw my head back and barked a laugh. "Oh, it is far too late for that. My oldest friend is going to die tomorrow. I don't think I'll leave the arena with a smile on my face."

"You don't have to watch the fight."

"I don't have to watch? Fuck you, Terrin. I will be in the front row." I poked my finger at him—or where I presumed he was. "If this will be your greatest achievement, then I will witness it. You may not be the man I need you to be right now, but I will be the woman you need. I hate this fucking planet," I seethed, "and I hate your awful rules, and all your ridiculous traditions... but

I love you." I shifted my head, speaking more to Genaro than Terrin. "And for love... I will do anything. Even watch my friend die."

Silence followed my admission. A long silence with no end in sight. My hopes of a happy ending slowly melted away into the reality I knew all too well.

I pushed away from the bars and stepped back until Genaro touched my back. I was shaking and seconds from becoming a volcano of wrathful tears, but I kept my chin held high as he guided me out of the cavern.

Genaro took my hand again, and I took Ayil's. He led us from one darkness to another, back into crooked rock and dank walls. When we reached our original entrance and the dim light of Genaro's lantern illuminated our faces, I turned to him. "I'm sorry I wasted your time. I really thought I could convince him to leave."

"You didn't waste my time. I didn't bring you down here so you could save him. I brought you down here to show you that my son's devotion to honor runs deeper than you think."

"Your son?" My eyes flickered over the red highlights in his eyes. I had seen the similarities before, but I'd mistaken it as a coincidence.

Genaro stared back at me, a small smirk growing on his face. He lifted his finger and grazed it along my cheek, where an errant tear had gotten away from me. "Don't mistake his dismissal as discord. My son cares a great deal for you, but he also cares about the condition he leaves his family name in when he dies."

FATHER

Genaro had graciously offered Ayil and me a pile of hay next to his fire for the night. We accepted, if for no other reason than avoiding a long walk back to the shuttle. Some time after Ayil had fallen asleep, and the firelight had died down, I began to cry.

It wasn't the first time I had cried for Terrin's death, but these tears were different. I felt betrayed. I felt abandoned. I knew my expectations for Terrin had always been a little higher than they should be, but I never expected him to walk willingly to his death. Not without considering what and who he was leaving behind.

"So, how long have you been in love with my son?" Genaro asked from the other side of the fire. I had assumed he was asleep. As it was, he hadn't opened his eyes to look at me yet.

I weighed my answer. I didn't dare admit to loving him at first sight. Even if that could be an excuse for my attraction, I couldn't claim a genuine connection to him without having met him properly. "Terrin and I have a long history."

"I know your history. He's told me a lot about you."

"What did he tell you?"

Genaro chuckled and rolled over to face me. He finally opened his eyes to look at me. "He told me about a spoiled young girl he intended to discipline into an obedient one."

I scoffed. "He really said that?"

"Oh, yes, he had high hopes for you. I think he imagined his superior strength would be enough to intimidate you. I told him my lessons on women must have been woefully inadequate if he believed that."

I smiled. "What else did he say about me?"

"For a long time, it was just the usual chit-chat about his daily routine. He talked about you occasionally. Something you did or said that amused him."

I snorted. "I'm sure I amused him a great deal in those days. He never thought much of my sense of humor." My levity died away. "What did he say after I ran away?"

Genaro's face dimmed as well. "He was very angry. More angry than I had ever seen him."

"I can see why if he had broken a blood oath."

"Oh, don't kid yourself. He wasn't angry because of the oath. Embarrassed perhaps, but not angry." Genaro propped himself up on his elbow. "You and my son are more alike than he would ever admit."

"How so?"

"Terrin was a very stubborn child. He was smart, which made him a target for other gattaw. Gattaw don't encourage intellectual status as much as physical status. Fortunately for my son, he had his father to instruct him in the ways of battle. Terrin learned early on to use his strength *and* wisdom to defeat his bullies."

"It's hard to imagine anyone picking on Terrin." I smiled at the thought of Terrin as a little kid, running from his enemies. "I never had any bullies. I didn't have any friends either, though."

"Terrin wanted to get off Miorita at the first chance he could get. In fact, he fashioned a fake I.D. to get himself into the military two years earlier than they usually allow. I was mad when I found out he was gone—by law, he was a runaway. But..." Genaro took a breath as if remembering the moment again. "I knew Terrin sought greater things than Miorita could offer him. I knew revealing his lie would not only hurt our relationship, but the deceit could have prevented him from re-enrolling at the correct age. I didn't want to sacrifice his future just because I was angry about his disobedience."

"That must have been a hard decision to make."

"The hardest of my life. Are you cold?" Genaro asked, noticing my arms tucked tightly around me. He leaned forward and tossed a few more dead cacti on the coals. The room immediately lit with the rising flames, but they died back shortly after. "As angry as Terrin was about your escape, I couldn't make heads or tails of the situation. All I knew was that he was putting together a team, and he was going to get you back. I believe there was a threat of dragging you back by your color-treated hair."

I smirked at him, though I was certain Terrin had not been exaggerating when he'd said it.

"I knew something had changed, though. Terrin's mother passed when he was a boy. After that, he became... reserved. I rarely saw any emotion on his face. He didn't cry anymore. He didn't raise his voice. A smile was even rare. It was as if her death had emptied him of everything he felt. It took me a while to figure it out. Once I did, it was obvious. Somewhere along the line, that spoiled little princess had burrowed her way into my son's heart. A difficult feat, I assure you."

I blinked at Genaro as if I expected him to scold me for making his son weak or interfering with his career.

"He called me when he had gotten a lock on your location. His intent was to assure me he would not need to deliver on his blood oath. He was very proud of himself. If I had been a good and faithful gattaw to our traditions, I would have congratulated him and ended the call." Genaro took a deep breath. "I didn't. I asked him if that was what he really wanted to do. Naturally, he was confused. He wasn't seeing what I was seeing. I reminded him of his own escape from his dissatisfying life. I also pointed out that there was a difference between wanting to retrieve you as part of his job and retrieving you because he missed you."

"What did he say about that?"

Genaro smiled. "He ended the call. He didn't like my interpretation of his behavior. He hated the idea of any emotional attachment, especially to a human. I must have gotten through to him, because you evaded his custody."

"Are you saying I owe my freedom to you?"

Genaro shrugged. "Once he was officially fired, I assumed he would be done with the chase, but that wasn't the case. He just started collecting other bounties along the way to pay his crew. Terrin would call me—usually after a close encounter with you."

"Close encounter?"

"Oh, yes, he kept you on a shorter leash than you may have realized. He claimed he was doing it for your mother, but I know he would have followed you, anyway.

"He commented on how resourceful you had become. And how quickly you were learning to adapt to life outside of your luxury. He was proud of you."

I smiled, feeling some relief that something I had done in the wake of my abandonment had made a good impression on Terrin.

"He would even update me about your hair color changes. That's when I knew his attachment to you had become more of an attraction." Genaro stared at me. Again, I felt as if I was supposed to apologize for breaking his son.

"What did you have to say to that nonsense?" I said with fake cheer. "No doubt you were disappointed."

"I was disappointed. Disappointed that he had distanced himself from every notable connection he'd ever had, only to entangle his heart with a woman he could never have."

I took a breath and laughed. "Well, I don't think his heart is too entangled. As evidenced by his behavior tonight."

"Don't mistake his demeanor for indifference."

"I don't, but I can't put on a brave face when my heart is breaking." With little to no warning, my voice cracked, and I was openly sobbing. I buried my head in my hands. After a moment, I felt Genaro's hand brush the back of my head. His sudden proximity made me jump. I looked up at his sympathetic eyes, which were glistening with tears.

"You are not alone in your sentiments, Kit. I do not wish to see my son die, but I must respect his wishes as I have always done. Tomorrow, you and I will say goodbye to Terrin forever."

"I'm not ready."

"We are never ready to lose the ones we love."

I tentatively raised my arms and Genaro opened himself up to receive me. I wasn't sure if I was hugging Genaro in place of Terrin or if he was standing in for my father, but I was relieved to have a shoulder to cry on.

Price

The next day, another round of competitions were scheduled throughout the afternoon, but the last match wouldn't be until near sunset—the battle between Terrin and Dagon, a fight that had gained particular attention from the gamblers.

After yesterday's run in with the "debt collectors," it was only a matter of time before the forced use of my credit stamp brought the Coalition to Miorita. The only thing protecting me now was the sheer distance between me and their nearest outpost. I knew I should make my escape while I still could, but short of a brigade of soldiers showing up at the arena, I wouldn't leave until I saw Terrin dead or damned.

Mr. Davis saw me sitting in the stands staring out at the arena in a comatose state and waved to me. When I didn't respond, he climbed up the steps and sat down beside me.

"Your gattaw friend has started quite a stir."

"I'm sure. Everyone around here seems to be excited about potential deaths."

"The stir is being caused because they think he has a chance of winning."

I looked at him and shook my head. "I've seen the guy he's set to fight. It doesn't take a professional gambler to see the odds are against him."

"Dagon is old. He's been watching those gates a long time. If anyone has a chance of beating him, it will be Terrin."

"I see what you are trying to do, Mr. Davis, and I wish you wouldn't."

"What am I trying to do?"

"Give me hope."

"Actually, I was pointing out that if he wins, whoever was brave enough to bet on him will make a small fortune."

"Mr. Davis, do you really think I give a damn about the money I could make?" I turned to glare at him and saw the small, subtle smirk on his face. My eyes moved from him to his betting tablet, which was open to Terrin's page. It contained several pictures of him, as well as a description of his measurements and a list of his wins and losses. To my surprise, there were no losses. In the short time since he arrived, he had rocketed straight to the winner's circle. I looked at Mr. Davis, eyes wide and expectant. "What are you saying?"

"Can't say much here. Eyes and ears, you know." He moved his eyes toward the tent at the top of the stadium, but not his head. "Let's just say Dagon has some weaknesses no one knows about." He leaned in a little closer. "Except me, of course."

"He has a chance? A real chance?"

"Of course he has a chance. He—" I leaned forward and kissed him on the lips. He smirked at me after I had moved away. "What was that for?"

"For helping Terrin. For telling him about his opponent's weaknesses."

Mr. Davis looked down at his tablet. "Oh, dear." He shifted and looked back up at me. "You've misunderstood me."

"What do you mean?"

Mr. Davis smiled and chuckled. "My secrets aren't free." His eyes froze on me, staring at me like I was the jerk of this conversation. "Nothing is ever free. Not even for you, Princess."

"But I thought we were allies."

"I've repaid your nugget of information and then some. I can only yield so much for the sake of gentlemanly conduct. If you want any more of my help, then it will cost you."

I laughed and looked out at the arena where a man was pummeling an animal to death. The strange creature looked like a kangaroo, but I was fairly certain kangaroos didn't have spiked tails, or nine-inch dew claws... or fangs.

Maybe *kangaroo* wasn't the best comparison.

I turned back to Mr. Davis and grabbed his tie. I pulled it toward me, along with his face. "Mr. Davis, are you really going to sit there and dangle the key to my best friend's survival in my face like a goddamn pork chop to a starving man? If you think I have survived dozens of attempts on my life only to be weaseled out by a smart suit and a cheeky smile, you have another thing coming."

Mr. Davis lost his *cheeky* smile. "Get a grip on yourself. You're drawing attention to us." I loosened my grip on his tie and he pulled away. He straightened it, smoothing down the fabric. "Meet me outside and we can discuss my fee." He stood and walked away.

I waited several minutes before following him. I plodded down the stairs of the stadium, getting angrier by the step. As I reached the soft sand at ground level, an arm reached out and pulled me under the wooden scaffolding. Mr. Davis pushed me back against the stone wall and braced his hands on either side of my head.

"Let's keep this civil, Princess."

"Stop calling me that!"

"Just as you said in the beginning, this is about business. Either you have something to offer me, or you don't."

"You son of a bitch!" I reached forward to rip his throat out, or at least scratch the hell out of it, but he pushed my hands back, slamming my wrists into the wall. "I will kill you!" I seethed.

"No, you won't." He spoke to me with his face only an inch away from mine. "Because one word from me, and your identity, will be around this stadium in two minutes flat."

"You wouldn't."

"Why do you think that?" His eyes squinted as he smiled. "Because in your mind I saved you from your wicked little life of privilege? That was just business."

"I don't believe that for one second. You lost money on that deal."

"I didn't do it for the money. I did it for the connection. Having you on my list of associates is far more lucrative than spare parts." He shifted, releasing my wrists. I pulled them down and rubbed them. "I'm not the bad guy, Kit, but I'm also not the good guy. I'm the guy who wants something in return for my help. Now, do you want my secrets or not?"

"Yes," I hissed through gritted teeth.

"Good. See how simple that was? Now we just have to agree on a price." His eyes glinted, thrilled by the prospect of negotiating the remainder of our back-alley deal.

"What do you want?"

"I guess that depends how much you have to offer"

"You know, the last time I revealed my location to the Coalition, a battlerunner blew up the ship I was being transported on. What do you think will happen to you if your name is on the other side of that exchange?" I threatened, even though I was prepared to use my credit. What was one more beacon to my enemies?

Mr. Davis's eyes fluttered over mine. "I'm not too worried about the Coalition, but I'm sure my employer would be none too pleased if I drew unnecessary attention to him. I'm not really interested in money, anyway. I can get that anywhere." Mr. Davis leaned into the wall behind me, bringing our faces close. He looked me over as he breathed in a long draw of air. "What else can you offer me?"

"You don't strike me as the type to extort a woman for sex."

Davis shook his head. "No, not usually, but I am curious how far you will go to protect your friend. How much is his life worth to you? Is it worth more than your pride? Your fidelity? Your virtue?"

As I stared at Davis's leering gaze, I couldn't help but think how many times Ayil had put himself between me and potential molestation. Gunther had called me a coward for not using my femininity to me advantage and he was right. As much as I wanted to save Terrin, I didn't want to get my hands dirty. Not really.

Davis leaned forward and kissed my neck. I swallowed hard, hopefully hard enough to swallow my pride. He continued to trail his kisses down my neck and tested my boundaries by groping my breasts.

I didn't stop him.

I didn't stop any of it.

Twenty minutes later, I stomped up the steps of the stadium and plopped down next to Ayil. "Where were you?" he asked.

"Where were *you*?" I bit back at him. "I was sitting on this step for an hour. Where the hell were you?"

"What's wrong with you?" He touched my shoulder, and I shrugged him away. "Kit," he whispered and scooted closer. "Why are you so mad?" I looked up as Mr. Davis rounded the corner and passed by below us. I leveled a glare at him, but he winked at me, smug and satisfied to have what he'd wanted from me.

Ayil caught the exchange and examined the look on my face. I wondered which of my mixed emotions was being broadcasted the most: anxiety, hatred, turmoil—or was it the shame? "Kit, where were you?" he asked, even more concerned than before. "Did something happen?"

"It's nothing, Ayil." I looked at him, tears pushing into my eyes. "I did what had to be done." I blinked and a tear dribbled down my cheek. "Anything for love, right?"

He nodded somberly and pulled me into a sideways hug. I explained the new information I had about Dagon and that we should bet our money on Terrin winning. As thrilled as I was about the prospect of Terrin living through his match, I wasn't happy about what it had taken to get it. I was glad Ayil hadn't asked for the details. I wasn't ready for that humiliation.

Finale

The moons of Miorita shone over the horizon as the sun descended on the opposite side. The sky was smeared with orange and the announcer made a comment about it being a sign of blood about to be spilled. It wasn't exactly a difficult prediction to make since it was a fight to the death.

Ayil caught me wiping away a stray tear and smiled at me. "Hey, he hasn't lost yet."

I shrugged. "I'm losing him either way. There's no way I'm leaving here without tears."

"Kit, you know we don't have to be here for this." I shook my head, and Ayil scooted closer to me. "If something goes wrong..."

I shook my head again, fighting back more tears. "If something goes wrong, I definitely need to be here. Since this miserable tradition means enough to him to die for it, then the least I can do is sit here and watch him do it." I looked at Ayil. "I have to see it for myself this time."

Ayil frowned and moved his lips, no doubt to form some words of solace, but nothing came out.

"It's okay, Ayil, because he won't die. He's going to win."

The worry in Ayil's eyes turned to pity, but he nodded at my delusion, as if he were agreeing with a child revealing the existence of an imaginary friend. Unfortunately, I didn't believe it any more than he did. I just had to say it—to put it out into the universe as a wish or a prayer.

Genero came into our section and scooted his cart up close to the railing below us. He glanced up at me, peering from beneath the shade of his brimmed hat. I couldn't help the scowl forming on my face. I knew it wasn't his fault Terrin was in this situation. The most expansive blame actually lay at my own feet. However, as much as I hated myself, I was still angry with him for raising a stubborn son.

The announcer introduced the competitors. Everyone cheered wildly for Dagon as he entered the arena. Whether he was the favorite or not, he had earned the right to be fawned over. I applauded quietly for the seven-foot mammoth man, secretly hoping he would drop dead from a heart attack or at least have a very violent gastro-intestinal attack. Anything that would keep him from fighting.

He was armored head to toe with copper shielding, including a head-encompassing helmet, which exacerbated the length of his horns to Freudian proportions. I should have known a battle this epic would be as much glam as gore.

After Terrin was announced, I watched him walk onto the battlefield in the same artistic armor as his opponent. I had never thought of Terrin as a small man, and by most comparisons, he was rather formidable, but standing next to Dagon, he looked diminutive. Nearly a foot shorter, he still stood proudly, shoulders back, chest bolstered, and chin high.

Terrin turned his head slightly and nodded to Genaro. The old man nodded back. His head shifted, and though I couldn't truly see his eyes from so far away, I knew he was looking at me. I took in a breath, wanting to shake my head or scream across the expanse between us. So many chastising words came to my mind, not one supportive of his actions. Instead of retaliation, I put my hands together and clapped for his arrival.

When the introductions were through and the applause subsided, Ayil took my hand in his and squeezed it. He leaned closer and whispered in my ear. "If I give the word, we will need to leave."

"What? No, I told you I want to stay," I whispered back.

"We may not have a choice."

I turned my head in the direction Ayil was looking, but he grabbed my face, cupping it in place to look only at him. "There is a bit of a hubbub going on in the tent a few doors down. I think your aunt just figured out who you are."

"Shit," I whispered. Between a blip on my credit stamp and my aunt tattling, my ticking countdown clock was turning into a fizzling fuse. I needed to get off this planet before every idiot with an empty wallet knew who I was.

The horn blew and all thoughts of self-preservation went out the window. I looked to the arena and saw the men drawing their swords and circling. It wasn't long before the *tink* of swords filled the air. In a cross between a sword fight and a fencing match, the men parried and dodged the strikes. Though the shorter blades were seen as a lesser choice to a long sword, they allowed the competitors to throw the occasional punch while their opponent was occupied.

Terrin's quick concise movements were more than Dagon's size could compete with. He was turning and twisting awkwardly to keep up with his fast threats.

Naturally, Dagon compensated with harder and harder blows, nearly knocking the short sword from Terrin's hand when he deflected the attack. Terrin ducked the swinging sword and kicked the man's shin. Dagon bellowed and dropped to the ground, seemingly in immense pain.

His only weakness, I thought. Terrin had gotten the information from Mr. Davis. Perhaps it had been worth the price after all.

Terrin took his opportunity and shoved his sword toward the man's chest. Unfortunately, the blade missed the gap in the armor and Terrin left himself open for his opponent's retaliation.

Dagon threw his fist and collided with Terrin's helmet. Terrin did a double pirouette before he regained his balance and orientated himself.

Dagon struggled to rise through his leg pain, but once he did, he hurled himself onto Terrin. They both toppled to the ground, their blades only a memory as they rattled each other's armor. Their fists punched at anything potentially vulnerable.

With hands bloodied, and chests heaving, neither had accomplished anything they had set out to do. As if they both realized the futility of the fight, they separated and rolled away in search of their swords.

They stood and raised their weapons again. The crowd cheered as they got back to the more gentlemanly method of killing each other—sharp, pointy objects.

Despite my enthusiasm for the match and the burdening ramifications for my heart, my eyes were drawn away from the fight to a darkness emerging from the stairwell. My breath caught in my throat and my heart instantly jumped up to jackrabbit speed.

My countdown clock just hit zero.

The *man* emerging into the stadium stood out from the crowd. He was dressed all in black, including an oblong helmet which obscured his face. Black was hardly the color for anyone on such a hot day. However, since the man inside that uniform was arguably dead, the heat wouldn't bother him, anyway.

Biomechanoids were the best choice for long-range military operations, or so the Coalition believed. The practice of allocating humanoid cadavers to warfare was as controversial as slavery, but it was far too advantageous to outlaw. There were always bodies available to recruit and since none of the soldiers required food, sleep, or compensation, it was a very cost-effective army.

I turned away to avoid the biomechanoid's scanning gaze. On the other side, at the next section break, another biomechanoid popped out of a stairwell. At the top of the stairs, he shifted his head and then his body before proceeding along the terrace level to observe the audience members. I could only imagine the details these things had stored in their data banks about me. There was no hiding from them. Not with purple hair, not even with a facelift.

I accidentally caught my aunt's gaze as she stared out at me from her tent. She was glaring, but she was also noting the soldiers. As angry as she was at her wretched little niece for abandoning her sovereign duties, she certainly didn't want me to be captured by the Coalition. That was a whole different kind of prison sentence.

"What the hell is that doing here?" Ayil asked when he saw the biomechanoid on his right. Despite the population being mostly gattaw, there was a noticeable shift in the crowd's temperament as the soldiers emerged at every available entrance. The reasons may have varied species to species, but as a rule biomechanoids were loathed.

"My father's army," I answered Ayil.

A look of horror flickered across his face. He looked at the soldier and then the stairwell. I already knew he was counting the steps for our escape and calculating the probability of being caught. For the time being, we were stuck.

Terrin was still fighting hard in the pit, but I could tell both men were getting tired. It was only a matter of time before someone fell. As much as I didn't want to see the end of this battle, especially if it wasn't in Terrin's favor, I needed an escape route and the exiting crowd would be my best chance.

Ayil looked at the soldier as he moved on to the next section, effectively opening the stairwell for us, but he didn't bother to make a move for it. He understood that where there was one militant biomechanoid knocking down your front door, there were at least a dozen more waiting at your back door.

Terrin swung his sword, and it collided with Dagon's neck. Blood spurted from beneath his helmet and the crowd cheered. I clasped my hands together, hoping the fight was over and the victor would be Terrin, but it was never that easy in the dogfights.

Dagon came after him, swinging his sword even harder. He had no concern for his wound, or perhaps he was too angry to feel it. Terrin backpedaled, stumbling over a rock.

Dagon wasted no time and drove the sword down at him. The sword penetrated Terrin's armor and hit the edge of his abdomen. He let out a roar, and Ayil had to hold me down as I tried to rise from my seat. It was all I could do not to cry out.

I knew I needed to keep control. I was already on the cusp of being discovered. My only reprieve was that biomechanoids were slow. The face-by-face search they were implementing was going to take them forever.

Dagon removed his sword from Terrin and stumbled back, the blood to his brain no doubt dropping to all-time lows. With some effort, Terrin got to his feet and charged the slowing champion. Dagon raised his sword to slash at his neck, a potentially mirroring wound, but Terrin dropped to his knee and shoved his sword up under the man's armor at the waist. His blade angled upward, burying itself deep in the man's body.

Dagon fell instantly, and the audience gave a standing ovation. I rose and applauded Terrin's victory. A joy unmatched by any other flooded my heart, and I hugged Ayil.

When the audience quieted, I returned my attention to the arena. Terrin was standing over his kill, panting and staring at the ground beneath him. The bloody pool seeping into the sand was not only from his opponent, but from him. He was bleeding a great deal more than from a simple flesh wound.

I had underestimated the danger he was in. Dagon had likely hit his kidney.

Terrin removed his body armor and dropped it to the ground. I shook my head. He kneeled down carefully and picked up his opponent's copper blade.

"No." I was moving before Ayil could get the grip he needed to detain me. I didn't even know what I wanted to do. Miorita wasn't the pinnacle of medical achievements. Suicide was as much a cure to them as a band-aid. They weren't likely to have a blood transfusion ready for Terrin, and they would hardly let me take him to my ship for proper treatment.

I pushed through the people ahead of us and reached the mezzanine. I hit the railing and opened my mouth to scream. To beg one last time, in futility, for love.

For my love.

For his love.

For a thousand more chances to say it and one more chance to get it right.

A green molting hand came from out of nowhere and clasped around my mouth, keeping me from disrupting the dramatic silence that had stilled the entire audience out of respect for a dying man.

I grasped Genaro's hand, pinching my nails into his skin. He pulled me back against his chest and pushed his face to my ear. He shushed me ever so quietly before slowly releasing my mouth. I sniffled and sputtered a bit before getting control of myself. I gripped the stone railing and watched Terrin as he looked over the crowd.

He kissed the sword that would soon bring his end. He spoke a quiet prayer that usually preceded a noble intentional death in the ring.

Terrin's eyes once again looked at his father, and he nodded to him. Genaro dipped his head slightly, as if giving him permission to die. When Terrin's eyes shifted to me, I felt the same question being posed. Would I release him? Would I grant him the permission to die?

I wasn't sure the answers running through my mind would have satisfied him. There was as much anger in my heart as grief, but I bit back both the sorrow and the resentment. I stiffened my back and nodded to him.

After a slight pause, he nodded back and raised the blade.

It was up and back down again without ceremony. I gasped as it entered his chest.

TRIBUTE

All my bravado melted, and I dropped forward, bending over against Genaro's arm. My head hit the stone wall railing, and I stayed there as I listened to the crowd cheer for the death of my friend. It was the second time in such a short time that I had mourned for him. The first time I had recovered with some dignity, but I wasn't sure I could do it again.

Genaro pulled me back up and I flopped against his chest. He shifted me around and held me close. I cried against him, into his shirt, as the hum of the crowd disguised my moans of despair.

Some people pushed past us, getting ahead of the exiting crowd while the announcer declared the winner and honored the dead with one last triplicate *"rah."* Genaro joined the cheer, but I couldn't quite muster the strength.

As the passersby increased, I heard them discussing the glorious outcome of the battle. I pulled away from Genaro and looked back at Ayil. He was still near our seats, patiently waiting for me despite the urgency of our situation. He looked down at me downtrodden and possibly even a little teary-eyed himself. *"I'm sorry,"* he mouthed to me.

I nodded and peeked around to see where our nosy biomechanoids were. They had not made it to us before the people started moving. They were all stuck along the railings, frantically documenting every face that passed by them. The lunacy of it was they were even inspecting people who were clearly not the correct race—another few seconds in my favor.

"I have to go," I rasped, despite being perfectly content to weep into his arms for another hour... or ten. Genaro looked around at the soldiers. He turned back to me and I looked up at him. "I'm sorry for... your... son." My words turned to stutters as I looked up at him. My mind was playing tricks on me. Cruel, cruel tricks.

Genaro's eyes glimmered with reddish highlights which bore a devilish glow to anyone caught in the path of their rage. The skin molting on his face looked gray, but beneath the peeling areas was a brighter green than I remembered.

I glanced down at where my hand touched his chest. There were few differences in young and old gattaw, but his body felt different from the one I had been hugging the other night. I looked back up to his face and a smile turned the edge of his lips. I shook my head. He nodded.

I shook my head again and his smile raised a little higher. I felt my broken heart twist with torturous hope. I was trying desperately to grasp what I was seeing. My fear of prolonged pain refused to let me believe it. If it was a dream, then it would surely flee with the return of my consciousness.

"Terrin?" I whispered as quietly as I could.

"Mallory," he whispered back.

My mouth dropped, but he squeezed me close and shushed me. I stared at him another long moment, words lost as my heart simply collapsed into a puddle, unable to keep up with the emotional transition the moment demanded.

As I stared at him, swallowing hard and embracing a life that now included him, and God willing always would, a thought occurred to me. I frowned and looked down at the arena floor.

Two men were dead.

I looked back at Terrin, eyes wide at the thought of what had transpired to allow this confusion of identity. Terrin looked out onto the arena and then back at me, a certain solemn calm in his demeanor. I didn't have to ask to know Genaro had taken his place, no doubt with an excess of drugs to sustain the energy required for the fight.

It was the perfect sacrifice. Genaro would save his son, be honored in battle, and revive the family name. The only flaw was he had to die. He could win or lose, but he had to die. There would be no question of his identity when it was all over. Gattaw weren't buried, they were burned. No one would question his identity post battle. He was likely bruised and swollen beyond recognition, anyway.

My stomach clenched, and an ache set into my chest. Genaro's generosity was awe-inspiring. I never wanted him to die, but I was so grateful he had been willing to. And if my suspicions were correct, it had had nothing to do with me. He had always intended to replace his son. That was why Terrin wanted me gone. He'd already had a plan, and I was getting in the way.

Terrin pulled a small knife from his pocket and pressed it into his palm. Blood seeped from the cut he created and filled his hand. He leaned forward and squeezed his fist over the railing, dripping his own blood onto the sand below.

I didn't know if it was appropriate or not, but I reached for the knife. He gave it to me and I sliced a cut into my palm. I held the blood for a moment, letting it build up before squeezing it out onto the arena floor.

"Kit, I'm sorry, we can't wait any longer." Ayil shoved in between us and ushered me to leave. I was about to explain the situation to him when I saw a bulbous black head bobbing through the crowd behind us. I ducked down, tucking in beside Ayil before the man could get a good view of my face.

Ayil pulled me into the flow of spectators. We shuffled along slowly, surrounded by gattaw. I dared a glance back to see how close the biomechanoid was to us. We made some leeway, but only because Terrin had shoved his father's food cart into the soldier's path.

"What about Rayne?" I asked as an afterthought.

"We'll figure out something later," Ayil said. "Right now, we need to get off this planet."

When we reached the wooden gates, the crowd scattered, some left, some right, and some forward. Through the breaks in the bodies, I saw a flickering view of the city and the surrounding landscape. I also saw black.

At least twenty biomechanoids had surrounded the arena and were carefully eyeing the exiting spectators. Everywhere I turned, I found a scanning face I had to hide myself from. Our shuttle was more than a quarter mile out. There was no chance I could get past them unnoticed. It would only take one of them to detect me and the rest would converge on my location like a swarm of insects.

As our barrier of people got thinner and thinner, Ayil veered us off course, back toward the arena. "What are you doing?"

"Buying time. We're surrounded." Ayil looked around. "I'm open to ideas. Any ideas."

My first thought was to find Terrin and beg for his help, but aside from putting him into jeopardy right along with us, I knew if he exposed his identity, it would undo everything his father had just done. I didn't want that. Terrin would need to leave the planet on his own terms to keep his secret safe.

Unfortunately, there was only one other person I could think of to give us help. I just didn't know how much more it would cost me.

Desperate

"I'm not asking this time, Mr. Davis." Ayil and I weaved through the city center, dodging vendor carts and avoiding cactus spines. Mr. Davis was walking briskly away from us as we tried to convince him to assist our escape. He knew as well as anyone how dangerous it was to be around me. I wasn't sure he was up for a life-or-death scenario, but he was clever. If he couldn't buy us a way out of this situation, then he could at least weasel us out of it. "There are already too many guns pointed at my head. Desperation does not make for friendly debate."

"Stop!" Ayil grabbed his arm and whipped him back around to face us. Mr. Davis yanked his arm free and wiped down the fabric. He glanced around at the passersby, but no one seemed concerned about the affairs of the humans.

"Even if I was inclined to help you, you have nothing more to offer. I've already taken what I want from you." I wanted to punch the smug smirk off his face. I was begging for my life and he was needling me for his own amusement.

"What is that supposed to mean?" Ayil snarled, pushing into Mr. Davis's face.

"I'm not offering anything, Mr. Davis," I snapped. "This is effectively a stick-up."

"You either help us or I pummel your face in," Ayil threatened him.

Mr. Davis hissed. "Oh, that doesn't sound fun at all... for you."

"You son of a bitch." Ayil threw his fist, nicking Mr. Davis in the jaw. It should have put the man down, but Ayil's fist bounced off it like he had punched a brick wall.

Ayil groaned and cradled his hand. I didn't see any blood, but I got the sense from the tears in his eyes that he hadn't merely bruised his knuckles. I looked at Mr. Davis, trying to understand what had happened. He smiled at me and shrugged. "I'm more of a lover than a fighter, but I do have the best toys." He lifted his chin and showed me what looked like a skin-toned band-aid. He tapped the center of it and I could see the shield skin over his face flicker off, then on again as he clicked it a second time. "It reacts to force and speed. Amazing technology. I would say it's ahead of its time, but I think everyone else is just behind the times. Good day, Princess." Mr. Davis turned to walk away.

"I'll give you a debt."

He stopped and turned back. "Excuse me?"

"You heard me." I ground my teeth together. "What's more profitable than that?"

"Kit, don't," Ayil grunted.

"What exactly are you saying?" Mr. Davis stepped back to me. His eyes lit with intrigue. "What are your parameters?"

"One debt. One favor. One errand. Nothing compounding—I won't date your cousin or be your maid or donate to your favorite charity in perpetuity. I will give you one debt, to be repaid at any point in time, so long as it doesn't result in someone's death, including my own."

Mr. Davis smiled. "That's a dangerous deal to make with a man like me. Are you sure you won't regret it later?"

"I regret it now. I regret ever meeting you, Mr. Davis, but since we are in this situation, I have no choice but to stoop to your level of money-mongering and give you something I know your fiendish mind can't refuse."

"Careful, that was almost a compliment."

"Do we have a deal or not?" I noticed a black body approaching in the distance. He was still searching every face he passed. I had just enough time to run, but my option for escape was now down to finding the entrance to the caves and hiding out until the soldiers left. Unfortunately, I couldn't tell the difference between one cactus house and the next. I doubted I could find the cave entrance before the soldiers caught me.

"Deal." Mr. Davis frowned and stepped closer to me. He yanked off the sticky tab beneath his chin. I could see the underside had a thin black screen. Mr. Davis tapped on it with his pinky finger, apparently changing the settings. He pushed my chin up and pressed the device onto the underside of my chin, pushing the tacky material onto my skin. He then pressed the center of it. I could see the force field rise, but it didn't feel any different. "For the record, I'm sorry you met me, too." Mr. Davis turned and walked away.

"Wait, what am I supposed to do?" I turned to Ayil, who was staring at me, eyes wide in disbelief. "What is it?"

"You... You aren't you. Your face is different."

"Different?" I grimaced. "How different?" I glanced at the biomechanoid coming closer to us. It took everything

I had not to run. I didn't know if it was wise to trust Mr. Davis, but I was certain if his little shielding could withstand a punch, it could hopefully fool a mechanically enhanced brain.

I waited with bated breath for the soldier to arrive. Ayil stood upright as the man paused momentarily on him. The quick identification no doubt confirmed he was male and not of interest. The soldier turned to me and paused. I could only imagine the little screens fluttering against the interior of his visor like virtual reality, except he never got to come out of it. After a moment of comparison, he walked away, no more interested in me than a family picture on the wall of someone else's house.

I looked at Ayil and smiled.

"Come on. Let's get out of here." He pulled me along and we set out on our journey across the desert—me with my unfamiliar face, and him with his old one. As we passed by several more soldiers, they examined me, but none of them attacked. I was pleased with my new toy, but once again it had come with a great sacrifice, one I was certain I would ultimately regret.

When we emerged from the forest of cacti to a clearing that was effectively long-term parking for the stadium, there were shuttles of all shapes and sizes sitting on the concrete platform. Among them were several long-nosed fleet ships—sleek black, streamlined, and ominous as hell. Even more foreboding was the thirty-plus biomechanoids standing near them. They all simultaneously turned to look at us as we arrived.

Ayil took my hand, and we walked on, facing forward as each of the soldiers analyzed us, one after the other. Step after step, a new *face* locked onto me, monitoring me with computerized precision, their movements as creepy as they were choreographed. There was definitely something wrong with mixing man and machine.

We made it through the crowd of soldiers monitoring the parking without a problem. Ayil and I stepped into our shuttle and we each began the takeoff process. There was no conversation between us except to announce when the thrusters were primed and the vents open. We jumped from land to air with the gentle g-force of gravity times three.

The farther we got from the planet's surface, the more relief I felt and the more hope I allowed for my foreseeable future. I clicked the button device under my chin to disengage my mask and sat back to enjoy the ascent.

The gravitational pressure reduced, and the atmosphere thinned. The clouds parted, and blue turned to black. It was a beautiful sight, one I could never tire of.

There was, however, one flaw in my view.

"No," Ayil whispered beside me.

The mothership to the ones on the surface of the planet was circling the planet. I recognized the battlerunner. It was identical to the one that had blown apart Sicily's ship. Off in the distance, I could see another huge carrier—not as modern, but definitely a military ship. I checked my readings for an insignia code, but I couldn't register anything. The battlerunner was most likely jamming the local signals, effectively blinding us.

"Where's Starla?" I asked, already pounding on the screen.

"Right there." Ayil weakly pointed out the view window to the tiny blip close to the Coalition's mammoth carrier.

"Aresties? Come in, Aresties." I tried the com several times, but nothing came through. We were blind and deaf.

"Hurry," Ayil warned me and I accelerated the shuttle up to top speed.

home

Ayil and I nearly fell over each other to get out of the shuttle and into the cargo bay. We ran straight to the cockpit where Aresties was frantically pressing buttons on the console. She looked back at me with tears in her eyes. Her tired eyes looked positively bloodshot, and her bouncy hair was matted down by sweat. "I tried to move the ship," she said. "But they booted our system."

"What the hell?" I switched places with her, and Ayil jumped into the copilot chair. I punched a few buttons, but came to the same conclusion Aresties had. The upgraded system may have made flying a breeze, but it also made us susceptible to autopilot hacks. "No, no, no," I murmured. I escaped out of the main screen and tried to override the system in the base code mode, but it rejected every command, immediately overriding it.

"They're talking to us." Ayil put the coms on speaker.

"Attention, H-class ship, you have been identified in connection with a fugitive," a computerized voice said. *"You have one minute to surrender and comply with our requests to search your ship."*

"One minute!" I screeched.

"They've been counting down from ten minutes," Aresties said. "I tried to warn you not to come back, but I couldn't get through."

"It's okay," Ayil assured her. "Where is Edric?"

"I put him in a pod. Just in case."

Ayil glanced back at her, a look of relief on his face. "Thank you."

Aresties nodded.

"Maybe we can turn on the weapons system," I suggested.

"They're armed with torpedoes," Aresties said quietly. After a few screen changes, I confirmed this as well.

"Forty-five seconds," the robotic voice announced without ire or enthusiasm.

I exchanged a look with Ayil before we both jumped up and ushered Aresties out of the cockpit.

"Okay, time to go." Ayil pressed on her back while I ran ahead to the closest pod. With only one on each deck, that left a grand total of three. I quickly programmed the pod for instant ejection, while Ayil strapped Aresties inside. I was about to suggest he join her, but her ample body didn't leave much room and we didn't have time to negotiate with the safety harness.

"Thirty seconds." The irritating announcement came over the speaker as I slammed my hand on the door close button. The pod launched from the side of the ship with a *woosh*. It wouldn't go far and it had very little steering capabilities, but it was virtually indestructible. The only danger of escape pods was how long the oxygen would last.

Ayil jumped the stairwell ahead of me and reached the next pod. By the time I arrived, he had it programmed and ushered me inside. I wanted to argue, but I was certain his intention was to join Edric in the third pod. "Good luck," he said and slammed his fist into the door close button.

The device bleated unhappily and would not close. I checked the interior gauges and saw the reason for its rejection. "There's a leak in the oxygen. It won't release," I reported as I unfastened my restraints.

"Fifteen seconds."

"Go, go, go!" I yelled and ran down the stairs with Ayil pounding right after me. I ran across the cargo bay to the back corner, where the last pod sat containing a frightened but safe Edric.

"Daddy!" he screamed when Ayil rounded the corner.

"Ten seconds."

"Get in!" I frantically punched on the keys, forcing the pod to activate.

Ayil paused at the door. "The oxygen tank is at half."

"It'll be enough for you two," I said without another thought and pushed his back. "Get in, now!" Ayil pinned me with a scolding gaze. "He's your son, he needs you," I whispered and pressed on his back again.

"Five."

"He has a better chance without me." Ayil moved out of the doorway.

"Ayil, no!"

He slammed his hand against the button, sending his son out into the universe frightened and alone... but still safe.

For barely a second, I stared at him in awe of his sacrifice and angry as hell at the same time. I wasn't sure what he thought he was accomplishing by staying to die with me. Now both our children would be orphans.

"Three."

Ayil's eyes widened with realization. "The shuttle, go!" He shoved me toward the other side of the bay. It was a long shot. The shuttle wasn't much stronger than the ship, but if it could hold oxygen for another minute, maybe it was enough time for our guardian angels to catch up with us.

"*Two.*"

"Kit!" Ayil yelled at me, begging me to move faster.

"*One.*" I leaped through the shuttle door and jumped to the panels to activate the shields. When I looked up, I came face to face with the view of death right outside the observation window. Two tiny sparks were there and gone on the surface of the battlerunner, barely enough to light the hull, but more than enough to shove two metric tons of devastation at my ship.

Ayil secured the door and stepped up behind me. He rested a hand on my shoulder. I reached up and gripped his fingers. For those last seconds, we watched the grim reaper coast through the vastness of space to reach my ship.

When the torpedoes hit Starla, the shuttle trembled and creaked. I fell against Ayil as our position suddenly shifted—a result of our anchor clamps involuntarily disconnecting. Shrapnel filled the view window. *Bangs* and *pings* echoed through the shuttle as debris rained down on us. I yelped as sparks burst from the control panel. The floor cracked beneath us.

"We're losing her!" Ayil drifted away from me as the gravity released. I reached out, but he was already too far.

"Ayil," I whimpered, still grappling for him.

I took my last breath before the shields gave out. The air was ripped away like a warm blanket. I pinched my eyes shut and huddled in a ball to preserve my body temperature. I was just another fragment of debris now. Remnants of a ship, floating out in open space, waiting to be drawn in by Miorita's gravity.

FELICIA JEDLICKA

Destiny Razed

BOOK 3 IN THE DESTINY SERIES

Destiny Razed

FELICIA JEDLICKA

Book 3

When Kit thinks things can't get any worse, she discovers a man who wants her DNA even more than the Coalition.

Trapped on a ship with a mad scientist, Kit discovers there is something more sinister at work in her biology. The grand altruistic prophecy, placed on her shoulders as a child, is nothing more than a murderous plot, with her as the linchpin.

When her struggles to survive, lead her right into the hands of her enemy, Kit discovers her baby is not the miracle her brainwashed empire has been waiting for.

She is an act of war.

With the empire now at stake, to prevent genocide, Kit must lay waste to her destiny and sacrifice her child.

Thank you so much for reading. I hope you enjoyed the ride and if you aren't getting off here, I encourage you to sign up for my newsletter so I can return your generosity with new release updates and special offers.

Sign-Up

You can also find me on Facebook or visit my website. Keep reading!

Website

Facebook

About the Author

As a Nebraska native, and a small-town girl at that, I have very little to occupy my time beyond imagining a world outside of my own reality. By the grace of God and the seat of my pants, I have kept my waning attention span on the task of becoming an author.

So here I am, an indie author, peddling my words in cyberspace and enduring my comeuppances with an unwavering determination. I may not be a professional, and I certainly am not perfect, but if you've made it this far, you have to admit, this smartass yokel does spin quite a yarn.

From the self-inflicted sweatshop conditions of my unairconditioned childhood home, to the arthritis reaping positions of a sedentary lifestyle, I bring to you: my sarcasm, my oddity, and my heart. Take it with a grain of salt or a teaspoon of sugar, but take it for what it is: a story born of the mind, translated to paper, and gifted to you.

I thank you for your readership and even more for your support. Please recommend this book to your friends and family via any social media you use. Word of mouth is still the best advertising and is greatly appreciated.

Most importantly, keep reading. I'll keep writing.